My Turn Now

LAUREN WELLS lives
The Simple Life, was pul
My Turn Now is her second novel, and she is currently at work on her third.

By the same author

The Simple Life

My Turn Now

LAUREN WELLS

HarperCollins*Publishers*

HarperCollins*Publishers*
77–85 Fulham Palace Road,
Hammersmith, London W6 8JB

This paperback edition 1999
1 3 5 7 9 8 6 4 2

ISBN 0 00 651179 1

Set in Plantin Light by
Rowland Phototypesetting Ltd,
Bury St Edmunds, Suffolk

Printed in Great Britain by
Caledonian International Book Manufacturing Ltd, Glasgow

For my son David Skinner,
another Gemini, with much love;
Bring me Sunshine

Deborah is humming; it sounds horribly like Mendelssohn's Wedding March.

Robyn, lying beside her on the short springy grass, leans on one elbow and looks at her. Deborah's face wears a soft smile, the expression it habitually falls into nowadays when she is not actively thinking about anything.

'Debs?'

'Hm?'

'How many men does it take to clean a lavatory?' Deborah, still smiling, doesn't answer. Robyn tells her anyway. 'Nobody knows – the attempt's never been made.'

Deborah says, 'Ha.' Like that – ha – as if it is a word in its own right, having nothing to do with the expression of amusement.

Irritated, for a wealth of reasons which culminate in a vast and inexpressible whole, Robyn lies down again. Shades her eyes with her arm, for the afternoon sun is bright. On the periphery of her vision is a thorny little tree, its trunk bent by the prevailing wind, green leaves brilliant as tropical feathers in the strong light.

Presently Deborah resumes her humming. Then she says, 'You can't compare coming home to an empty house with coming home to a loving husband.'

Robyn lights on three possible replies: one, so who's to say a husband will turn out to be loving?; two, an empty house will be precisely as you left it when you went out, whereas a house with a husband in it will have been rearranged according to his own unique pattern.

And three, what about coming home to someone *not* a husband? A good friend, for example?

But it is too hot for rancour. And, in any case, what good will it do?

Robyn has been twice married; once divorced, once widowed. She has borne four sons. She calculates that, for the past twenty-five years, she has lived with no less than one and no more than five males.

Although it is, she believes – indeed, hopes – only temporary, she is at the moment rather tired of men.

But Debs appears to be in love. In what is surely the ultimate triumph of optimism over experience – for she has a track record of being horribly wounded in relationships – it seems that Debs could actually be contemplating getting married again.

Robyn's conscience is disturbed over this. As if it is up to her to point out to Deborah the possible pitfalls. No. *Possible* is understating the case. 'Lots of people don't bother with getting married nowadays,' she says, trying to make her tone light. The sort of voice one would use for a general discussion of the topic, where neither side holds strong personal views. Achieving this tone is not easy, for she is all too aware that both she and Deborah hold very firm views. And, unless dear old Debs is teasing, these views are diametrically opposed. 'Couples just live together. After all, there isn't a great deal of point in marrying unless you're going to have –' Going to have children, she is about to say. But stops in time, for Deborah has recently been speaking of children as if they are a distinct possibility. Does she – *can* she – mean it? All right, she made her startling statement when she and Robyn were polishing off a very acceptable bottle of Muscadet, and before that each had drunk a large G and T, but there must, nevertheless, have been a grain of truth? *In vino veritas*, and all that?

2

Robyn tries to remember the exact exchange. She had remarked to Debs that babies definitely got better once it became possible to reason with them, and Debs replied that she didn't care about the non-reasoning, she just loved holding them, caring for them, adored the delightful, soapy, clean-soft-skin smell.

Perhaps, Robyn now thinks, I'm worrying about nothing. Debs's comment didn't *really* suggest she was about to rush out and get pregnant there and then. Did it? Anyway, reflects Robyn somewhat grimly, she hasn't got to grips with the truth about babies if she thinks they habitually smell of soap and clean skin. Far from it.

She tries to recall what she was saying. Remembers. Says, 'I mean, when both partners have careers, do people really need an old-fashioned institution like marriage? It's not as if you, of all people, need the security.'

She senses Deborah stirring beside her. Looks down, sees the large brown eyes open, a slight frown disturbing the smooth brow. Replacing another, fleeting expression that is there and gone too swiftly for Robyn to catch. '*You* got married,' Debs points out reasonably. 'Twice.'

'I know, but I was pregnant the second time.' In the heat of the moment, Robyn is not sure whether this fact weakens or strengthens her attempt to put the anti-marriage case.

Neither, apparently, is Deborah. The frown has melted away, and the tender expression is back. 'I was married in a shocking pink suit, when I married Br – . . . the first time,' she says.

Robyn notices that she does not inflict upon herself the pain of mentioning her first husband's name unless it is absolutely necessary.

Debs shoots Robyn a quick glance, her face full of humour. Had Robyn only caught that look, she would have realised without a doubt that Debs is teasing. 'I know that forty-six is too old for the full bridal bit' – it's also a bit old for contemplating having babies, Robyn thinks – 'but what do you think about a creamy-coloured, chiffony dress thing? And a big hat? Could I get away with it? And loads of cream flowers . . .' Her eyes close, and Robyn is horribly certain that some highly charged romantic scene is being enacted behind their lids. After a moment, the quiet humming of the Wedding March resumes.

Robyn stands up. The temptation is strong to pack up the picnic and pull the rug out from under Deborah's recumbent form, her bad temper putting a sharp edge on every gesture. But she restrains herself. What *is* the point? Deborah will do what she wants to do, being free, single, and over twenty-one. Well over.

Robyn walks away, down the slope of the meadow towards the fence which marks off the danger area, where the ground begins to crumble towards the cliffs. She leans on the top rail of the fence, eyes narrowed against the glare off the sea. Eastbourne to the left, Seaford off to the right. And up there, on the top of Beachy Head, a telephone with a direct line to the Samaritans. People sometimes put flowers on the spot from which the dead had leapt.

Robyn wonders why her thoughts have turned that morbid way. Suicide is as far from her own mind as the rings of Saturn; she is not, she tells herself, the suicidal type. Perhaps if she were in great pain, yes. Mentally she composes what she would say to her sons.

With a distinct effort she makes herself stop.

It is a glorious day, she reminds herself. Saturday, so no work tomorrow. Not that she dislikes her work – far from it. She only works part time – intermittently, actually, is a more accurate description – and just recently she seems to have fallen into the happy position of having sufficient engagements when she wants them. Her current account contains nearly eight hundred pounds, which gives her a nice warm glow whenever she thinks about it. She has decided she can definitely afford the jacket she's seen in Hoopers' sale. The bills are all paid, clean sheets are on the beds, house left tidy, supper in the freezer for when she and Debs get home this evening. Nothing awful looming on the horizon, no more traumas in sight.

God willing.

Superstitiously she crosses her fingers. Nemesis never sleeps; she is always alert for the smug attitude that says, I've had my share of bad luck, it's going to be plain sailing from now on!

Deliberately Robyn turns her thoughts to the bland contemplation of what colour she will paint the downstairs loo. And, eventually, she returns to Deborah.

PART ONE

Beginnings

CHAPTER ONE

When Robyn was widowed and, her family grown up, left to manage a large home all on her own, her decision to take in a female lodger surprised her mother.

'Why do you want to live with another woman?' Frances had asked, not for the first time, as Robyn put a plateful of salmon mousse and fresh vegetables in front of her; knowing that announcing her intentions to her mother might well be a sticky moment – Frances, happily married for fifty-plus years to Robyn's father, was a founder member of the marriage appreciation society – Robyn had put her heart into the meal. Salmon mousse was one of her mother's favourites. 'Nice mousse, darling,' Frances went on, poking it with an inquisitorial fork, 'the consistency's just right.'

'Thank you.' There was crème brulée to follow, and Robyn had bought a small box of very expensive Belgian chocolates to go with the coffee. Frances had a sweet tooth.

'I mean,' Frances went on, returning to the subject of Robyn's proposed lodger, 'it's not as if you've gone funny, is it, darling?' She laughed lightly, a melodious, tinkly sound, like bells; Robyn recognised it as a relic from her mother's days on the stage. In the well-thumbed but fairly thin album containing Frances's reviews, there was more than one reference to 'Frances Holly's beautiful musical tones'. Holly hadn't actually been Frances's maiden name, it had been her middle name. But with a surname like Buggins, you could hardly blame her for adopting a soubriquet. Marrying

Robyn's father and becoming Frances Swift had, no doubt, come as a great relief.

'Gone funny?' she repeated, privately amused. 'Mum, whatever do you mean?'

'Oh, you know!' Frances, quite unembarrassed, reached for the mange tout peas. 'Are these fresh, darling?'

'Yes. Are you suggesting that, merely because I'm not instantly out there hunting for a new man, it must mean I've turned into a lesbian?'

Frances smiled, then laughed again. 'No, sweetie, I'm suggesting you're not. I said, if you recall, it's *not* as if you've gone funny.'

'Well, I haven't.' Robyn felt it was necessary to say so. 'I need a lodger because I can't afford to run this place on my own, and the property market is so depressed at the moment that I won't get a decent price for it if I sell.' The estate agent, walking round the huge house with a clipboard and a turgid expression on his face, had kept saying things like, 'Six bedrooms! Dear, dear. You don't really get those big families any more,' and, 'Of course, a working woman doesn't thank you for three toilets and two bathrooms, not when it's her who has to clean them.' *She*, Robyn had silently corrected him, tense with the strain of fuming at his dismissal of her loved home and not letting it show.

'You should sell, darling.' Frances looked sympathetically at her daughter. 'Haydon Hall must be full of memories. Zach did have a way of marking his territory, didn't he?' She smiled indulgently. She had been very fond of her second son-in-law.

'You make him sound like a terrier,' Robyn remarked mildly.

'Oh, darling, I didn't mean to!' Frances, who was possessed of a strong sense of what could and could not be said to new widows, looked upset. 'Of course I didn't mean to imply –'

Robyn reached out and took her hand. 'I know you didn't, Mum. And you're right, Zach had a strong personality and yes, he did put his stamp on the house.' She looked around her, remembering. When Zach had first become ill, they'd installed a shower in the downstairs loo to save him having to go upstairs. He'd insisted on having the altered cloakroom painted a nice, bright colour; Robyn had returned from a shopping trip to London to find the decorator finishing the second coat of deep turquoise blue. It did look good against the terracotta colour of the basin and the loo, but the shade was far too dark.

'I wanted it to look like home,' Zach had said, a catch in his voice. 'I will not see my beloved Crete again.'

Sometimes, Robyn had reflected ruefully, it was like living with Cassandra and a miserable, doom-laden chorus rolled into one. It was, she supposed, one of the penalties of being married to a Greek.

'Shouldn't it be a brighter blue, if you want it to be like the Cretan sea?' she suggested. 'It does make the room look awfully small.'

'You don't like it.' Zach clapped a dramatic hand to his forehead. 'Ach! You preferred your pale cream. Your *magnolia*.' He managed to invest the innocuous word with considerable venom. 'You can redecorate when I'm gone.'

She had tried to reassure, to say, I love it! It was just a bit of a surprise!, but he had gone, shuffling off into his study with the invalid's gait he had adopted since his stroke.

She sat now at the lunch table with her mother, remembering. Wishing, as she often did, that she could put the clock back and act differently. Do better. Run after Zach, throw her arms round him and tease him out of his pessimism. Reassure him, make him smile, force him to realise that a stroke might be a warning sign but was not necessarily going to lead to imminent death.

Only, in Zach's case, it had done.

Frances cleared her throat. 'Robyn?'

'Sorry, Mum, I was miles away.' She noticed her mother's empty plate. 'More mousse?'

'I – yes, please, darling.'

Spooning out mousse and new potatoes, Robyn reflected that her mother's discreet idea of how to behave to the new widow must include the directive, don't put in a request for more grub when she's remembering her dead husband.

'We have to eat,' she said, thinking what an idiotic remark it was.

But her mother seized on it with relief. 'Yes! And, darling, you must never think Zach would want you to pine away. You must get on with your life – why, he'd hate to think of you grieving!'

He wouldn't, Robyn thought. He would virtually expect it. But I am grieving, in my own way, so that's all right.

'Getting on with my life is why I'm advertising for a lodger,' she said. 'But don't worry, I'm being very careful. I've spoken to my solicitor, who put me on to a man who specializes in the law as applied to letting. Everything'll be water tight.'

'The legal side wasn't what was bothering me,' Frances said, 'although it might concern your father. It's the idea of your living with a woman, when up till now you've had so many men.' She could, Robyn reflected, have phrased it less ambiguously. 'Darling, how will you *adjust*?'

Robyn cleared the plates and put them down rather too firmly on the draining board. 'That,' she said, with a finality meant to imply the subject was closed, 'remains to be seen.'

*

Robyn had been born, educated and had lived most of her married life in or around the same town, only leaving it for short spells to live in London with her first husband and in Athens and Crete with her second. Some people found

Tunbridge Wells over-fussy, with its self-consciously pretty Pantiles and its wealth of Decimus Burton buildings that were bound up solid with preservation orders and Neighbourhood Watch, but Robyn liked it. It might have been that she was merely used to it, or, more accurately, had grown used to it; she hadn't appreciated plus points such as elegance, the Common and proximity to Channel ferries and airports when she was a teenager, roaming the streets with nothing to do except go to the cinema or hang around Forté's café. Then it had seemed an elderly town, over-full of middle-class, disapproving people who complained, as the raucous sixties got into their confident stride, that 'youths' hadn't behaved like that in *their* day. Once, an acquaintance of Robyn's father had come across her lying out in the sun in Calverley Grounds, entwined with a boyfriend and smoking. She had lived in trepidation for many days in case he passed his obvious disapproval on; thankfully, he hadn't.

Her friends then had included a wild child or two: in the second form at grammar school, one friend hadn't known whether the continued absence of the onset of menstruation had been because she was a naturally late starter or because she was pregnant; Robyn, innocent still, had none the less thought that explained why her mother had refused to allow her to stay overnight at that particular friend's house. It quite definitely explained some rather odd sounds Robyn had heard coming from behind the sofa when, at the friend's house for an unsupervised tea party, she had thought the mixed group of boys and girls were meant to be playing sardines.

She did better at A level than anyone had apparently expected; her university application, filled in dutifully despite the fact that she wasn't at all sure she really wanted to go, had resulted in five rejections and a waiting list. Bs for English and French and a C for History had nudged Keele into thinking she might be an adjunct, after all, and she went apprehensively off to Staffordshire the October after she left school.

She realized just how thorough had been her failure to impress herself on her school when, on making the formal visit to the headmistress to say her farewells, the woman had said, 'And who, actually, are you?'

She had always sung. Primary school concerts, grammar school choir, and, at university, a folk group; on graduation, in the absence of any enticing career offer, she took a daytime job driving a delivery van and, several evenings or Saturdays each month, sang with a band who hired themselves out to weddings and dances.

She met her first husband at a wedding. It was a lush do, the reception held by the bride's parents at their huge house in deepest Sussex, candy-striped marquee on the lawn, a hundred and fifty guests in morning dress and expensive frocks milling about ooh-ing and aah-ing over the wildly expensive presents and the bride's fifteen-foot train.

The band was installed in a particularly ill-ventilated corner of the marquee. Belting out 'Secret Love' – a special request from the bride, who admitted coyly that it was 'our tune' – Robyn reflected that, for all the notice anyone was taking, they might as well have put on records. The second vocalist, who also played sax, put aside his instrument and came to join her, harmonising easily; between verses, he said in her ear, 'Hear them braying, down there? Like a load of fucking donkeys, aren't they?'

Trying and failing to suppress a laugh, she agreed that they were.

And it was at that moment, laughing at the loud guests whose upper-class manners didn't include polite appreciation of a live performance, that she first set eyes on Paddy Kingswood.

Squeezed into a grey morning suit that couldn't quite accommodate his broad shoulders, he looked more like a bouncer than a guest. She told him so later, when, the bride and groom having left in a flurry of confetti that would be hell to clear off the smoothly-raked gravel drive, he approached her with two glasses of champagne and the opening remark, 'I don't suppose you've had any of this?'

She realized fairly soon that he was quite drunk. She, on the other hand, was sober; he'd been right, the band had somehow been missed out by the waiters circulating with laden trays of Veuve Cliquot. She was contemplating whether or not it would be fun to get drunk with him when he said suddenly, 'Can you drive?'

'Yes.' Actually, she could have added, I earn my living driving.

'Feel like driving us somewhere nice for dinner?' He was lying on the flattened grass in front of the small stage where the band had been playing; conscious of her new apple-green dress, she was perched on the edge of the stage. He looked up at her, and she noticed how very long his eyelashes were.

'Okay,' she said, trying to sound casual.

'We'll finish this' – he up-ended the champagne bottle he'd removed from a waiter's tray into his mouth; it would have been more accurate, she thought, to say, *I'll* finish this, '– and we'll go.'

She insisted on collecting her fee before they left, which was just as well since Paddy discovered he hadn't got any money. She offered to lend him a fiver, which paid for their supper. She drove him home in his car – it turned out not to be one of the great array of sports cars she'd spotted on the field being used as a car park for the wedding reception, but was a sedate grey Austin Cambridge – and he kissed her goodbye on his own doorstep.

It was, fortunately, only a ten-minute walk from his house to hers. And it was a fine night.

She hadn't expected to see either him or her five pounds again. But a week later a card arrived, and, on opening it, a brand-new fiver fluttered out.

Paddy had written inside the card, which was actually a Christmas card and thus quite inappropriate for September, 'I'm in T. Wells on Friday. If you'll agree to have dinner with me again, I promise I won't touch you for another loan. If you're free, phone me on this number at around six on Friday.'

She was free, and she did phone him.

It was the start of a lively courtship, spent mainly in pubs and rugby clubs, which led to her moving in with him after six months and marrying him within the year.

Paddy had a flat in London, where he worked for an import company. The Tunbridge Wells house was his parents' home; he had been in the habit of returning each weekend to play rugby for the local fifteen. When Robyn moved into the London place with him, she tried to encourage the development of a new, joint circle of friends in the vicinity of the flat, but her suggestions of inviting this or that couple for dinner, of joining one or two local clubs and associations, fell largely on stony ground.

They married quietly in the local register office, and, after a honeymoon in Italy, returned to the flat. It was very small, and looked even more so now that it had to accommodate the wedding presents; Robyn's parents had given them a large leather sofa, which was lovely and very generous of them, but which made it almost impossible to open the living room door widely enough to get through the gap, especially carrying anything larger than a book.

For eighteen months, they continued in their carefree ways. Being married didn't make much difference to their social life; despite having a very acceptable home of their own, if anything they seemed to spend even more time in the clubs and pubs. They travelled quite a lot; Paddy's job took him to places like Amsterdam, Marseilles and Naples, and sometimes Robyn went with him. She had given up driving her van since moving out of Tunbridge Wells, and was now working only as a singer; a contact of one of her old band members had put her on to a record producer looking for session singers, and she regularly provided the *ooo-eeees* and the *sha-la-las* which backed some of the seventies' best-known stars.

Their first child was born in June 1973. They called him Timothy Patrick, after Robyn's grandfather and the baby's own father. After a few months of taking him around everywhere with them, they – or rather Robyn – realized that the old life must now come to an end. A rugby club bar, swilling with spilt beer and thick with cigarette smoke, was no place for a baby.

She started to let Paddy go out on his own. It was a shame – she'd enjoyed the carefree life – but then things were different, now. There was Tim to think of.

And the flat, it was rapidly becoming obvious, was far too small for the two of them plus infant. Although Paddy didn't seem to appreciate the problem, Robyn worked away at him until, reluctantly, he agreed they should move.

In April 1974, when she was three months pregnant with her second child, they left London. They moved into a terraced house in Tunbridge Wells, and, with enormous and understandable reluctance, Paddy became a commuter.

The terraced house lasted them until their second child, Stephen, was almost six months old. Then Robyn's great-uncle conveniently died and left her £10,000, an unexpected piece of good fortune which, combined with Paddy's recent promotion, gave them enough to sell the terraced house and buy Haydon Hall. It was a shambles when they bought it, which was why they got it so cheaply; it was still mostly a shambles eighteen months later, when Robyn and Paddy's third son, William, was born.

Robyn had realized by then that, if she was ever to have the cosy and comfortable family home she craved, she was going to have to make it happen herself. In four years of marriage, Paddy had painted one door and put up two small shelves in a pantry. Robyn had had to re-do the door, and one of the shelves – the one which didn't have a large nail banged in underneath it – was crooked.

Tim and Stevie were old enough to be left at home with their father, but she was still breastfeeding Will when she enrolled on the DIY course. It might have been less awkward had the majority of the people on the course not been men, but the chaps were very sweet, and soon got used to her nursing Will in the coffee break. One of them proved to be better at winding babies than Robyn; it became a regular occurrence, during the first ten minutes of the second lecturing session, for him to walk up and down with Will on his shoulder until the necessary burp was produced. Once, the lecturer, a middle-aged man with a weary expression that seemed to suggest he'd seen it all, said, as the burp resounded round the room, 'Ah! There 'e blows.'

Family life finally became too much for Paddy, and he moved back to London. He said it was because he was spending such long hours in the office that it just wasn't practical to keep coming home to Tunbridge Wells every night, especially when the company were offering help with London accommodation, and Robyn accepted his reasoning.

But they both knew it was an excuse. Paddy wasn't cut out for parenthood; he had neither the patience nor the skill required for dealing with very small children.

And he must have known – Robyn certainly did – that apart from financially she could manage without him. Manage better, for when he was home he felt the need to impose his way of doing things, which wasn't necessarily the way in which they were done when he wasn't around.

He had been living in London for several months before Robyn realized that he wasn't living there alone. He was a frequent visitor to Haydon Hall, usually bringing presents and sometimes a bottle of wine for him and Robyn to share. Often, when he did that, they would end up making love. Which was, she reflected during that strange period of being married yet *not* being married, only to be expected, really.

During his 1976 Christmas visit he told her about Karen. After the initial shock wore off, Robyn realised she was neither particularly surprised nor particularly hurt.

They were divorced in January 1978.

Life at Haydon Hall went on largely as it had done before; Paddy earned enough to be able to support them adequately if not luxuriously, and Robyn, disliking the dependent role, started part-time work. The boys were so used to their father not being around that they didn't appear to miss him; once he came to visit accompanied by Karen, and that seemed to be all right, too.

In 1979, when the boys would be six, five and three, Robyn decided that she would take them away for a real summer holiday. She would work flat-out for four months, saving every penny, and she would fly her sons out to some sunny spot and install them in an apartment for a fortnight, longer, if she could manage it.

She chose Crete because the boys had liked the illustration of the bull-leaper in the holiday brochure; Tim said the bull had its horn through the acrobat's body, and all three sons seemed to find this gory enough for at least two minutes' undivided attention.

She booked them into a small and pretty basic family hotel, which was heaven as far as the boys were concerned because it had a little swimming pool. Tired from the exacting life she'd been living for the past few months – it wasn't easy, she had found, combining two part-time jobs with running a home and three young children – Robyn was content to lie beside the pool with a succession of lighthearted novels.

It was there, one morning soon after the start of their holiday, that she met Zacharias.

CHAPTER TWO

He had tripped over another sunbather's outstretched leg, and his foot had landed squarely in the small of Robyn's back.

When apologies had been offered and reassurances given that she was quite all right – a lie, actually, since her back hurt like mad and she subsequently developed an enormous bruise – he said gravely, 'My name is Zacharias Kazandreas, but my foreign friends call me Zach.'

'Robyn Kingswood,' she said, glad that she was to call him by the short form, since his full name seemed to contain rather a lot of sounds which the average English person would find embarrassing to express. A bit like clearing one's throat in preparation for a good spit.

He had insisted on installing her at a table beneath an umbrella, where he clicked his fingers at a distant barman and procured for her a tiny cup of very strong black coffee. It was, she discovered on tasting it, extremely sweet; maybe it was the Greek equivalent of a nice cup of hot, sugary tea. She had, after all, had a shock. A very slight one.

He leaned forward, watching her intently as she drank it. 'Mm, lovely,' she said, trying to chew a mouthful of grouty bits without it being too obvious, 'thanks very much.'

He had removed his sunglasses as they sat down in the shade of the umbrella, and she noticed that his eyes were very dark brown. He was quite short, wiry-looking, and, she guessed, in his mid-forties, some fifteen years older than herself. He looked rather like a world-weary, greying Al Pacino. 'You are better now,' he observed, 'your cheeks have more colour.'

For some reason his remark made her self-conscious; she was not used to being minutely studied by middle-aged strangers with disturbing dark eyes. Especially when she was wearing a bikini and he was dressed for the street. 'I feel fine,' she said, laughing nervously. 'Honestly, there was no need for the coffee!'

'You do not like it?'

'Yes! It was lovely!'

'Hah! You want another?' He was already looking round for the waiter.

'No! I mean, it did the trick.' He frowned slightly. 'Made me feel all right again.' This was getting silly. She had never seriously felt *not* all right, but if he bought her another cup of coffee, she might throw up.

'Did the trick,' he muttered. 'It did the trick. Thank you, it did the trick.' Then, obviously pleased at having learned a new English idiom, he flashed her a marvellous smile and asked her to have lunch with him.

*

She didn't accept; not that time. She explained about Tim, Stevie and Will, pointing them out as they played in the pool. Will was in armbands in the area reserved for the very small – the water was only inches deep and a smiling young Greek sat on the edge keeping an eye on the little ones – but Tim and Stevie were out in the main pool, preoccupied with their new masks and snorkels. She had hardly seen their faces all morning, and they must by now be familiar with every single square centimetre of the bottom of the pool. Zach watched the boys for a few moments, then nodded approvingly, remarking that they were fine, strong sons.

Nothing is guaranteed to go more directly to the heart of

22

a mother than praise for her offspring. Robyn, in two minds as to whether a lunch or dinner date with this man was a good idea, waved a swift goodbye to her reservations and agreed to meet him that evening for a drink in the hotel bar.

*

He was forty-six, divorced – his wife had gone to live in Sweden, which had puzzled Robyn until Zach had added that she was in fact Swedish – and he owned a hotel and several blocks of holiday apartments. Or rather, it became clear, he owned them in conjunction with his two brothers. The hotel in which they sat was actually owned by the family, but, being rather small and humble, had been given to a younger cousin to run. Rather, she thought, in the manner in which a rich man might give a poor relation his cast-off overcoat.

He had a house in the country outside Rethymnon and an apartment in Athens. When he had arrived that evening, she had noticed – she had been watching out for him – that he drove a large Mercedes.

The Kazandreas family, it became apparent, were not short of a bob or two.

He did not take her out that night, because she could not leave the boys. 'I will arrange for someone to care for them,' he said, staring into her eyes in a way that made her feel a strange tightening right in the middle of her body. 'My cousin has a daughter, several daughters – I will tell him to make one go to sit with your sons. Tomorrow night.'

She wondered how this unknown girl would feel about being summarily ordered to give up an evening to babysit three small English boys. How, indeed, the boys would feel about it, although this was actually of lesser importance since they were usually asleep soon after seven and she could wait with them until then. And, quite an important consideration, would this girl be expecting to be paid?

23

'I – perhaps I could meet the girl?' she said. Intent dark eyes and melting insides notwithstanding, she must remember that the most important consideration was the boys' welfare.

'Naturally.' He was looking at her with approval. 'You would not wish to leave your sons with an entire stranger.'

She tried to suppress a laugh and failed. 'Sorry,' she said. He raised an eyebrow. 'Entire is not the right word. Total stranger is better.'

'Total stranger,' he repeated. 'Okay. I will tell Elara to come to see you tomorrow. Then she will call me if you agree to her as a child minder of your sons.'

She took another sip of her drink. Accepting this girl – this Elara – would be, it appeared, the prelude to accepting Zach's invitation to dinner. Since that was at the same time a thrilling and an alarming prospect, something she both wanted very much to do and yet was afraid of doing, she had another sip. Finished her drink.

And found that he had ordered her a fresh one.

Some time later – she had been upstairs twice to check on the boys and found them fast asleep – Zach announced he was going home. Slipping off his bar stool, he held out his hand to her, and she took it. On shaky legs – quite a lot to drink plus fierce sexual attraction packed a heavy punch – she walked out to the car park with him.

He had left the Mercedes in a dark corner beneath an awning which, during the day, gave much-needed shade. Now, it provided privacy; as he drew her to him and kissed her, she wondered if he had foreseen this moment and had deliberately parked his car in a secluded spot.

As the kiss continued, she decided there was no *if* about it.

*

Elara turned out to be a friendly, self-assured young woman in her late teens or early twenties; she was round and very

24

dark, with more than a suspicion of facial hair, and Robyn's three boys took a shine to her straight away. She suggested, sensibly, that she spend the morning with the boys in Robyn's company, explaining in halting English that they would more readily accept her as a friend if their mother was there with them too. By lunchtime Tim and Stevie had persuaded her to go and put her swimming costume on so that she could have a go with the new snorkels, and Will said he loved her and could she go back to England with them?

As if fate were taking a helping hand, in the afternoon Tim and Stevie made friends with some children who had recently arrived, a brother and three sisters from Norwich whose parents had bought them an inflatable boat. The newcomers' parents, a relaxed couple who apparently wanted to do nothing more on their holiday than lie flat-out on loungers, occasionally stirring to re-oil each other, took the view that three extra children didn't make much difference when you had four already. They obligingly strolled into Rethymnon in the early evening and bought a second inflatable boat, to avoid, they explained to Robyn, too much squabbling over whose turn it was.

With minimal effort on Robyn's own part, her children now had a babysitter for the evenings and a ready-made family of playmates for the daytime.

When, five days later, the family from Norwich asked if Robyn's three would like to go with their lot to spend the afternoon on the beach, it seemed like a gift from the gods. Robyn was hesitating – Will was so little! supposing he got into difficulties? – when the wife, as if reading her mind, said not to worry, she would keep a special eye on the littlest one. 'He can sit with me, we'll build a sandcastle,' she suggested comfortably.

It seemed like a heavenly gift because, the previous evening, Zach had hinted there would be nobody at home that afternoon. If Robyn could arrange for her boys to be looked after, they could have his house to themselves . . .

By now, after nearly a week of furtive kisses in the car park and a very brief session on their own in Robyn's room, with the door to the boys' quarters ajar and Robyn tense with fear that one of them would wake up and come stumbling in, the sexual tension between her and Zach had become almost unbearable. She tried to appear normal for the boys' sake, although the very sight of food made her feel sick and she couldn't eat any lunch.

The Norwich people swept the boys up soon after two o'clock, and Robyn's three raced away without a backward glance. Robyn showered and dressed, then went downstairs to wait for Zach.

The two hours they spent entirely alone, in the thick-walled, cool old house hidden away in the hills, was a time that Robyn never forgot. When the first wild lovemaking was over, and they had temporarily assuaged their hunger, he fetched a bottle of cold retsina, climbed back into bed beside her and, lighting a cigarette, said, 'Now, talk to me.'

It was not only she who did the talking; once his direct and penetrating questions had extracted from her more about herself than she had believed she knew, he began to reciprocate. To tell her, in exchange for the full run-down on life with Paddy and the birth of her three boys, about the Swedish ex-wife and the progeny of the marriage. He had, he told her expressionlessly, only one child. And she was a girl.

Robyn didn't notice, at the time. Or, if she did, the fleeting impression was quickly subsumed by other things. By intimate, lighthearted conversation, by passionate and highly satisfying lovemaking. Only later – years later – did she remember. Or, more accurately, *think* she remembered. That expression of regret. That frown as he explained, with cruel frankness, that his former wife, not wanting more children, refused to have sex with him after the birth of his daughter.

It was only later, too, that she saw the significance of that exchange, in his bed just after they had made love for the first time. She, so she had revealed, had conceived and borne three strapping sons, one after the other, in under four years. It had been – and she recalled her own words – just like shelling peas.

It was tactless, she subsequently decided, to declare her male-orientated fecundity quite so freely to a son-hungry divorcé with one daughter and a frigid ex-wife. Not only tactless, but far more significant than she could have imagined.

*

She had assumed it was just a holiday romance. Had thought, as the happy days with the children and the wonderful, snatched moments alone with Zach continued, that, although thrilling and highly enjoyable, their affair would burn itself out. That, when the time came for her to return home to Tunbridge Wells, she would kiss him goodbye with perhaps a tear but with no regrets. And, more crucially, no promises to come back next year.

It didn't turn out that way.

She missed him. Badly.

He telephoned, one evening in September when she had had a row with Tim over his new trainers (he had gone paddling in the stream and their pristine whiteness was now an irrevocable, dirty beige) and was trying to make Stevie switch off the telly and learn his spellings. Picking up the receiver, she said angrily, 'Yes?'

There was a pause, and then Zach's deep voice said, 'I think maybe this is a bad moment.'

Her heart gave such a violent thud that she wondered if she'd done herself some harm. She said softly, 'Zach.' Then, before she could stop herself, work out whether it was sensible when, up till now, they had both played it cool, burst out, 'It's so lovely to hear you! Life's shitty here, I'm really pissed off and I wish I'd never left Crete!'

'Shitty,' he murmured. 'Life is shitty.'

She did not think that particular expression was one he should add to his rapidly expanding collection of well-known English phrases. 'I didn't mean –'

But he interrupted her. 'Life here, too, is shitty,' he said solemnly. 'It is because you are no longer with me. I wish, Robyn, to see you again.'

To have what she had desperately longed for so suddenly expressed by him, too, made her want to sing. It also prompted a small voice of reason to whisper: watch out!

The little voice was easily annihilated.

'Oh, I want to see you, too!' she said. 'Can you come here?'

'To England? To Tunbridge Wells?' He said the name of the town slowly, making it sound absurd. She could hear that he was smiling.

'It's quite a nice place.' She was smiling, too. Laughing, from sheer happiness. 'I told you, didn't I, that it has many fine buildings and much interesting history?'

'You told me, yes. I said you were speaking like a guide-book.'

The exchange had taken place in his bed. He had interrupted a spell of licking the golden down on her stomach to ask suddenly where she lived. She wondered if he remembered the moment as vividly as she did.

'Do you still have your suntan?' he asked, his voice husky. 'And the beautiful line where the tan ends and the skin is pale, like cream?'

She swallowed. 'Yes.' The word came out in a slight squeak. 'Zach, you didn't answer. Can you come to Tunbridge Wells?'

'No. Robyn, it is not possible for me to be away, when

28

still the tourist season is occupying me. And, also, there has been a problem with one of the apartment blocks – a shower was broken, and nobody thought to tell me, so that a floor is flooded.'

'Oh, dear.' Her response was, she felt, unsatisfactory, but broken showers and floods did not seem to be able to compete with her disappointment. To be speaking to him, and to imagine, if only for a moment, that they might be about to be reunited, then to have that brilliant prospect snatched away!

'But, Robyn, what is to stop you returning to Crete?' he said.

God! Three children and no money for starters, she thought angrily. She said, fairly coldly, 'It's not easy for me, either.'

He sighed. She heard it, quite distinctly, over the however many hundreds of miles separating them. 'Your children have a father, is it not so? You have taken them on a holiday, so does this father not want to take a turn, too? So, it is simple.' It bloody well isn't, she thought. 'You ask this man to look after them, and you fly out to see me.'

She said dully, 'I can't afford it.' There was no obvious point in pretending otherwise.

He hesitated. 'Then I will pay your fare.'

'You mustn't do that!'

'Robyn, do not be *English*. I will not miss the price of an air ticket, but you will. Since we both want to see each other, is it not as much for me to pay for the ticket as for you?'

His logic was hard to refute. 'I suppose so.'

'Ach! It is fixed, then. You send your sons to their father, and you fly out to me.'

'But –'

He waited. Almost as if he could hear the cogs in her brain turning round, throwing up objections then racing to overcome them, he sat patiently out there in Rethymnon until she was done. 'Okay,' she said quietly. 'I'll let you know when I've arranged everything.'

He said something in Greek.

'What was that?'

He laughed. 'Never mind. I will tell you when I see you. Perhaps.'

They said brief farewells, and she put the phone down. Going back to the living room, to Tim's spoiled trainers and Stevie's spellings, she wiped her wet hands on her skirt and hoped the hectic flush she could feel in her face would not be noticeable in artificial light.

*

She flew back to him at half term. Paddy, after initial surprise and detectable reluctance, had come round to thinking it wouldn't hurt to see a bit more of his children. Had, in his own inimitable style, convinced himself the whole thing had been his idea.

The boys were excited at the prospect of a week or so with their father. Robyn wondered if the excitement was more at the list of activities Paddy had promised them, but she told herself that was unfair. Paddy collected them after school on the Friday evening, setting off for London with minimal delay to avoid the worst of the traffic; ten minutes later, hurrying out of the house before she could start missing them, Robyn set off for Gatwick.

*

She and Zach had ten days of bliss. He was kind, generous, and he put himself out to entertain her and introduce her to his friends and family. They, too, were kind, welcoming her to join in the fun at a couple of parties, treating her at the same time like an honoured guest and like one of the family.

His daughter, whose name was Cliantha, treated Robyn neither like an honoured guest nor one of the family; in fact, after the first brief and uncomfortable meeting, she didn't reappear. Zach said, when Robyn asked, that she'd gone to stay with friends in Chania.

He took her on a three-day trip to Athens, and showed her the Parthenon and the archaeological museum. He also showed her his flat. It was luxurious in the extreme, and she did not allow herself to be disturbed by her discovery of what were clearly a woman's toiletries in a drawer in the sumptuous bathroom. So Zach had entertained other women in his flat. Why not? The women, whoever they were, weren't there *now*. Now, Zach was devoting himself to Robyn.

And at night, whether alone in his house near Rethymnon or in the Athens flat, they made love. Again and again, each time precious, each time an enhancement of what they felt for one another. There was no doubt of it now; they were in love.

*

He came to England at Christmas. On Christmas night, after the boys had gone to bed, she told him she was pregnant.

On 14 February the following year – it was a Thursday, but they both liked the idea of doing it on St Valentine's Day – they were married.

On 6 June 1980, Robyn's fourth and last son was born. At Zach's insistence, they selected Greek names, and he was christened Jerome Christopher.

Robyn, exhausted after nine months of an unplanned pregnancy and, for the first time, sore after a difficult birth and suffering from the back pain that was to plague her for the rest of her life, observed Zach holding the two-day old Jerome in his arms.

She didn't think she had ever seen a man look quite so ecstatically happy.

Robyn flumps down beside Deborah, who has fallen asleep with her mouth open. Despite this temporary handicap, Debs still looks beautiful. Robyn studies her. Dark hair, thick and naturally wavy. Olive skin, with a faint pinkish flush to the cheeks. Probably it's cosmetic rather than natural in origin – Debs is skilled at make-up, taking to heart Helena Rubenstein's dictum that there are no ugly women, only lazy ones. Still, Debs would be beautiful even if the world was still in the age of thick kohl lines all round the eyes or dead-white face paint like the first Queen Elizabeth.

Robyn, prompted to think about her own appearance, finds a hairbrush in her bag and tugs it through her hair. The wind has taken liberties with this morning's careful arrangement of scrunchie and pins; perhaps, Robyn thinks, Debs is right and it's time I had it cut.

Zach had loved her long hair. But Zach is dead. Possibly a new external image will assist the development of the new person inside.

'Debs, shall we –' Robyn breaks off. It is a pity to wake Debs, who looks so happy. So peaceful. She who has had so much in her troubled past that is *un*happy, *un*peaceful. Robyn's dilemma returns, hitting out hard: Deborah, who has survived her own past only through developing a courage she did not originally possess, is poised on the very brink of plunging herself back into the maelstrom. Or so Robyn believes.

Yes. It *is* time to wake Deborah up. For Robyn needs to talk to her.

'Debs?' She shakes the thin shoulder – really, Debs is far too skinny, it's clear this whole business isn't really making her happy or she'd be eating like a horse from sheer contentment and putting on weight like a Sumo wrestler – and says again, closer to Deborah's ear, 'Debs!'

'Mmmmmmmm,' Deborah says by way of response; her eyes are still shut, but a beatific smile has spread across her face.

Possibly it is not the right moment to come right out with it and say, look, Debs, you've got a diabolical track record with men, you should no more be contemplating remarriage than flying to the moon without breathing apparatus. Maybe, thinks Robyn, the subtle approach is more appropriate?

Robyn is not very good at being subtle. She thinks on her feet, hits from the shoulder. Such is her self-image. She admits ruefully to being blunt, unimaginative, but there is more to her than this.

Deborah is now awake. She sits up, stretches her arms above her head, the slim, graceful fingers extended as if she is practising spanning an octave. The right hand bears a small ring – five cabuchon garnets set in gold, the garnet being Deborah's January birthstone – but the left is bare. Deborah's wedding and engagement rings were sold to pay off some of her shit of a husband's debts. A very small part of them.

Another legacy from Deborah's husband is the scar she bears above her right eyebrow. He threw a spanner at her.

Filled with sudden powerful affection – an emotion containing a good deal of protective love – Robyn sits down on the rug and flings an arm round Debs's shoulders.

'I've had an idea,' she confides.

Deborah smiles. 'Oh, yes?'

'Mm. I've got fifty pounds in my purse, so let's not bother

33

about cooking anything tonight, let's stop at a pub and let someone else do the work. I'm driving, so you can have a few drinks. It's Sunday tomorrow, so we can sleep in, and if we – what's the matter? Why are you laughing?'

Deborah reaches up to take hold of Robyn's hand. 'Oh, it's just you!' She smiles at Robyn, giving the captive hand a squeeze as if to indicate that there is no malice in her laughter. 'Robyn, your motive is as clear as crystal. You're setting out to suggest to me that two women can have a good time living together, that it's perfectly possible to enjoy a full and satisfying life without s—' Without sex, Robyn imagines she is about to say. But Deborah has difficulty with sex. Difficulty, even, with saying the word. It is, like the absence of wedding ring and the scar, a left-over from the ex-husband, who did not believe that a married woman had a right to say no. '– Without men,' Debs substitutes, 'and this flurry of cheery outings is your way of proving it.'

Robyn is slightly hurt. Deborah, sensitive to the smallest nuance of body language, feels the reaction in Robyn's hand. 'I'm sorry I'm so obvious,' Robyn says neutrally.

Deborah twists round and hugs her. 'Don't be a prat,' she says affectionately. Then, more seriously, 'Robyn, I *know* what you think. I'm grateful, more than I can ever say, for what you've done for me – it's only *because* of you that I could even be contemplating getting involved again. But –' She pauses, the lovely face tense with concentration as she tries to put her deepest feelings into words; as ever, it is not easy. 'Could we not accept,' she goes on gently, 'that I'm better? That, recognizing my past mistakes, I'm not about to make the same ones again?'

There is a grain of truth in that, Robyn has to acknowledge. But she still has this dread fear that once a victim, always a victim. That Debs's past experiences have etched too deep a groove for her ever fundamentally to change.

Is it right for her to point this out?

Can she bring herself to do so, when Debs is apparently lit from within with the joy of what she believes is the newly found love of her life?

Robyn stares for a moment into the luminous face.

Then, unable to answer her own questions, turns away.

PART TWO

Departures

CHAPTER THREE

Had Zach lived, Robyn would not have advertised for a lodger. Would not have needed to, for, until Zach's death, the house had always seemed full. Apart from Zach, who, as Frances intimated, did have a talent for imposing his personality on a place, there was Jerome, still at school, and the temporary but frequent presence of the three older boys. Tim, equipped with an engineering degree, worked in the north, but his job was close enough to home for him to return most Saturdays and play for the second fifteen; Stephen, in his last year at university, liked to breeze in when he had nothing better to do and present his mother with a bin-liner full of dirty laundry; Will, in the middle of his degree course, found that Haydon Hall provided an atmosphere more conducive to study than his student digs in London.

But within days, almost, of Zach's funeral, suddenly everyone had to be somewhere else.

Hence Deborah.

*

As a husband, Zach, like most, had his strengths and his weaknesses. Marrying him after so short a courtship, Robyn was aware of few of either to begin with, and consequently she was in for both pleasant and unpleasant surprises.

Being an optimist, she preferred to dwell on the plus points. Until, that is, they were all but obliterated by the minus ones.

He continued to be generous, and, usually, kind. Only when his own desires conflicted directly with hers was he not kind: when that happened, his own wishes always prevailed. He adored Jerome, and was acceptably friendly to his stepsons; they, as far as Robyn was aware, liked him. They certainly liked the fact that he was married to their mother, because they had worried about her being on her own and could see for themselves that Zach made her happy.

They knew he made her happy, because she did not let them see any evidence to the contrary.

On the practical – and, let us admit, the mercenary – front, Zach was a first-rate husband. He was wealthy, certainly by Robyn's standards and probably by those of most people, and he enjoyed his wealth. The flat in Athens and the country house in Rethymnon were kept on even after Zach had bowed before common sense and agreed that they'd have to live mainly in Robyn's home, at least until the boys left school. The whole family made enthusiastic use of these exotic foreign homes; one year, when Tim, Stevie and Will had not yet reached the stage of wanting to do different things in the holidays, the family had spent every single school holiday in Greece; all four boys came back to England speaking basic but understandable Greek.

In the course of her marriage to Zach, Robyn received many extravagant presents, the majority of which could in some way be displayed about her person. Zach took an interest in her appearance, and, when she was wearing a new outfit or piece of jewellery, enjoyed watching the effect she – or, more likely, thought Robyn, *it* – had on other people.

The fact that Zach had to spend considerable time away from home, attending to hotel and apartment business in Crete, might have appeared to be a minus point but was, in fact, a plus. Before Zach, Robyn had been used to managing her home – and her children – virtually alone. She made her own decisions, brought up her sons in her own way. Zach, it soon became apparent, was not about to let that state of affairs continue while he was in residence; he had very strong views on how Jerome should be raised – most of which, fortunately, coincided roughly with Robyn's – and he usually had something to say about the majority of other domestic matters, from the minor, such as whether Stevie should have the most expensive football boots given that he never cleaned them, to the major. Such as, should Robyn go back to work? She lost that one. And, should they have another baby?

That one, she won.

It suited her that he was away so much. It meant she was free to revert to being captain of her own ship. And, more positively, it meant she could be genuinely welcoming, truly delighted to be with him again, when he returned to England.

And, as sailors and their wives are reputed to say, frequent absence made the heart grow fonder. Not to mention the more earthy parts of the body. After ten years of marriage, Robyn still enjoyed sex with Zach almost as much as in the hectic days when they were first together.

*

The trouble with Zach was that he allowed himself to grow old. Not so much allowed, positively encouraged it.

When Robyn celebrated her fortieth birthday, she still felt young. Her children were sixteen, almost fifteen, thirteen and nine; her husband was fifty-five. He should have felt young, too, Robyn told herself in irritation; why, he was active, lively-minded, still fully involved in the family business, still commuting between Crete and England, albeit not quite so frequently.

But he seemed to have resigned himself to age. Not middle age – that might have been tolerable – but, apparently, old age.

For a long time, Robyn did not understand why this was.

The reason, when she finally began to uncover it, was complex; was, really, two separate elements rolled together. And their combined effect, so it appeared, was too strong for Zach to resist.

Robyn had never fathomed out Zach's feelings towards his daughter, because he did not let her. His relationship with Cliantha, who, when he met Robyn, had been a rebellious sixteen-year-old, was uncomfortably stormy, so much so that, as soon as she had been old enough to get her own way, Cliantha preferred to live in her grandmother's house instead of her father's. Robyn would have liked to ask Zach how *he* felt about this, but, the one time she tried to broach the subject, had been met with such determined and angry stonewalling that she hadn't tried again.

However, there is always gossip in families, and, over the years, Robyn picked up enough loose threads to weave a fairly substantial garment. Cliantha, she gathered, had adored her Swedish mother, and had been devastated when she had left Crete and gone back to Sweden, promising to send for her daughter when she had found a place to live but, in fact, never fulfilling that promise. The best she had ever offered Cliantha was the occasional two-week holiday in some neutral location such as London or the Costa Brava. The holidays, according to Zach's sister-in-law Sophia – the most outspoken gossip of them all – were usually spent in such humble accommodation that Cliantha – 'and *that* one is not a child who will settle for second best!' – soon announced she preferred to stay at home.

There was, Robyn sensed, some basic malfunction in the father–daughter relationship, some element which made Cliantha constantly strive for her father's attention, only, it seemed, in order to do something outrageous and deeply upsetting when finally she got it. There had been many such incidents in the past, most of which were relayed in whispers to Robyn at various family gatherings, and, after Robyn and

Zach were married, they not only continued but, if anything, grew worse.

It was not that Cliantha wasn't invited to share her father's new family: quite the contrary. Robyn suggested she might think about coming to England, possibly to enrol in sixth form college, possibly to look for a job, and she offered not only help in finding Cliantha something suitable but also – and, she felt, more importantly – a welcoming home.

Cliantha received both offers with a stony silence. Prompted, not, in fact, by her father but by her clearly embarrassed grandmother, she turned a deceptively calm face to Robyn and announced she would not live in England if it were the last country on earth.

At eighteen, she was too old to be sent to her room. Or – as Robyn longed to do – be given a good smacked bottom.

And all of them – Zach, Zach's mother, his two brothers, Sophia, Robyn – meekly sat and watched as she took a cigarette from her father's packet, calmly lit it with his lighter, and, without a backward glance, sauntered out of the room and closed the door.

They saw little of her after that. She broke off diplomatic relations with Zach and Robyn, who had to find out how she was and what she was doing via Zach's mother. Zach, Robyn thought, probably made an effort to see her whenever he was in Crete on his own; once, when she had gone with him, they arrived at a party to find Cliantha ensconced in a corner with a man who looked only one up from a moron. She – and he – had left as soon as Robyn and Zach arrived.

The affair with the moron, if that was what it had been, did not last long. But, a year or so later, Cliantha left Rethymnon to set up home with some young man somewhere near Heraklion. Since she never wrote, Zach was not able to contact her; any communication had to originate from her, and she didn't choose to communicate.

Cliantha, then, was an abiding sorrow in Zach's life. So

Robyn believed. As such, she must surely account, in part, for Zach's air of pessimistic resignation.

The other element eroding his *joie de vivre*, which surfaced in the summer of 1998, when Zach was sixty-four, was his health.

*

In May of that year, Robyn had managed to persuade Jerome that it really would be fun to spend the whole of the summer holidays in Crete. Jerome, offered the carrot of being allowed to take his best friend Charlie with him, had finally agreed, and the four of them had flown out at the end of July.

Jerome and Charlie had quickly established a life of their own; Jerome was entirely at home in Crete, and long familiarity with his Greek relations meant that he was welcome in anything up to ten households in and around Rethymnon. He had a cousin with a boat, another cousin with a farm in the hills, and having uncles who ran hotels, bars and restaurants meant that he and Charlie never had to pay for a beer, a coffee or a meal. They didn't always come home to Robyn and Zach even to sleep, although Jerome faithfully kept his father's rule of always telephoning to say if he was staying out, and telling him who he and Charlie were staying with.

They were away from home the night Zach had his stroke.

Robyn and Zach had spent a lazy day. Zach had said he was tired, and he had a long sleep up on their bed during the heat of the afternoon. He appeared at six, and they went for a stroll, stopping to have a couple of drinks in one of the bars by the harbour. He ate hardly any supper; unusually for him, he complained of a headache.

At two-thirty in the morning, Robyn was woken from deep sleep by the sound of retching. Shocked into alertness, she sat up in bed, noticing that the bathroom light was on.

Running out of the bedroom, she reached the landing.

And saw him, slumped on the bathroom floor.

She fell on her knees beside him, shaking him, calling his name. His face was pale – bluish – and he was unconscious. A trickle of saliva ran from the corner of his mouth. He did not respond to either her cries or her shaking.

She had learned, years ago, how to summon the local emergency services. Now, her panicky inner being observing how calmly her hands performed the task, she rang for an ambulance.

The remainder of the night passed in a sort of trance. Rushed to the clinic, Zach was wheeled away on a trolley and she did not see him again for a long time. A nurse brought her a terrible cup of coffee, and a doctor appeared briefly to say that Zach was still unconscious but now less deeply, whatever that meant.

At some point she got up, found a phone and called Zach's mother. She would not have done so – the phone was a bad medium via which to break such news – except that Jerome was there, and it was awful to think of him returning home to an empty house with vomit on the bathroom floor.

Zach survived his first stroke, with only a very slight impairment of function in his right hand and arm to remind him of it.

To remind him physically, that is. But, to Robyn's great distress, he became, from that night on, an invalid.

She insisted that he consult her own doctor when they arrived back in England. There was no question, now, of spending the summer in Crete; Zach, pathetic in a chair under a checked blanket, had said feebly that he couldn't stand the light.

The English doctor confirmed what the Greek one had said: that Zach had suffered no lasting harm, and that, provided he heeded this warning sign and lived calmly and sensibly, keeping his blood pressure down, there was no need to fear that another stroke would occur.

But all the reassurances in the world could not get through

45

to Zach. He resigned himself to disability, worrying over every sneeze and shiver, refusing utterly to contemplate any form of exertion. Any form of exercise, even; he asked Robyn to enquire about getting him a wheelchair.

Assuming he was making an unnecessarily high mountain out of a molehill, Robyn tried to jolly him out of it. She had many private talks with the doctor – fortunately, a friend – and he encouraged her to take a 'nice, positive attitude – don't let him get morbid!'

She did her best. Even suggested they ask Cliantha to come and stay, thinking that a visit might cheer Zach up. Unfortunately, he seemed to think she was making the suggestion because she had been secretly told he hadn't long to live.

He now leaned on her for everything, demanding her arm to help him shuffle from his chair to the lavatory, ordering her to stand outside the little shower cubicle while he washed, assuming she had nothing better to do than sit taking notes while he went about the apparently mammoth task of putting his affairs in order. Their quarterly telephone bill was vast, and recorded that he had spent hours on the phone to his family in Crete.

There had been one very long call to Cliantha. Robyn never found out how he had managed to track her down – perhaps she had been at her grandmother's house when Zach had been talking to his mother, and obeyed the old woman's order to speak to him. The result had not been happy; Zach and Cliantha had obviously argued, and he had finished by shouting at her, slamming the receiver down so hard that the plastic cracked.

He insisted Robyn make him up a bed in the living room; he would not even climb the stairs last thing at night. She slept alone in their great double bed, suffering the anguish of loving him, being angry with him and sorely missing his physical presence, all at the same time.

'Oh, *Zach*!' she would yell aloud when, unable to stand the strain in the house any longer, she had taken herself out for a long, hard walk on the Common. 'Christ, what am I going to *do*?'

She didn't have to do anything. In the autumn, shortly before Robyn's forty-ninth birthday, Zach suffered another stroke. This time it wasn't a mild one: he died an hour and a half later, in the casualty department of the local hospital.

★

A huge delegation of Greek relatives came over for the funeral; Cliantha, who did not say a single word to Robyn for the entire duration of her visit, and who appeared strangely unmoved, was at all times flanked by aunts or female cousins. Some of the younger family members were emotional, but the old guard took their cue from Zach's mother, blank-faced in her grief and reserving her tears for the privacy of her room. Robyn had offered accommodation at Haydon Hall, but the family had kindly said she had enough to cope with already, and they checked into one of Tunbridge Wells's better hotels.

Tim, Stevie, Will and Jerome were with Robyn all the time. The older boys, although shocked, did not suffer as badly as Jerome, for their attitude towards Zach had been more one of respect than deep love. Jerome, though, had adored his father, sensing Zach's pride, sensing also, Robyn suspected, the indulgent attitude which meant that, had Jerome asked him for it, Zach would have given him the world.

Jerome, of all of them, would miss Zach most sorely.

Robyn kept a special eye on her youngest son in the painful, limbo days between Zach's death and his funeral. For herself, she appeared to be on automatic pilot: she would forget, sometimes, that he was dead, then have to go through the distress of remembering. Life was put on hold, as it always is until the dead are buried; accepting this, she did not demand too much of herself, instead quietly going about simple domestic tasks and, when she was tired, re-reading one or two of her favourite novels.

The older boys, taking their cue from her, tried to walk the tightrope of offering Jerome comfort and a shoulder to cry on when he needed it, and leaving him alone when he didn't. It wasn't easy.

★

The day of the funeral was bright and warm; as if the weather were giving to this son of Greece a final blessing, the sun shone down all day without interruption. The family had found a Greek Orthodox priest to hold the service, and the crematorium chapel was filled with unfamiliar sounds as he intoned the ritual.

When the coffin had disappeared, and the priest at last finished his interminable prayers and dismissed them with a blessing, it was a relief to go outside into the sunlight. Robyn stood in front of the great array of flowers, shaking hands, kissing cheeks; afterwards, she could not have said who was there, what remarks they made, how she replied.

She was swept up by the family. Her father, grave-faced, brisk and efficient, shepherded people out towards the car park, while Frances, in a very becoming black hat with a wide brim and a feather, employed her considerable charm to steer mourners away from her numb daughter before their supply of sympathetic small talk ran out.

With Tim and Will holding her hands and Stevie putting an arm round Jerome, Robyn was escorted away to what appeared to be a sort of wake, held in a large reception room at the hotel where the Kazandreas family were staying. A drink was thrust into her hand, trays of food were wafted under her nose. She felt detached, uninvolved, and quite dry-eyed; she wondered what had happened to her emotions.

48

Jerome was sitting with his paternal grandmother. She was talking quietly to him, and, although he was crying, he had a faint smile on his face. He was, Robyn thought, in the best place; she had enormous respect for her mother-in-law.

The Greeks were closing ranks. It was not that Robyn felt excluded; several of them had approached her, asked if she was all right, had all she needed. It appeared that they were expecting something of her, although she did not know what.

After some time, Stevie came to sit beside her.

'Are you okay, Mum?'

'Yes. I'm fine.'

He studied her for a few moments. Then: 'Mum, I was talking to Andreas – Zach's brother, you know?'

'Yes.' Andreas was a nice man.

'I – Mum, it's a bit awkward, but apparently they're wondering why you're not being like Grannie and Grandad. Why you're not joining in more.'

'Not – Stevie, I'm sorry, but I don't know what they expect.'

'No, no, I know that. They're not getting at you – it's just that . . .'

'Just that I'm cramping their style?' The remark was unjustified, when they were all trying so hard to be kind and considerate. 'Sorry. I didn't mean that.'

'No, I know. It's okay.'

They sat in silence for some minutes. Then Tim joined them. He put his arm round Robyn, the same brief intense hug he'd been giving her since he was tiny. 'Mum, why don't you go home?'

She looked up at him. 'Oh, Tim, *could* I?'

She had not realized, until he suggested it, that it was exactly – uniquely – what she wanted to do.

'Of course. The old lady suggested it, actually.' Robyn's affection for her mother-in-law went up a notch. 'She says

Grannie and Grandad are your representatives, and that you look stunned and would be better alone.'

How right she is, Robyn thought. 'Should I say my good-byes?' Suddenly she was the child, Tim the wise parent telling her what to do.

'No,' he said, gently helping her to her feet. 'I should just slip away. They'll understand.'

Stevie said, 'Do you want me to run you home?'

'No, darling. I'd rather walk, and it's not far.'

Stevie kissed her, then returned to the chattering group in the centre of the room. Tim walked with her to the door, then he, too, bent to kiss her.

'Look after Jerome,' she said.

Tim glanced across to where his half-brother was still crouched beside his grandmother. 'I don't think that'll be necessary.' He smiled briefly.

'No. Quite. I meant, see him home later. When he's ready.' She smiled, too, even more briefly. '*If* he's ready.'

'Don't be upset, Mum.' Tim hugged her again. 'It's good that she's comforting him. It doesn't mean you couldn't do it just as well.'

What a nice son you are, she thought. 'Thank you, darling.'

She gave his hand a pat, then hurried away.

*

Haydon Hall was quite silent. And it felt, as she crossed the cool hall, serene. Welcoming.

She kicked off her black patent-leather shoes – they weren't very comfortable – and threw her hat on to the stairs. Going into the kitchen to make a cup of tea, she wondered what to do next.

There was going to be a mountain of things to see to in the wake of Zach's death. She decided, as she squeezed the tea-bag and chucked it in the bin, that she might use this no doubt brief period of solitude to have a preliminary look through his desk, and make sure she knew where all the necessary bits and pieces were.

An hour later, she had done all that she felt she could for the time being. Zach had left his desk tidy, and everything she was going to need was there and, moreover, clearly labelled.

She leaned back in his big leather chair, propping her feet up on the edge of the desk and observing that she had a small run in one heel of her black tights. Staring at it, she noticed the handle of the little drawer under the desk top, where Zach kept special treasures. The key was in the lock; she turned it, and opened the drawer. If there was anything precious in there, she ought to . . .

There was a small package, wrapped in navy-blue tissue paper. The gold braid tied round it had a label attached; on it, in Zach's writing, was her name.

She picked up the package. Turned over the label. Read, 'To my beloved wife on her birthday, with gratitude for eighteen years of her love. For ever, Zacharias.'

Her hands were shaking.

Slowly she unwrapped the tissue paper. In its folds lay an eternity ring, of heavy gold, eighteen large diamonds set around its circumference. One for every year they had been married.

Zach.

In a flash of brilliant memories, she rewound through their life. First meeting, first lovemaking, marriage. Jerome, and Zach's radiant joy. Family life, with all its ups and downs. His moods, and his sense of humour. His generosity. The fun they had, the sheer variety of life with him.

Slowly she put the ring on her wedding finger, next to her gold wedding band.

She closed her eyes.

For a strange moment, it was almost as if he were standing

behind her, his hands on her shoulders. After a while, the sensation went away.

She opened her eyes again. Tears had spilled down her cheeks, and she wiped them away.

It was going to be hard, learning to live without him.

CHAPTER FOUR

Deborah Warne, forty-five years old, divorced, scarred and anxious, made herself sit up straight and look the woman in the lettings agency in the eye.

'I'm not prepared to waste my time going to look at properties which are outside both my price range and my preferred area,' she heard herself say firmly, 'so, please, don't keep suggesting that I do.'

She could feel her heart beating uncomfortably quickly. The lettings woman, who had raised an ironic eyebrow, allowed her glance to drop, and Deborah felt a small thrill, as if she had just won a minor but significant victory.

'Very well, Mrs –' The woman made a show of going through her notes.

'Not Mrs.' Deborah kept her voice level. 'I am divorced. Ms.'

'Mzzzzz,' the woman echoed, drawing out the unpleasant buzzy sound. 'As I was about to say, Ms Warne, you are tying my hands rather, and . . .'

Deborah lost it then. Tying hands. Tying my hands. For an awful moment she was back in the luxury bedroom in the house in Worcester, and Bruce was . . .

Stop. *Stop*.

'. . . feel you're not prepared to go farther afield, I can only suggest you go and have a look at Haydon Hall,' said the lettings agency woman.

'What's that?' Deborah felt cold sweat on her forehead,

and hoped her new fringe hid it. She wiped her palms on the straight skirt of her suit; it, also, was new. She had read in a magazine in the fracture clinic waiting room that a dramatic change in lifestyle was a good occasion for new clothes and a new hairdo. Also, it seemed only common sense to boost her desperately low morale by making every attempt to make herself look smart. Efficient. As if she were in control.

If only they knew.

'Haydon Hall,' the woman repeated. 'The one I mentioned first, if you remember.' The smile was too swift, surely, to be sincere.

'Indeed,' Deborah said neutrally. 'Perhaps you would show me the details again?'

The woman reached for a buff folder at the bottom of the small stack on her desk. 'Haydon Hall is the property of a Mrs Kazandreas,' she said, opening the file and extracting a photograph, 'a widow whose grown-up family have left home, so that she rattles around in there like a pea in a drum, ha, ha.' She pushed the photograph across to Deborah. 'It's a lovely house. Nice position, too. Parkland on one side, easy reach of the station and shops.'

Deborah studied the photograph. Haydon Hall looked as if it was Victorian, a large, brick-built house set in rather overgrown gardens (what would you expect, she thought, when the family has left home and this little old Mrs Kazandreas has to cope alone? She's probably too feeble to push a lawnmower), with a conservatory tacked on to one side.

'The accommodation being offered comprises a bedroom, sitting room, kitchenette and bathroom, with loo,' the agency woman said. 'For the price, it's good value, you must agree.' That was fair comment; the price was only just outside Deborah's budget. 'And' – the woman's voice took on a distinct wheedling tone – 'it has the *great* advantage of having its own, quite separate, entrance.' She leaned forward conspiratorially. 'Nobody'll know about your comings and goings,' she said, 'nor about who comes to visit you!'

Deborah thought the last comment was a little suggestive. 'I don't imagine that any comings and goings of mine would entertain anybody anyway, I live very quietly,' she said, regretting almost immediately that the woman had managed to goad her into confiding something about her personal life. Even something as innocuous as that.

'You'll love Haydon Hall, then.' The woman sat back, arms folded. 'It's as quiet as anything. Mrs Kazandreas is a widow, like I said, and hardly one to be kicking up her heels.'

'Quite.' Deborah forbore to say that she hadn't meant *that* sort of quiet. 'Well, then, I'd better go and view this flat. Have you a key, or do we have to make an appointment with Mrs what's her name?'

'Kazandreas. It's Greek.' Once more, the woman studied her notes. 'And in fact I see it's by appointment, so, if you'll bear with me a moment, Mzzz Warne, I'll just ring her up . . .'

Deborah listened to one end of the ensuing conversation. The agency woman wasn't talking especially slowly, so Deborah concluded that this Greek widow must speak good English, which was a relief.

'There!' The woman put down her phone. 'This afternoon at four – you *did* say you were free all day?'

'I did.' Deborah almost wished she hadn't; it might have been nice to have the opportunity to take a preliminary look at the outside of the house, then the chance to sleep on it before actually meeting the owner of Haydon Hall. Still, on the other hand, the sooner everything was settled, the sooner she could relax. 'Four o'clock, then. Will you explain to me how I find it?'

*

At ten to four, Deborah was standing on the other side of the road looking up at Haydon Hall.

In reality, it looked rather more attractive than in its photograph. The beech hedge had been cut quite recently, and the trees in the front garden gave an attractive dappled shade over the flower beds and the lawn. Someone had mowed the grass since the photo had been taken; perhaps Mrs Kazandreas employed a gardener? There was a Peugeot estate car in the drive; it was parked neatly, square onto the garage doors in front of it.

Deborah walked slowly up the road and back again until some church clock near at hand struck the hour, then she went up the drive and rang the doorbell.

A woman of around her own age answered. She had thick hair of an indeterminate reddish-fair colour, with lighter streaks which could either have been grey or the effect of sunshine. The loose bun was in the process of unravelling itself, and the grubby overall worn on top of the jeans and sweatshirt suggested that the woman had been interrupted in the middle of some domestic chore.

'My name is Warne, Deborah Warne,' Deborah said, 'and I've come to see Mrs Kazandreas about the flat that's to let.'

The woman smiled, and held out a square, sun-tanned hand. 'That's me,' she said. 'I'm Robyn Kazandreas.'

'Oh! I –'

'I know, you imagined some little Mediterranean type in a shawl with hardly any teeth' – the smile widened, showing the woman's own teeth, white and regular – 'and dressed in widows' black. Everyone does.'

'Well, I had sort of expected someone foreign,' Deborah admitted, 'although I didn't actually go as far as the shawl and the teeth.'

'I was born and bred in Tunbridge Wells. My late husband was the foreigner. He was from Crete. Come in' – the door was opened fully.

'Thank you.' Deborah looked around at the hall, whose parquet floor was covered by a worn rug. A large display of

flowers stood on a chest, and a wide staircase with an elaborate wooden bannister led to an upper storey.

'The flat's up here.' Mrs Kazandreas led the way along a
passage towards the back of the house, and up a smaller staircase. 'There's an entrance from my side of the house, but the
connecting door is quite stout and you can lock it if you want.'

Deborah, disarmed by such frankness, nodded. 'I see.'

'Through here,' – she flung open the door on to a landing
and led Deborah into a large, sunny room – 'the flat comprises this bedroom, the little sitting room, and the bathroom
at the end.'

'I see,' Deborah said again. The bedroom was large, with
a wide window overlooking the garden. The bed was wide,
too. Maybe she could get it changed for a single? Double
beds were . . .

Don't think about that.

'I understood there was a kitchen,' she said, far more tersely
than she had intended; it sounded as if she was accusing this
nice friendly woman of deliberately misleading her.

'Yes.' Robyn Kazandreas looked faintly surprised. 'It's in
here.' She opened another door, revealing a tiny room with
a single drainer sink, a Baby Belling beside it and a gap
where, presumably, a fridge and washing machine could be
installed. 'It's hardly more than a cupboard, I'm afraid, but
it'll do for preparing a snack.' She frowned suddenly. 'Unless
you're a Cordon Bleu or anything?'

'No, I'm not.' Wanting to make up for her gaffe, Deborah
added, 'I hate cooking, actually, so this would be more than
adequate.'

'I dare say you eat out a lot,' Mrs Kazandreas said, turning
to look at her. Her smile seemed to freeze; she's just noticed
how skinny I am, Deborah decided.

'No,' she admitted, overcome with the desire to tell the
truth for once. 'I don't eat a lot anywhere, in or out.'

'Have you been ill?' The voice was kind.

Deborah looked into the blue eyes, bright in the tanned face. 'Sort of.'

Robyn Kazandreas seemed to realize it was a delicate subject. 'Look, shall I leave you to have a poke round on your own? It's terribly difficult to assess a place with someone breathing down your neck, isn't it? Especially when the someone happens to own it.'

'Well, if you're sure you don't mind.'

'Not in the least. Take your time, then when you're through, come back down to the main hall and give me a shout.' She headed for the connecting door. 'I'm clearing out my husband's study,' she said over her shoulder, 'and it's quite frightful.'

Deborah stood staring after her for some moments – what was frightful, the study or the clearing out? – then pulled herself together and began to look around.

★

It wasn't so much the flat itself that decided her, although it was pleasant enough, being adequately roomy and with enough cupboard space for Deborah's possessions. It had a good atmosphere, too, she thought. Sort of cheerful, welcoming. She wondered if the bedroom had belonged to one of Mrs Kazandreas's grown-up children; the walls had clearly been painted recently, so perhaps the bright, sunny paint covered places where football and pop star posters had recently hung?

No. What made up her mind was Mrs Kazandreas. Robyn. She is, Deborah reflected, just what I need.

Not pausing to elaborate on exactly what she did need, or why she was so instantly sure Robyn Kazandreas was it, she hurried through the connecting door and back down the stairs to announce her decision.

★

58

'I should have explained straight away,' Robyn said as she stood in a fresh-smelling, airy kitchen, pouring out two cups of tea, 'but I can't actually give you a firm okay at the moment.'

Deborah, devastated, sank down on one of the stools in front of the worktop. She said, 'What do you mean? I thought – I mean, your flat's on that agency woman's books, I assumed we could firm up arrangements straight away.'

Robyn muttered something; it sounded like, 'Oh, *shit*.' Then her eyes met Deborah's and she said, 'It's that bloody woman. I'm sorry if this looks as if I'm monumentally passing the buck, but I did actually tell her to make absolutely certain that any prospective tenants knew the position.'

'Which is?'

Robyn drew in a breath. 'This will sound as if I'm chronically untrusting as well as a buck-passer, but I'm actually trying to please my father, my eldest son, Uncle Tom Cobleigh and all,' she said ruefully. 'To a man, they're advising me to get everything sewn up legally before I go ahead with the let, and I'm still waiting for one or two details to be finalized.'

'But surely the letting agency makes sure everything is properly done?' Only her anxiety, Deborah thought, could have made her speak out so boldly. It *was* a lovely flat. It could so readily feel like the home she so desperately needed. And, now that it appeared it might not after all be available, she wanted it all the more.

'Yes, that's what I thought,' Robyn agreed. 'Only my father's gone and come up with this wretched but no doubt well-meaning friend who had a shocking tenant he couldn't get rid of, and –'

'And the let was arranged through the same agency,' Deborah finished for her.

'However did you know?'

'Just guessing.'

Surprisingly, Robyn started to laugh. Even more surprisingly, Deborah found herself joining in.

'I *am* sorry,' Robyn said again. 'All I can do is reassure you that it is, I'm sure, only a matter of waiting for the final go-ahead. And I promise I won't let it to anyone else – in fact,' she reached for the phone, mounted on the wall at the end of one of the kitchen worktops, 'I'll ring the agency and tell them to stop circulating the details.'

Deborah drank her tea. Eyed the tin of biscuits which Robyn had proffered, decided she couldn't manage one.

'Hello, Mrs Hope?' Robyn was saying. 'Robyn Kazandreas. I've got Deborah Warne here, and she's going to take the flat, if I decide to go ahead, so I'm calling to ask you to take it off your list of lettings.' There was a burst of chatter from the other end, and Robyn said once or twice, 'Yes,' and, 'Quite so.'

When it sounded as if the call was being wound up, Robyn, looking as if something else had just occurred to her, gave Mrs Hope a distinctly chilly reprimand for not having given Deborah the full picture. 'You have caused her distress by misleading her – yes, all right, by *unintentionally* misleading her,' she finished, 'and you ought to have been more careful and remembered your instructions.' Replacing the receiver with a bang, she muttered, 'Bloody woman.'

Golly, Deborah thought. It was good to have someone take up arms on her behalf, even over a relatively minor matter. Watching Robyn, Deborah felt warmed, somehow. It was illogical – especially for one such as she, who had learned the hard way not to trust first impressions or subjective, emotion-prompted judgements – but she felt drawn to this Robyn Kazandreas.

And, as if Haydon Hall offered a haven, a lighted window in a lonely, dark night, Deborah knew without a doubt that she would do all that was in her power to live there.

CHAPTER FIVE

It was getting chilly in the little yard behind the village post office stores. When the sun went down behind the surrounding brick wall, as it did around three-thirty nowadays, you could tell it was October, and definitely autumn. There was, as Mr Kippings was always saying, a bit of a nip in the air.

Jerome ground out his cigarette and threw it in the dustbin; Mr Kippings was also always saying that tidiness, even in little things, was part of God's plan for a beautiful world. An admirable sentiment, no doubt, but it lost some of its power when you knew, as Jerome did, that, for one thing, Mr Kippings didn't go to church and, for another, had never done a Christian thing in all the sixty-odd years of his life.

Jerome had been working for Mr Kippings for almost three months. Having achieved modest success in his A Levels, he had secured a university place for the following year. For now, he was having a gap year, intending to go off travelling and see something of the world; working in Mr Kippings's shop was meant to be earning him the money for his fare. The plan, conceived with his friends Charlie and Ben, had been to save every penny between now and next February, then, in time for at least some of the Antipodean summer, to set off to spend four or five months in New Zealand. Ben's family had connections in the North Island, and it was very likely that the boys would be able to work out there, too, to supplement what funds they took with them.

Two things had happened to upset the plan. While Ben

and Charlie were earning decent money – Charlie was in an office where they paid him £5 an hour, and Ben was doing three different jobs, so his average pay came out at slightly more – Mr Kippings was a mean bastard and stuck to the minimum wage like a limpet to a rock. Quite often, he would tell Jerome to drop an order off 'on your way home', except that it never was; when Jerome had diffidently asked about overtime, Mr Kippings's boot-button eyes had bored into him as he said, in a horribly patronising tone, 'Jeremy, when *I* was your age, a youth was grateful for what he got in his wage packet – and, let me tell you, young man, it didn't amount to anything *near* the sort of money I have to pay you, oh, dear me, no, not by a long chalk!' Momentarily convulsed at his own humour, Mr Kippings lost his thread. 'Where was I? Ah, yes, overtime. Overtime!' Shaking his head, he turned his back and walked away.

The other thing that had happened was that Jerome's father had died. Nobody seemed to have expected it – Jerome's mother had explained to him that, while Dad had had a slight stroke, the doctors said he'd made an excellent recovery and should soon be back to normal. Jerome, trying to reconcile those cheerful sentiments with Dad's increasingly halting step, with his yellow-pale face, with the lacklustre mood which never seemed to lift, had done his best to believe what his mother told him.

But Dad had died, anyway.

Mr Kippings had magnanimously given him the week off – without pay – but Jerome knew that was only because Mum had told him to. He smiled faintly; Mum was more than a match for Mr Kippings. He wished, really wished, that he and Mum could change places, just for a day. Mum would know how to cope with the snide remarks, the petty cruelties, the outright unfairnesses, that were the lot of those who worked for Mr Kippings.

Mum.

Oh, hell, he hadn't meant to start thinking about Mum.

He leaned back against the wall. His afternoon tea break was almost over – three and a half minutes to go – and he had told himself he wasn't going to go back inside the shop until he had finally made a decision.

Eighteen years old, he reminded himself, I'm an adult now. I can vote, I could die for my country, if we were fighting anyone. I'm in charge of my own life. Okay, those things were all true, but they didn't tell you how to cope with Mum's reaction when you informed her what you are thinking of doing.

He stared up at the brown leaves steadily being blown off Mr Kippings's birch tree. There weren't many left. One, two, three . . .

'Oi!'

It was Mr Kippings's usual way of summoning him. He had finally been persuaded that Jerome's name was Jerome, not Jeremy, but apparently couldn't bring himself to say it. Anything remotely foreign-sounding was, in Mr Kippings's book, definitely to be avoided; Jerome sometimes reflected that Mr Kippings probably wouldn't have taken him on at all had he known Jerome had a Greek father.

He pulled himself away from the wall, consulted his watch, and said, 'Yes, Mr Kippings?'

'Tea break's over, young man,' Mr Kippings said self-righteously, tapping his own watch.

Jerome stayed where he was. 'Actually, it's not. I still have forty seconds to go.'

'I do not think so.' Mr Kippings's face wore the unpleasant smile which it had worn the morning he reduced a new young girl employee to tears; he had told her she was late for work, and, when she protested that the church clock was in the process of striking nine right at that moment, as she was walking into the shop, he had said smugly, 'Ah, yes, but I expect you to be here, hat and coat hung up, standing behind your till, at nine o'clock, not sauntering through my door!'

It was the girl's first day, at her first job. She said dumbly, 'But – but –'

'You're in the real world now, my girl!' Mr Kippings's nasty little grey moustache, always carefully trimmed so that its lower edge had the pristine straightness of a new tooth-brush, stretched over his thin smile. 'You present yourself here at five minutes to the hour, and you get yourself ready for work in your own time, not mine!'

The poor little thing had survived for a week, and Jerome had not seen her again.

'Fifteen minutes you have for your afternoon break,' Mr Kippings was saying now. 'Ample time, I think you will agree, for a cup of tea and –' his beady eyes quartered the yard – 'a cigarette.' He pronounced the word as if cigarettes were a brand-new, highly suspicious commodity.

'It's all right, I put the butt end in the dustbin, wrapped up in at least three sheets of newspaper,' Jerome said blandly.

Mr Kippings spun round and fixed him with a hard stare. 'I do hope you are not being lippy with me, young man,' he said unpleasantly. 'If you are, I shall –'

'You'll what?' Suddenly Jerome made up his mind. About the job, about his future; indeed, the two were not unconnected. He'd had enough; much more than enough. In a heady moment of abandon, he felt the long pent-up words fly to his lips. 'What will you do, Mr Kippings? Dock my pay, like you did the week when I was half an hour late one morning because my mother had a migraine and I went to the pharmacist to get her some of her special tablets?'

Mr Kippings opened his mouth to reply, but Jerome didn't let him. Advancing across the yard – he was both broader and taller than Mr Kippings – he backed his employer into a corner. 'Or will you do as you're always threatening every poor sod who has the misfortune to work for you, and make a note of it in your little black book, to be resurrected and trotted out if ever I'm stupid enough to ask you for a reference?'

Mr Kippings, recovering from his amazement, rallied. 'I do not know what has got into you, Jeremy, but –'

'*Jerome!*' Jerome yelled. 'My fucking name is *Jerome!* My father, you may care to know, was Greek, and my name derives from the Greek – it means "of holy name". Okay, Mr Kippings? And I'm *proud* of it!'

Mr Kippings had gone quite pale. 'Young man, if you do not stop this dreadful abuse, I shall have to call the police!'

Jerome's temper left him as quickly as it had come. 'Don't bother, I'm going,' he murmured.

'But it's only half past three! You can't *go!*'

Amused, he turned back to Mr Kippings. 'You'd like me to return to work? Ha! Tough! I'm no longer an employee of yours, Mr Kippings. I've had enough of you and your shop – life's just too short to spend another day of it in your company.'

He was congratulating himself on the dignity of his exit line, when a small devil prodded him to throw dignity to the winds. At the back entrance to the shop – where he realized belatedly that the door had been open and the rest of the staff, now standing staring towards the yard with their mouths open, couldn't have helped hearing every word – he stopped and spun round to face Mr Kippings.

Enunciating clearly, he said, 'In case you haven't got the message, Mr Kippings, you can poke your job right up your arse.'

★

It took him about fifteen minutes to cycle home. Nowhere near long enough to work out how he was going to word what he had to say to Mum.

He put his bike in the garage and went into the house.

65

He was assailed by the smell of clean washing; a rack of towels and pillow-cases stood by the hall radiator.

He stopped, smiling involuntarily. Home would irrevocably be associated with the evocative aroma of warm detergent; his mother was hot on cleanliness, and, given the choice, would always opt to do the laundry rather than the cooking. He, like his home, had always been clean; bath-time, linked in his earliest memories with laughter, splashy games, and the comforts of hot water and soft, enveloping towels, had always been fun.

Haydon Hall had a special area for laundry, where his mother had washing machine, spin dryer, drying racks. But she stubbornly refused to buy a tumble drier: 'I managed when I had three little boys and a sports fanatic husband,' she'd been saying in recent years, whenever Jerome's dad had offered to get her one, 'I can *certainly* manage now it's just us three.'

Consequently, whenever, like today, it was too wet or cold to hang washing outside, there would be sheets, shirts, trousers, towels, draped on bannisters and over radiators.

Jerome liked it. It meant home. Meant Mum.

He squared his shoulders and went to find her.

*

Robyn was on her knees on the floor of Zach's study when she heard footsteps in the hall.

'Who's there?' she called out.

'Me.' Jerome appeared in the doorway. 'Mum, what are you doing?'

She sighed. 'I've got to sort this lot out.' She waved a hand over the stacks of ageing papers that covered the floor. 'Your dad was a bit of a hoarder, darling, and I'm having a job separating the small amount of essential from the mountains of unnecessary.'

'Oh. D'you want a hand?'

'Sweet of you, but no, thanks. I've got something of a method up and running, though you'd hardly credit it.' She tucked a long stray lock of hair back up into her bun. 'How do papers put away in boxes and drawers manage to get so filthy? My skin feels all itchy, and my hands are black.'

'The black's probably ink, off the papers.' He knelt down beside her, picking up a file at random. 'This one's full of stuff about some election back in the sixties . . .' There was a pause, and Robyn watched as he studied a few lines. 'My Greek's not up to reading it,' he said, smiling. 'But I see what you mean about Dad and the hoarding.'

'We'll have to have a mammoth bonfire,' Robyn said. Then, looking closely at her son's face, 'You don't mind, darling?'

'Huh? No.' He seemed preoccupied.

'Jerome? Are you all right?' Suddenly she remembered what time it was. 'You're home early – is everything all right?'

He was fiddling with the file of papers, extracting paper clips and putting them in a little pile on the dusty carpet. 'No.' He took an audible breath. 'Mum, I've jacked it in. I'm not going off to New Zealand, I'm not sure I'm even going to take up my uni place next year.'

'But –'

'Mum, while all Dad's lot were here for the – for the funeral, I got talking with Uncle Andreas and Uncle Costas, and they were really cool, I got on really well with them, and they said if I wanted I could go out to Crete and stay with them.' He looked at her, a brief glance, as if ascertaining how she was receiving this. 'Well, not exactly stay with them, sort of live with them. Work with Uncle Andreas in the family business. They'd train me, they said, and teach me all about it, and they said I'd be welcome because I'm Dad's son.'

Abruptly he seemed to run out of steam. His shoulders

slumped, and he began tidying the pile of paper clips with the flat of one hand.

Robyn would have been far more taken aback by her son's bombshell had she not suspected that something of the sort was in the wind. She had observed how well Jerome got on with the Greek side of his family: despite the fact that he looked far more like his tall, fair mother than his short, dark father, the Kazandreas relatives had taken him under their collective wing with a demonstrative affection which had clearly charmed him. And why not, Robyn thought, they're loving people, they appreciated what he was suffering at the funeral and they tried to help in the best way they could think of. It *would* be a consolation for him, to go out to Crete, live among his father's people.

That was all very well in theory. Watching his hand busy with the paper clips, she was hit by such a surge of protective love for him that, for a few moments, she did not trust herself to speak.

'Er – you think this might be a long-term thing, then?' she asked eventually. 'A proper career thing, and not just a holiday or gap-year job?'

'I don't *know*!' No, of course he wouldn't. 'Mum, I can't think that far ahead.' His head came up, and the bright blue eyes met hers. 'I just know that I want to go. Since Dad – I can't settle here, with him gone. I think I'd be better out there, with his lot. They're nice. Aunt Sophia said I could have George's room, now that George is working in Heraklion.'

The plans had got that far, then. 'I think,' Robyn began carefully, 'that at times like this, it's sometimes best to act on instinct rather than try to work things out logically. If you really feel you'd be happy going to live in Crete, then I think that's what you ought to do.'

His head flew up. 'Mum! Do you really? But what about you, don't you need me here?'

She reached out and took his hand. Held on to it, squeezing hard. 'Yes, I need you because I love you, you're fun to be with and you've always made me laugh. But you can't do that now, because you're too sad.' She forced a smile. 'So you may as well bugger off to Crete.'

He eyed her steadily, then, apparently deciding there was a deep sentiment behind the flippant words, squeezed back. 'But what about all the sorting out?' he said, as if wanting to make sure he had covered every aspect. 'Couldn't my strong arms and willing back be of invaluable assistance in carting bonfire fuel out to the garden?'

Deliberately keeping the tone light – it was becoming increasingly difficult – she said, 'Well, I don't suppose you'll be getting on a flight first thing tomorrow. You can help me with the bonfire before you go.'

He lunged towards her, throwing his arms round her neck. She returned his hug, and, while he couldn't see her face, recovered her equanimity.

As he released her, a thought struck her. 'What about the post-office job? Did Mr Kippings let you come home early?'

A grin spread across his face, culminating in a hoot of laughter. It was, she thought detachedly, wonderful to hear him laugh again. 'I told him to poke his job up his arse.'

'Oh, Jerome! How superb!' She felt like laughing, too; Mr Kippings was an obsequious little shit, even if he did run an efficient shop. Straightening her face, she added, 'Of course, you know what this means, don't you?'

'No.' He looked worried. 'What?'

She smiled. 'I'll have to buy my stamps somewhere else from now on.'

*

After a momentous change in their lives such as that one, they both needed something positive to do; Robyn pushed all the papers and boxes destined for the bonfire to one corner of the room, and instructed Jerome to ferry them out to the end of the garden. Provided the wind didn't get up, she would go out with him when he'd finished and they'd have their fire.

They worked quickly – he'd always been the best of her sons at that sort of task, indeed, at *any* sort of task – and, in under two hours, the room that had been Zach's study was clear of the great majority of its clutter. She'd had the desk and the bookshelves out from the wall, hoovered and cleaned behind them and pushed them back into place, and Jerome had taken the curtains down and put them into the washing machine, which could be heard faintly in the distance on fast spin.

Together they had rearranged the room. It had been a sad task, for, in removing Zach's vast collection of detritus, they had also, it appeared, removed the remaining tenuous aura of his personality. Standing side by side surveying their handiwork, she sensed that Jerome felt as emotional as she did.

Suddenly he exclaimed – she didn't hear what he said – and hurried away along the hall. She heard him bounding up the stairs, and soon he came down again. He had a framed picture in his hands; without seeing the front, she knew what it was.

'Jerome! Oh, what a brilliant idea! But are you sure?'

He was kneeling on Zach's bare desk, removing a calendar from a hook in the wall above it and replacing it with the picture he had brought downstairs.

'Quite sure.' His voice was firm. 'I'm not going to be in my room, and, anyway, this is as much Dad's as mine, so it's just as appropriate here.'

He straightened the frame, adjusting it once or twice till he was satisfied, then jumped down and came to stand with her.

Together they looked at the enlargement of Jerome's

favourite photograph. He and Zach were standing side by side on a quayside, a small boat waiting for them on the smooth blue waters beneath. Zach had his arm round his son's shoulders – Jerome would have been about ten – and both father and son were smiling, their happy faces alight with excited anticipation. The moment had been so faithfully captured that you could, Robyn thought, almost smell the salty sea, hear the sound of Greek voices and distant laughter.

'It's a goodie, isn't it?' she said softly. 'Dear old Dad.'

'Dear old Dad,' he echoed.

Neither of them said any more. After a few seconds, they turned, closed up the room that was once more filled with Zach's spirit, and went outside to their bonfire.

CHAPTER SIX

Robyn suffered several days of disturbingly mixed emotions between the afternoon when Jerome announced his plans and the morning when she took him to Gatwick for his flight to Heraklion.

They kept busy, which helped; there proved to be considerable valeting necessary on most of his clothes, and she took him shopping to buy him a new holdall and some trousers and shirts. His feet were the same size as his father's; she had watched as he carefully polished three pairs of Zach's shoes and put them in his room ready for packing.

There was something heartbreakingly poignant about a dead person's shoes.

When the sadness struck her, she told herself she was glad Jerome was going, because undoubtedly he would not feel it so badly away from home.

She was also assailed by guilt, because she knew that Jerome mourned Zach more profoundly than she did.

She had loved him – hadn't she? – but, now that the initial shock had worn off, she had to accept that she was not devastated by his death. There were days, yes, when some small, potent memory would floor her, but, in the main, she thought she was managing rather well. And she *shouldn't* be! Her guilty feelings were augmented by the memory of how she had treated Zach in the time between his first stroke and the one that killed him; he had been quite right, he *was* sick, an invalid who should have had the necessary care and attention, not been the object of a doubting wife's merciless attempts to jolly him out of it.

Guilty.

She tried herself, judged herself, pronounced sentence. Your punishment, O, unfeeling one, is to see your beloved son off on his journey away from you with a smile and a cheery wave.

Whatever it might cost you.

*

Neither she nor Jerome had remembered that it would be her birthday the day after his flight. When they did, Jerome wanted to postpone his departure, but she wouldn't let him.

'The others are coming,' she said brightly, 'so it's not as if I won't see some of you on the actual day. You and I will have our own celebration two days early. Okay? I'll take you out to lunch.'

'No, *I'll* take *you*.' He took out his new wallet, thumbed across the top of a small wad of notes. 'Mr Kippings paid me up to the moment I left – honestly, I got my calculator out, and it's exact to the minute.'

'I suppose we should be thankful for small mercies,' Robyn murmured.

'*I'm* not thankful,' Jerome replied. 'I only got what he owed me.'

'But you told him to poke his job up his bottom,' she pointed out.

'He wouldn't *not* pay me because of something like that,' Jerome said perceptively. 'He'd only withhold pay for something covered by his precious regulations. He's a bastard.'

'The other staff will miss you.' Robyn diplomatically changed the subject. 'Wasn't that nice of them, to buy you a present?'

The people at the shop had bought him the leather wallet;

73

it was the sort that goes on a belt and can be concealed under clothes. They were, it appeared, of the opinion that Crete was a place bursting with muggers, pickpockets and other insalubrious characters out to separate a young man from his passport and his money. Nevertheless, it was a very kind gesture; Jerome, she observed, had been touched to think they had liked him enough to want to give him something.

As well as treating her to lunch, he gave her a birthday present. It must have knocked a considerable hole in the wage packet from Mr Kippings: he'd bought her a new, high-tog-rating duvet.

She knew why. She was always cold at night, and it had been a standing family joke that she used Zach as a hot water bottle for her chilly feet.

'It's brilliant!' she exclaimed when she tore the wrapping off the large box. 'Darling, it's honestly just what I needed!'

He said briefly, 'I know.'

*

They played one of Jerome's compilation tapes on the way to Gatwick, singing along with 'He ain't Heavy, He's my Brother', 'American Pie', and 'Mr Tambourine Man'. At Gatwick, she came in with him to make sure the flight wasn't delayed, then left. Too emotional, for both of them, if she hung around.

She didn't play the tape on the way home.

*

Tim, Stevie and Will were all coming home for her birthday. She was expecting Tim at lunchtime, and the others were arriving in the evening.

She made herself crawl out from under her new duvet and go to take a shower, washing her hair and determining to take trouble over her appearance. Not that she felt like it;

74

with Jerome gone, she had slept alone in the big house for the first time, and the strangeness of that was disturbing. The temptation was to say, sod the world, and stay in bed.

By midday, she was feeling much better. She had received a handful of birthday cards and Frances had come round for coffee; Robyn's father was going to look in later.

Robyn had ambiguous feelings about being with her mother. Frances's company was usually stimulating, but she noticed things – noticed virtually everything – and sometimes made remarks that Robyn found uncomfortable. Such as hinting that Robyn seemed to be coping very well with her grief. And saying, apparently without irony, that it was just as well Robyn had been 'the strong one' in the marriage, the 'coper' – both phrases were Frances's – since to lose a husband on whom one depended for the practicalities as well as for the love was even more devastating.

This morning, possibly because it was Robyn's birthday, Frances had kept her comments on a less controversial level. They had discussed Jerome's departure to Crete, talked about Frances's roses, laughed over Frances's description of her husband's round of golf with a hapless friend. 'Really,' Frances said, 'John ought to have known better, the man's got an enormous handicap.'

John Swift had been, before retirement, a solicitor. He had a large circle of male friends, most of whom he had known in his long years in practice in Tunbridge Wells. It seemed to Robyn that he spent far more time out of the house, golfing, lunching or otherwise whiling away the time with his friends, than he did at home with Frances. Presumably, she had long ago concluded, that was how they both liked it.

Frances had been gone for about a quarter of an hour when Tim arrived. 'Darling, I'd love to stay and see him,' she'd said, 'but I shall be late for my hair appointment, parking's murder at lunchtime. At *any* time, in this poor traffic-choked town!'

Robyn went out to meet her eldest son on her own.

Tim's car – a new one, she noticed – swept up in front of the house and came to a halt beside her. Tim flung open the door, jumped out and hurried across to her, wrapping his arms round her in a warm hug. 'Mum! Many happy returns!'

She hugged him back. He was not much taller than she was, but, if anything, he felt even more solid than the last time she'd hugged him. Like his father both in build and in pursuits, the rugby, the running and the work-outs had turned him into the sort of man people just didn't like to annoy.

'Come in,' she said, 'I've got lunch ready.'

Tim straightened up from reaching into the back of the car; he had a small parcel and an envelope in his hand. 'Don't say you've been cooking, Mum. I won't believe it, especially on your birthday.'

'I have removed some slices of smoked salmon from their wrappings and taken the lids off several boxes of delicatessen salads,' she replied with dignity. 'There is a granary loaf and a large Brie which you may operate on yourself.'

'Sounds wonderful. Any beers?'

She glanced at him. 'Timothy, is it likely I should invite you to lunch and not have a cupboard full of beer?'

He grinned. 'Not in the least. Here' – he handed her the card and present – 'happy birthday.'

They were in the kitchen, and she fetched Tim a beer and poured herself a glass of white wine before sitting down with her present.

He had bought her a pair of opal earrings. She held them in the palm of her hand, staring down at them and fighting the tears that, irrationally, were stinging her eyes. Gold surrounded dark opal studs, from which hung delicate chains in which were set other opals and what looked suspiciously like tiny diamonds. 'Tim, darling, these are quite exquisite,' she said.

'You're crying!'

'No.' She raised her head and gave him a brilliant smile, the tears on her cheeks underlining the absurdity of her denial. 'It's just that I'm so touched. But, Tim, you shouldn't spend this sort of money on me!'

'You spent it on me,' he pointed out. 'And I thought you ought to have something a bit special, because of – well, you know.' He turned his attention to his beer. He also took after his father in his reluctance to touch on what Paddy had been wont to call 'smushy stuff'.

Acknowledging this, willing to accept it in her son when she hadn't been in her first husband, Robyn reached out for his hand. 'I'm thrilled,' she said quietly. 'I'm going to put them in . . .' she went to stand in front of the mirror in the hall, screwing in the new earrings and observing the effect, '. . . There!'

'Lovely.' He looked slightly embarrassed at her obvious delight. 'Got another beer?'

*

Stevie and Will arrived in the early evening. Stevie had driven down from Ipswich where, having finished his degree, he was, in the absence of anything better turning up, working in an estate agents' office. He had collected Will from his London digs, and, as they got out of the car, they appeared to be concluding a fairly amicable argument about football.

'No change there, then,' Tim observed to his mother as they stood on the step to greet the new arrivals.

'Quite.' She smiled, somewhat grimly; the memory of Stevie and Will's fights was something she was not quite ready to laugh about yet. Two years separated them, and they had been rivals since Will was old enough to crawl.

Will's first memory, in fact, was of Stevie teaching him how to get out of his cot. In view of their subsequent behaviour, Robyn had sometimes wondered if Stevie had encouraged him purely to provide Stevie with someone to thump.

The silly thing was that, as well she knew, they were devoted to each other. Let anyone else usurp Stevie's fraternal thumping rights and they soon knew about it; he had once floored an older boy who had taken the piss out of Will when a temporary stiff neck made Will walk with his head on one side. And they were only seven and five at the time.

The younger brothers helped themselves from the beer store – Robyn was glad she'd lugged home the extra dozen – and, when the initial catching-up chat was done, they all set off to walk the half-mile to the pub where the boys were going to treat their mother to dinner.

*

Over the starter she told them about Jerome. She had explained his absence only briefly on the phone, merely saying he was away. Now, she went through the whole thing, concluding – quite earnestly, since both Stevie and Will were looking dubious – that it was vital for Jerome to do what felt right at this dreadful time for him.

'It's a dreadful time for you, too, though, Mum,' Stevie said. Quite crossly, as if, with the three of them away, it was Jerome's duty to stay with his widowed mother. 'You ought to have one of us here, and we . . .' He trailed off.

'You all have your own lives to lead,' she finished for him. 'Quite right, and I wouldn't dream of asking any of you to come and hold my hand. But by the same token I don't want to cramp Jerome's style, either.'

'But he's Zach's son,' Will said. 'That sort of makes it more important for him to be with you.'

'Perhaps.' She wasn't sure about that. 'But, darling, he's terribly cut up at losing his father. Going to Crete does actually seem the best thing for him at the moment. Not so many memories there.' She smiled, trying to impart to the three of them the message that *she* could live with Haydon Hall's more immediate memories and survive.

'Don't you get lonely there on your own?' Stevie asked. 'Honestly, Mum, I think one of us ought to come home, even if it's only for a month or so. But I just can't, I –'

'I said, darling. I don't want you to.'

'I can't either,' Will said. 'Work's a bugger this year, I'm thinking of giving up rugby.' As if suddenly realizing he had suggested that, at present, he had time for rugby but couldn't think of giving any extra attention to his mother, a furtive look crossed his face. 'I *could* start coming back for weekends, Mum, if it'd help.'

Frustrated, she said firmly, 'I don't want you to. I don't want *any* of you to make any special arrangements. I'm really perfectly all right on my own.'

She had spoken too loudly; people at other tables were staring.

'You'd better repeat it, Mum, that man at the bar didn't quite hear.' Tim was smiling.

She realised that, alone of the three of them, he hadn't thought it necessary either to suggest she needed company or to explain why he couldn't supply it. 'What do you think, Tim?' she asked.

'This isn't just to appease my guilty conscience, but I do actually think you'd be better on your own,' he said. 'You've had years of looking after other people, and, towards the end, I know Zach wasn't easy.'

'I didn't mind!' she protested. 'He needed me, and I – well, it was okay.'

Tim was watching her. 'Maybe so, but it must have been a strain. And, even if you only had Jerome, you'd still be in the looking-after role, when it's really your turn for a bit of peace. And Jerome –'

'I still think Jerome should stay with her,' Stevie interrupted. 'And what about uni? Presumably he's coming back next autumn?'

She looked from face to expectant face, then said, 'No. Not necessarily.'

'What?' Stevie looked astounded.

Tim said, 'Mum's got three sons who have or will have degrees. That's more than the national average.'

'So you'd be happy for Jerome to waste his life working in some tourist business on a Greek island?' Stevie said forcefully, apparently forgetting that this was exactly what Zach had done.

Tim, who hadn't, smiled briefly. 'There are worse ways of earning a crust,' he observed.

'A crust quite thickly spread with butter and jam,' Will said, looking at the diamond eternity ring on Robyn's finger.

She thought it was time she drew the discussion to a close. This wasn't how she had planned to spend her birthday evening. 'Chaps, I appreciate your concern, and I'm grateful that you all feel so involved.' Stevie started to say something but she held up her hand. 'I have made my decision – in as much as there was one to make, it was really more a matter of just giving Jerome my blessing – and that's that. Now, if we've all finished, I'll signal the waiter that we're ready for our main course.'

*

They had had too much to drink for either Tim or Stevie to think of driving back, so she had all three boys under her roof again that night.

And for breakfast the following morning; for an hour or so, rushing to retrieve toast from under the grill, to stir porridge and to turn eggs in the pan, she was transported back to some school-day morning from the past.

It was – although she couldn't bring herself to admit it – actually quite a relief when they had all gone.

Irrational again – I must pull myself together! she ordered herself firmly – relief didn't stop her from sitting down on the bottom stair after the dust had settled and crying her eyes out.

★

During the afternoon, she thought a lot about Deborah Warne.

The reason she had given for not agreeing to the let of the little flat there and then, when she had met and liked the woman, was not entirely honest. Okay, there were one or two minor points outstanding, but she had also been suffering from second thoughts. Having a stranger there in her own house, a stranger who would, if the thing went ahead, have the right of abode in Haydon Hall, had made Robyn question what had, up till then, seemed absolutely the right thing to do, the most sensible solution to the problem.

For a brief time, Robyn had wondered if she wouldn't rather live entirely alone. She could manage without a bit of rent, couldn't she? She wasn't exactly a pauper!

But, with Zach dead and all the boys away, Haydon Hall did seem terribly big. And, as she had pointed out to Deborah Warne, the flat had a stout lockable door separating it from the rest of the house. Locks could, after all, be operated from both sides . . .

Just before five o'clock, she telephoned Mrs Hope at the lettings agency and said she wanted to go ahead. 'And, Mrs Hope, I'd like to tell Mrs Warne myself, so –'

'It's Mzzzzz,' Mrs Hope interrupted.

'Fine. As I was saying, I'd like to tell her myself, so, if you could give me the number?'

Grudgingly, Mrs Hope did so, suggesting by her attitude that such a call was normally *her* prerogative.

'Thank you so much,' said Robyn. Irony or what? she thought, amused.

*

At seven, she dialled Deborah Warne's home number.

'It's Robyn Kazandreas,' she said.

There was a slight intake of breath. 'Oh. Hello.'

'The flat's available for you, as soon as you want it. *If* you still want it?'

'Oh, *yes*.' The fervour was a little disturbing; as if Deborah Warne realized, she added, in a far less emotional tone, 'Perhaps I could move in at the weekend? Saturday, say?'

'Saturday's fine,' Robyn said. 'I'll be here all morning.'

'See you then.' Ms Warne's tone had gone from dramatic to calm to, now, almost indifferent.

As Robyn put the phone down, she wondered, just for a second or two, exactly what she was getting into.

Deborah leans across and tugs at the sleeve of Robyn's shirt.

'Robyn?'

'Hmm?'

Deborah senses that Robyn is still feeling slightly hurt. That, intending only to make it crystal clear to Debs that she is still there, standing right behind her, willing and more than able to fight Debs's battles, her stalwart championing is suddenly surplus to requirements.

'Robyn, remember Mrs Hope?'

For a moment Robyn frowns, and it seems she doesn't. Then abruptly she laughs. 'Yes! The agency woman! Wasn't she awful?'

'Well, I guess she was only doing her job.'

'Doing what she thought was her job,' Robyn amends. 'She must have written her own job description, and it was largely a work of fiction.'

'Remember that Saturday, when I moved in?' Debs prompts. 'She came round to tell you that you had to read some document or other, and sign it there and then, and you said, bugger off, I'm busy.'

'I didn't say bugger!' Robyn protests.

'Did.'

'Didn't.'

'Okay, maybe it was *sod* off, I'm busy.'

Robyn grunts a grudging acknowledgement. In her book, it seems, *sod off* is a lesser offence than *bugger off*.

Deborah remembers a lot more about that afternoon. Including why Robyn did not want to turn her attention to reading and signing documents. She is quite sure Robyn remembers, too. It is not the sort of episode anyone could forget, having been involved.

She leans forward so that she can look into Robyn's face. The eyes are on some object out to sea, screwed up against the bright light. The set of the mouth is pretty grim.

You remember, Deborah thinks. I hope that my making you remember has done the trick. Made you realize how I appreciated you then and, equally, have gone on doing so throughout the months of our friendship. As, indeed, I still do now, even though I know what you refuse to accept. Which is, dear Robyn, that I am not what I was. That, although you flew to the rescue of a woman whose spirit was broken, you and I between us have begun to put it back together again. Have very nearly completed the job.

Now it is Robyn's turn to lie down on the sun-warmed blanket. Flinging an arm across her face so that Debs can no longer study her, slowly the tense lines of the body relax. After some minutes, Debs imagines she has slipped into a doze.

Debs draws up her knees, rests her folded arms on top of them. Out there in the Channel, a small craft of some sort is making its steady way from east to west. Debs idles over where its destination might be.

This, unfortunately for Debs, leads straight to a contemplation of Br—. Of Bruce the Unmentionable. For he, as Debs cannot have forgotten, used to sail. Naturally, the sort of craft in which he put to sea was nothing like the one Deborah is now watching with an increasingly fixed and steadily more unseeing eye, for the boat down there in the Channel is a dirty old coaster, whereas Bruce could, and did, afford to treat himself to the best.

Or he *convinced* himself he could afford it, which is not quite the same thing.

Their first quarrel happened on board Bruce's boat, when they had been married for six months. Not that quarrel is really the right word for something so one-sided. As poor old Debs was to discover, Bruce's rages invariably followed the same pattern: she would do something to annoy him (often she never discovered what), he would tut, then begin on the verbal slanging, then, finally boiling over, would either hit her or throw something at her. On the boat – her name had been *Celestial*, highly unsuitable in the light of what Debs had to endure on board her – Debs's mistake had been to confuse port with starboard. Quite a predictable error, one would have thought, for a novice sailor? Ah, but even predictable errors were not exempt from Bruce's tutting, yelling and hurling: as well-meaning, dove-like peacemaker Debs's apologies echoed out across the sea, Bruce called her, in ascending order, a silly cow (this almost indulgently), a typical fucking woman (he was getting into his stride now), and a crazy cunt who shouldn't be allowed off dry land. Then he swung his fist at her. She ducked, and, in shock now, instinctively curled herself up in the farthest corner of the boat. Since it was only a small boat, the corner wasn't really far enough away. The half-full Thermos flask which he threw at her hit her on the back of her bent head, with sufficient force to raise a lump like a ping-pong ball.

The next phase of Bruce's rages was the remorse. The first time, innocent Debs had been fooled. 'Oh, my darling, I've hurt you!' as, with a tender hand, he touched her lump. And, a little later when she had been fed with hot, sweet tea containing a tot of whisky, 'Darling, dearest Deborah, let me take you to bed, and you must lie down with your eyes closed until your brute of a husband' – here a light, carefree laugh, to reassure her he was only in jest – 'can join you.'

It sounded lovely. Sounded, to Debs's optimistic ear, as if he were truly repentant. Truly wanting to make it up to her.

That was before he did what he had promised, and got into the narrow bed beside her.

Then, as if some relic of his desire to dominate, to overpower, to humble and humiliate, still lingered, he ordered her to lie absolutely still while he worked on her. 'My darling, you've been hurt, so hurt, and I'm trying to make it up to you by giving you physical joy. Let me, dearest one, do let me!'

Did she accede too readily? Was she a contributor to her own suffering? The police counselling woman seemed to suggest it, although that was not for years to come. Debs does not know. Certainly, she did not know *then*, on board the *Celestial* in a south-coast harbour, as her husband tied her hands to the rail behind her head, brought her quickly to climax then, when her body was pleading no! enough! took his own pleasure on her for what seemed like hours.

She cried out once, but, sweating with effort, veins bulging, a dread odour of sexual mastery emanating from him, he threatened to cover her face with a pillow if she so much as squeaked.

In the morning, he acted as if nothing had happened.

Maybe even then Debs acted like the victim they subsequently told her she was. For, sore and with a thumping headache, she followed his lead. She stitched on a smile, spoke pleasantly, went along with his happy planning of how they would spend the day ahead.

What would have happened if she had acted differently? If, that very first moment that he began to tut, she had stood up to him? If, when the bad-mouthing started, she had said, 'Now you just stop that! Either you accept my apology for what was, after all, a very minor matter, or you let me off this fucking boat *this instant*!'

If, the morning after he had raped her for half an hour or more, she had quietly gone ashore, returned to the marital home in Worcester and changed the locks, then phoned her solicitor?

I'll tell you what would have happened. Deborah would have escaped what lay in her future, and some other poor woman would have been on the receiving end in her stead. Bruce was a bully, and, as everyone knows, bullies are fundamentally cowards, and deflate when someone with a stronger will turns the tables on them.

But Deborah, sadly for her, did not have a strong will. Could not even have turned the tables on Mickey Mouse.

Bruce died in a spectacular aircraft crash over Normandy. He and three colleagues were being flown back to England by executive jet after a business trip – he was in the wine trade – and all four of them, plus two crew and an off-duty pilot hitching a ride back to Gatwick, were killed outright.

Debs's instant reaction – ecstatic, unbelieving joy – was swiftly replaced by guilt. Not because she was so glad he was dead – she never for a split-second felt guilty about *that* – but because he had taken with him into death six innocent men. At least, she assumed they were innocent, and, certainly, the widows and the children at the funerals had all appeared genuinely heartbroken.

Debs had sent money, anonymously, to each family. It made her feel marginally better, even if it did knock a bit of a hole in her account.

And that was before she discovered Bruce's debts.

*

And now for Deborah's mother. Edith Warne, or, as she usually whispered when asked her name, 'Mrs Warne', was widowed a few years after the birth of Debs, her only child. Left alone to cope with what she perceived as a universally hostile world, Edith turned in on herself, made the small semi-detached house in Evesham a sort of fortress from which she only ventured if she was right out of food, and from which she only allowed Deborah to go for essentials such as school. Not well off – her late husband had carried modest life insurance, and there was a small company pension – Edith Warne lived from hand to mouth and did not buy herself any new clothes for twelve years.

Deborah could no more have gone to her mother, for either moral or financial support, than have been elected Pope.

Edith's inward-turned psyche was faithfully reproduced in her daughter. When Deborah's troubles began, she found herself physically incapable of asking for help. Of demanding, as a more confident person would have, 'Something must be done! I *will not* endure this!'

In the doctor's surgery, she excused the black eye, the fractured wrist and the suspected broken ribs by, 'I fell.' And he, too rushed to have the limitless time it would have required to search out Deborah's terrified, cowering soul, pretended he believed her. Told himself, ah well, if she won't ask for help, I can't help her. Prescribed tranquillizers, assured her he was always there if she needed him. Meant it, as he said it, even if Debs drifted out of his mind as the rest of the day pressed in.

She first went to the police when Bruce threw her down the stairs (suspected broken ribs). Too uncertain, too willing to be deterred by the first obstacle, her nerve failed when the duty officer murmured, 'Domestic.' It was not, surely, his fault. Busy – nearly as busy as the doctor – he cannot have meant to sound as if being thrown down the stairs by one's husband was in any way a lesser crime than being mugged outside the supermarket or having one's house broken into or one's car stolen.

Unfortunately, though, that was how it sounded to Deborah. When the policeman looked up to ask her to spell her married surname – Bruce had Huguenot ancestry, and everyone found his name difficult – Debs had gone.

She went again when Bruce threw the spanner at her. Indeed, the people in the hospital had virtually made her; a terribly affronted young houseman – in fact, house*woman* – had offered to go with Deborah when she made her complaint, volunteering that she, the professional medical authority, would be happy to testify to the severity of Debs's wound.

It was a bad one. He'd flung the spanner so that it spun viciously through the air, whoomp-whoomping like a boomerang, only, instead of returning to him, it went straight for Deborah's right eye. Ducking – she'd got good at ducking over the years – it did not blind her. Instead, one end caught her just above the eyebrow, bursting open the flesh so that the two edges sprang apart exposing soft, red innards like a sea anemone. Drenched in her own blood, she had stumbled outside and caught a bus to the hospital, clutching to her wound a tea towel depicting Westminster Abbey and trying not to faint. (Echoes of Edith, yes? 'Don't make a fuss, never make a nuisance of yourself, don't draw *attention* to us!')

The wound required nine stitches.

The nurse's kindness and horrified sympathy had started Deborah's tears, and she did not know how to stop.

*

Nurse, doctor, police desk sergeant, detective, counsellor. Lots more sympathy, lots more horror.

But horror fades. Sympathy, no matter how strong and genuine initially, grows less intense. Diverts to other, needier causes. Reins itself in, indeed, when its object appears to do nothing to help herself.

Deborah, realizing that the lovely, heartwarming, strengthening support was slowly and steadily ebbing away, quietly let the whole thing drop.

He beat her up again, raped her again. Several times. Then – praise God, who, had His attention not been busy elsewhere with things like wars, famines, pestilence and Northern Ireland, might have relieved poor suffering Debs of her burden rather sooner – bloody Bruce died.

*

When the house (and most of its contents) had been sold, when Bruce's car and boat, the TV, video, and the hi-fi had all been reclaimed by the relevant hire purchase firms, when Debs had paid what she could of the debts and, so she fervently hoped, washed her hands of the whole thing, she was left with £1,235.07.

And, unless she went back to Edith, a move which she found herself unable even to contemplate, she had nowhere to live.

She left Worcester. Answered an advert for a PA in Tunbridge Wells, of all places, in a small firm of accountants. She had trained in secretarial skills, had, before her marriage to Br— (no need to mention him again now he's dead) had a first-class job working for a family building firm in Dudley. Liking the idea of Tunbridge Wells – she'd read an article about the town in another waiting-room magazine – she applied for and got the job. And the woman she was to work for – a high-powered confident soul called Maria Fletcher – suggested she go to the letting agency on whose books was the flat in Haydon Hall.

*

The day Deborah moved in – when hopeless Mrs Hope came along with her form, and Robyn told her to bugger (or, alternatively, sod) off, remember? – she had another of her flashbacks.

It wasn't Robyn's fault. She was trying to be kind and welcoming, and, naturally, she didn't know.

She was showing Debs the double-glazing in the flat. She was quite proud of it; she and Zach had only joined the general stampede and had it done a year or so ago, and it was still something of a novelty.

'The sound-proofing's great,' said unknowing Robyn, meaning well, trying to set this tense stranger at her ease. 'You could scream your head off in here, and, with the windows shut, no-one'll hear you!'

Scream your head off.

Already unnerved by the presence of the double bed in what was to be her new bedroom, Debs suddenly saw herself on another bed. Hands held in a relentless grip, her own nightie stuffed in her mouth so that she could not even breathe, let alone scream. He had almost killed her that night. She'd lost consciousness – probably through lack of oxygen – and, when she'd come to, found him practically hysterical at her side, slapping her face with a wet flannel, shaking her so hard that it was in itself a further assault.

Scream your head off.

I'll stop you screaming your head off, you bitch! Bite on this!

While Robyn wittered on about how to operate the radiators and where the airing cupboard was, Deborah quietly fainted.

*

She told Robyn, over the restorative cup of tea in Robyn's warm and welcoming kitchen, a little of her past. Only a little; the rest was to emerge, in dribs and drabs, over the next few months.

What she did say – 'I was married, only not successfully', typical Debs understatement, 'and then my husband died in an air crash' – moved kind-hearted Robyn to tears. Debs was in Robyn's arms, indulging in the unfamiliar feel of a bracing, sympathetic, morale-boosting hug, when Mrs Hope knocked at the half-open kitchen door waving her form.

*

Deborah watches the coaster gradually sail out of sight, and she smiles.

On further reflection, it was, quite definitely, *bugger* off.

PART THREE

Expansions

CHAPTER SEVEN

To begin with, Robyn saw little of her new tenant. Deborah, perhaps embarrassed by both the fainting episode and the subsequent confidences she'd made on the day she moved in, kept herself to herself. The connecting door remained closed but not, as Robyn discovered when she tried it after Deborah had left for work one morning, locked.

Finding that the door opened, Robyn instantly closed it again. She hadn't intended to go and have a poke around – even though the temptation to do so was quite strong – only to see whether Ms Warne's apparent nervousness extended to doing as Robyn had indicated she might, and securing the door from her side.

Robyn took this as a sign that Deborah wasn't entirely averse to some sort of communication between them. She hoped she was right; she was intrigued by Deborah Warne, and the hugging and comforting session had left her with a residue of kindness towards Deborah which, she was aware, was ripe to develop into friendship and affection.

*

Robyn bided her time. And, on her own side of the Great Divide, accustomed herself to living alone.

To her surprise and, indeed, to her shame, she discovered she loved it.

Sitting with her feet up one evening, a large gin and tonic in one hand and a bag of Brannigan's beef and mustard crisps within reach of the other, she switched on the early-evening news and tried to analyse why she felt so happy.

She wrote a mental list.

One: I can eat all the crisps myself.

Two: no-one's going to know if I have another, equally huge, gin. More importantly, I'm not going to be one sip into it and have someone come bumbling into the room asking for a lift to Charlie's/the station/the rugby club/the cash machine, because they just *have* to have a tenner tomorrow since it's been owing a week and the bloke it's owed to is threatening to get physical. It used to be dreadful – and a real triumph of maternal devotion – to leave that wonderful glass of gin, get up, get the car out, drive off along roads inevitably heaving with home-going traffic, turn round and come home again. And a gin and tonic, left standing for twenty-five minutes, loses the fine first flush of its seductive, blueish, bubbling appeal.

Three: I can watch what I like on telly. All evening. No boys to say, oh, I thought we were watching the footy, England's playing Estonia/Puerto Rica/Timbuctu Wanderers, no Zach to look snootily at *Casualty* or *EastEnders* and say, in a decidedly superior tone, what time is the news? Are we not missing the headlines? In eighteen years of marriage, Zach never mastered the *Radio Times*.

Four: when I've had enough telly, I can go upstairs, lie in a hot bath – from which I won't first have to clean a tide mark – for as long as I like without anyone rattling the door and saying, Mum/Robyn, how much longer are you going to be? Then, when I'm nicely red and pruneish, I can get out, get dry, put on my most frumpy nightshirt, get into bed and read, till dawn if I like.

Another marital art Zach never mastered was going to sleep with the light on. He was also relentlessly scathing about her choice of night attire; he preferred her to sleep naked, which she disliked for inexplicable reasons, or, failing

96

that, to wear one of the skimpy, lacy little whimsies with which he regularly presented her at Christmas or on their anniversary. Five such garments lay in one of her drawers, expensive, beautiful fabrics, subtle colours, and as unsatisfactory to wear as a piece of string. Thin shoulder straps might look sexy, but when one wound itself round an upper arm in the night, bedding in and all but cutting off the circulation, it wasn't very comfortable. And, besides, she felt absurd, dressed in something whose frilly hem only just covered her backside.

Five: five she was unwilling to dwell on, even in the privacy of her own thoughts. Five had to do with no longer having to endure what used to happen when, reluctantly abandoning her book, she would give in to pressure and turn the light off. Five concerned living with a man who, desperate to persuade himself he was still young and vigorous when actually he wasn't, tried to make love to his wife. Tried to encourage her to make love to *him*, to bring about an erection that didn't lose heart almost as soon as it had appeared. She had said gently, when repeated attempts failed, 'Darling, let's give it a rest, shall we? This isn't doing either of us any good. And they do say that to do without sex when you really want it is a good aphrodisiac!'

He'd gone along with her suggestion, but only for a month or so. Then the whole thing had begun again. Frustrated herself, she'd suggested seeing a sex counsellor; he had feigned outraged surprise that such people existed (although surely he must have known?) and utterly refused even to contemplate it. It was as if, Robyn realised miserably, to go public and admit failure would be the last straw. In vain she informed him that most men suffered in the same way at sometime in their lives, it was terribly common! Everyone else learned to cope!

Crushingly, he'd turned his pained dark eyes on her and said, 'How do *you* know?'

Six: returning with relief to life outside the marriage bed (a friend in her days with Paddy had referred to it as the Marital Pit), she thought, no ironing to do. No laundry of any description, no hurried attempt to get two, three or even four rugby jerseys clean, dry and aired and ready for school in the morning.

How *did* sports masters imagine one coped? One of Stevie's teachers had once had them practising tackles in the wettest, muddiest corner of the pitch, presumably on the grounds that it provided a softer landing, and Stevie's entire sports kit had been absolutely coated in dark brown mud. Furiously bashing shirt, socks and shorts in the sink, on the eighth lot of water and *still* with mud weeping out of the fabrics, Robyn had cursed both the sport and the sports teacher. She had written a note, suggesting that *if* the man had to get the boys so muddy, couldn't he at least make them stand under the shower afterwards in their kit, which would remove the worst of the dirt? She didn't receive a reply. She wondered, in fact, if the embarrassed Stevie had actually delivered it.

Eight.

She felt very relaxed. Eight, she repeated to herself, what was I going to have for eight?

Noticing that her glass was empty, she got up and made herself another drink. Returning to her chair, she found that the holiday programme was just beginning, and they were talking about Nile cruises . . .

Eight, and, for that matter, nine, ten, eleven and twelve, drifted gently out of her mind.

*

Up in her flat, Deborah often heard the happy sound of her landlady's laughter.

Accustoming herself to the lovely novelty of living in her own place, with her own front door to lock – and bolt, if she so desired – and an interconnecting door that she *could* lock, only it seemed a little untrusting, she felt, for the first time in years, *safe*.

For the initial few days, she did nothing more than revel in it. The little flat had been decorated, and there were newish curtains at the windows. The colours would not have been Deborah's choice – Mrs Kazandreas liked the yellows, rusts, strong oranges and ochres of autumn, set against a creamy background, whereas Deborah had been brought up on quiet pastels – but that was a minor complaint.

Deborah had exchanged the threatening double bed for a single. Her request, greeted with not so much as a raised eyebrow by Mrs Kazandreas, had been accomplished on that first day; between them, they had moved the double bed through the connecting door and into a room that Mrs Kazandreas said was Tim's, whoever Tim was, replacing it with this Tim's single.

Deborah had treated herself to new bedlinen. Pale minty green, with sprigs of snowdrops, the pretty white flowers embroidered on by hand. It had cost a bomb, but, secure in the knowledge that there was now a salary cheque being paid into her account at the end of each month, she felt she could afford the occasional luxury.

She had also bought make-up and a new outfit, a trouser suit with a long jacket and beautifully cut trousers. That had cost quite a lot of the £1,235.07, and she had been obliged to pay a deposit of £350 to Mrs Kazandreas. Fortunately, she had begun her new job in the second half of the month, so there was only now a week or so to wait until payday.

She was of the firm belief that one should get out of the workplace during the lunchbreak, if only for half an hour, and she was using these sessions to get to know Tunbridge Wells. Her office was up at the top end of the town, from where the whole urban area seemed to slope away downhill.

There was a common, which had attractive walks, mature trees now turning gold, and a huge outcrop of rock (sandstone, she was informed) where, every day that the weather allowed, groups of pre-school children gathered to play, watched by well-wrapped-up mothers.

Down in the town, there was a large covered shopping mall, and a traffic-free precinct, where there were usually at least two people busking and three selling *The Big Issue* ('Why did the chicken cross the road?' someone in the office had asked. 'Because he'd just seen someone selling *The Big Issue*.').

I am, Deborah told herself as she left work one evening, having exchanged friendly 'cheerios' with all five of the other staff, settling in. I am, I think – she did not quite dare probe too deeply – happy.

*

Mrs Kazandreas, as Deborah had deduced this evening from the laughter coming from the other side of the house, was quite definitely happy.

This was strange, for Mrs Hope at the letting agency had informed Deborah of her new landlady's circumstances. Told her she was a widow, and added, in a subsequent conversation, that the bereavement was quite recent. A dread suspicion crossed Deborah's mind as, relaxing one evening in her little sitting room, she abandoned her novel to ponder the matter: had Mrs Kazandreas also been a prisoner in a terrible marriage? Had this Greek husband been another Br—?

Almost as soon as it had occurred to her, she dismissed it. Women who shouted 'Bugger off!' at unwanted callers were not likely to be the sort who would cower before a bullying, brutal husband. Had Mrs Kazandreas's late spouse tried any of those dreadful tricks on *her*, she would have had his balls on a plate.

Deborah emitted a snort of laughter, swiftly suppressed. *Wherever* had she heard *that* phrase? Goodness, it wasn't like her at all! What would Mother say?

The thought prompted her to remember that she owed her mother a letter. Edith had written to her, a long, depressing sermon full of warnings and dire prognostications. Deborah had telephoned from work to thank her, hoping a phone call might be regarded as sufficient reply, but, with a martyred sigh, Edith had made it perfectly plain that *she* didn't think it was.

Edith, Deborah reflected resignedly, had turned the sigh into an art form.

Suddenly she got to her feet and, going through into the kitchenette – horrid word, she thought, horrid *estate agent* word, I shall from now on refer to it as my *kitchen* – she made herself a mug of hot chocolate. She decorated it liberally with whipped cream and chocolate swirls, then headed back for the sitting room.

From the other side of the connecting door, another burst of laughter rang out. Deborah stopped to listen; after a moment or two, Robyn laughed again. She was, undoubtedly, watching something on TV – Deborah had noticed there was a comedy show on that night, *French and Saunders*, she thought it was.

Deborah *hoped* that her landlady was watching television. If not, if she was sitting there in her spacious, echoing house, laughing so uproariously at nothing, then Deborah was in for trouble . . .

She was scraping the last of the chocolate residue out of the cup a little later when she heard a soft tapping. Freezing – and telling herself simultaneously not to be so daft, there was nothing to be scared of! – she put down the cup and stood up.

The tapping was repeated, and a voice called quietly, 'Deborah?'

She opened the connecting door. Robyn was standing on the other side.

'Oh! Hello!' Deborah said brightly, as if it was a pleasant surprise to see the only person it could possibly be.

'I forgot you were here,' Robyn said, with an embarrassed grin. 'I've been watching *French and Saunders*, and I was laughing so much, I quite forgot there was anyone else in the house. I hope I didn't disturb you?'

'Not in the least.' Should she be honest and say she'd heard, or diplomatic and pretend she hadn't? 'I *did* hear, actually, but it was lovely.'

A genuinely pleased smile spread over Robyn's face. 'Really? My husband used to say I laughed like a jackal, although actually I think he meant hyena. But, since you heard through three closed doors, then maybe he was right.'

'Two closed doors,' Deborah amended. 'I only heard when I was out here in the corridor.'

Robyn chuckled. '*That's* all right, then.'

They stood looking at each other. Deborah, feeling a sudden glow of well-being, found herself smiling widely.

Robyn responded. 'You've got chocolate all round your mouth,' she observed.

'Oh, Lord!' Deborah felt in her sleeve for a handkerchief, wetted it with her tongue and hastily scrubbed at her mouth and chin. 'Better?'

'Better.' Robyn was still smiling. 'Actually, it was quite interesting – you looked like Groucho Marx.'

Deborah giggled. 'Just what I've always wanted.'

Changing tack, Robyn said, 'Does your telly work okay?'

'My telly? Oh – I think so, yes. I've only watched BBC1 so far.'

'Not a telly addict, like me?'

'No.' Deborah had got out of the way of watching television. There had been little point, when she never got her choice of programme.

Robyn was watching her closely. 'It can be a good companion, the old telly,' she observed. 'I don't only watch comedy – there was a brilliant programme about badgers earlier, and there's a new Jane Austen adaptation starting tomorrow.'

'Is there?' Deborah loved Jane Austen.

'Look,' Robyn appeared hesitant, an expression, Deborah noticed, which did not often appear on her face, 'why don't you come through the Great Divide' – she patted the connecting door – 'tomorrow evening, and we'll watch together? That is, unless you have other plans, which you probably will since it's nearly the weekend and –'

'I'd love to,' Deborah said gently.

She observed all sorts of thoughts flash through Robyn's mind – really, she did have the most open, expressive face. Had she overstepped the mark by inviting her new tenant into her own side of the house? Was she herself going to regret it? Had she offended, by seeming to assume that Deborah had nothing better to do in the evening than sit watching television?

Deborah could reassure her, at least on the first and the last; she said again, with as much warmth as she could muster, 'Thank you. That'd be really nice.'

CHAPTER EIGHT

One morning in November, Robyn's post contained two airmail letters, both bearing Greek stamps.

One was from Jerome. Robyn had received one or two brief phone calls from him since he'd arrived in Crete, but had not managed to glean from them much more than that he was okay, was being made very welcome by all the uncles, aunts and cousins, that the weather was terrific (he'd been swimming, sailing, sailboarding, and his cousin George was teaching him to waterski), and work was cool.

His letter was considerably more expansive. He said he spent quite a lot of time with his grandmother – 'she's not as busy as the rest of them and she's a great cook' – and Robyn gathered, reading between the lines, that Zach's mother was deriving as much comfort from her grandson as her grandson was from her. Robyn regretted, fleetingly, that, for her sake, Jerome didn't look more like his father.

Jerome also told her a lot more about the work. He was being shown all the Kazandreas properties: the large and the small hotels, the apartment blocks and – a new venture for the next season – a small boat for brief cruises around Crete's coast. He had just spent a fortnight in the main office in Heraklion, where his uncle Andreas was giving him a thorough grounding in the economic realities of the tourist business.

He sounded, Robyn concluded, quite happy.

He only mentioned his father once, although she knew this didn't indicate that Zach wasn't constantly on his mind.

He said, towards the end of his letter, 'Grandma and I go often to the house. Dad's things are just as he left them, and Grandma said we could leave it that way if I wanted. I said I thought we should, and she seemed to think it was a good decision. She did say I should feel free to take anything of Dad's that I wanted, so I've got his Swiss army knife – you know, the really expensive one he bought when we were in Italy? – and also some other small stuff, like sunglasses and trainers and a couple of really thick beach towels (I think they're new). I know some of this stuff, like the towels, is actually yours too, and not really Dad's personal possession, so I hope this is okay. Grandma said she didn't think you'd mind.' How right she was, Robyn thought. 'The house was sad, at first. It was much more Dad than Haydon Hall, which feels like all of us. But going there often, I really like it now. I sort of talk to Dad, if you don't think that sounds odd.' No, my love, of course I don't. She stroked the page, Jerome vivid in her mind.

As if he didn't want to end on an emotional note, he finished by telling her his cousins had got him drinking ouzo with hardly any water, and he didn't like it much: 'I'm going to stick to beer in future!'

Right at the bottom of the page, after his artistic signature, even, he'd written: 'Love you, Mum', and followed it with the row of noughts and crosses (for hugs and kisses) with which he'd been signing notes to her ever since he could write.

She tucked the letter away in her desk drawer. She would reply to it in a day or so, longer, if she could make herself wait, since, if he got a letter back from her straight away, he might feel she was hinting that he should reply to hers equally quickly.

She picked up the other letter. The postmark was Athens. It was from Zach's solicitor. He said, in strange formal English which suggested he wasn't terribly familiar with the language, that Mrs Kazandreas would wish to know that certain possessions belonging to her late husband, Zacharias Kazandreas, required her esteemed attention. Mention was made of the Athens apartment, and the emotive word 'irregularities' was used; he finished by saying Mrs Kazandreas was not to discommode herself (his Greek–English dictionary, Robyn thought, must date from the last century) and that it was undoubtedly a matter that had been subjected to a misunderstanding.

It was all rather confusing and slightly alarming. Robyn, feeling more than a little discommoded, decided she would do what the man – who, she saw at the end of the letter, signed himself N Efstathiadis – seemed to be hinting at, and fly out to see for herself.

*

She was both excited and alarmed at the prospect of setting off for Athens on her own to investigate this legal irregularity. As soon as she'd booked her flight, she instantly regretted it, and wished she'd at least made an attempt to sort the matter out by phone and by letter. But then, Mr Efstathiadis had hinted – more than hinted – that it was a delicate matter, one on which he did not appear to know how to proceed. There was a strange, ambiguous sentence in his letter in which he seemed to say that there were two interpretations of the late Mr Kazandreas's wishes, and that 'considerable contemplation' was needed.

Robyn looked up the Athens weather in *The Times*. Sunny, nineteen degrees.

It was raining in Tunbridge Wells, and there was a spiteful easterly wind. Athens began to look more attractive.

She told Deborah she would be away for a few days, adding, and trying not to sound pretentious, that she had to go to Athens to sort out some legal muddle over one of her husband's properties there.

'Golly,' Deborah had said. 'How lovely! Oh – or not lovely?' The brown eyes looked doubtful, as if she feared she'd trodden on Robyn's sensitive, grieving toes.

'Lovely, I hope and expect,' Robyn said lightly; Deborah, it seemed, had sufficient problems to bear on her own account, without taking on anyone else's. Particularly when they weren't actually problems at all. Robyn could, she was quite confident, visit the Athens flat and tackle whatever hiccup had occurred without it bringing back incapacitating and undermining sorrow.

So she hoped.

Deborah offered to keep an eye on Robyn's bit of Haydon Hall, agreeing to water the plants and make sure mail wasn't left sticking out of the letter box. One of the plus points, Robyn thought, of having a tenant.

She telephoned Tim and Will, telling them what she was doing. Some unknown woman answered Stevie's phone, and agreed to pass on the message. She had toyed with the idea of flying on from Athens to Crete to drop in on Jerome, but she had reluctantly abandoned the plan. It might have looked as if she were checking up on him.

Robyn packed a small bag, bought herself a couple of new paperback novels, and, on a bleak November afternoon, flew out to the late-autumn sunshine of Athens.

*

Sitting in the taxi blasting its way through the early-evening traffic, she wondered if she should have seen Mr Efstathiadis before going to the flat. He would surely not be at his office *now*, although one never knew how late they worked; it all depended on how long a siesta had been taken. Did solicitors take siestas? And did they take them in November?

Still, even had he still been at his desk, she didn't think she was up to tackling a meeting with him at this moment. She'd have to find her way to his office first, and that wasn't going to be easy, she didn't know Athens very well. No. Better, by far, to phone him in the morning.

It had not even occurred to her to check into a hotel. Why should it, when she had a perfectly adequate – more-than-adequate – flat at her disposal?

When they'd arrived at the flat, she paid off the taxi, hefted her holdall over her shoulder and walked up the short path to the apartment block. It was in a quiet suburb, and there were trees to give shade from the fierce summer sun; some optimist had even laid down a lawn between the flower beds from which late roses put out a heady scent.

The entrance hall was cool and dim. She pressed the button that summoned the lift, and, while she waited, reached in her handbag for the flat keys.

Going up in the lift, she could hear the bass thump, thump of rock music, being played somewhere in the building. Being played pretty loudly; she hoped it wasn't going to go on all night.

She emerged from the lift, turned right along the corridor; their apartment was second to last, facing away from the street.

With each step, the music got louder.

It was coming from her own flat.

She stood in the corridor, mouth dropped open in dis-belief.

She wondered afterwards why she hadn't been afraid. Why she didn't turn back out of the block and summon help. Probably, she decided, because anyone with nefarious inten-tions would hardly advertise their presence by blasting out music on Zach's prize stereo.

A door opened behind her. A grey-haired man poked his head out, nodded to her in recognition, and said something in Greek, miming distress, putting his hands over his ears. Trying to bump-start her brain into recalling what Greek she knew, she nodded, smiled, said, in Greek, 'Sorry. Too much noise, yes. I will stop it.'

Grunting something, he went back inside his flat and slammed the door.

Robyn put the key in the lock and quietly let herself in. The music was now deafening. She needn't have bothered being quiet; whoever it was wouldn't have heard the Seventh Cavalry. The flat smelled strange – joss sticks, was it? There was also the echo of some well-known scent . . . Opium, she thought. Or maybe Coco?

She walked steadily down the short hall. The door to what had been her and Zach's bedroom was ajar; the bed was unmade, and quite a lot of clothes were strewn across the little tapestried nursing chair that Zach's mother had given her when Jerome was born, spilling on to the floor. Most of the clothes seemed to be hers, a selection from the summer-weight wardrobe she kept in the flat.

She went on. The kitchen looked as if a bomb had recently gone off in it: every one of the surfaces was loaded with dirty plates, overflowing ashtrays, bags of rubbish. Out of the corner of her eye she saw something scuttle away – oh, God, not cockroaches!

On past the other bedroom, whose door was also ajar. The room was empty, the bed covered with nothing but a cream linen bedspread; nobody in occupation there.

And into the large living room; it was from here that the music was emanating.

Cliantha was standing in front of the French windows that opened on to the little balcony. She was singing along with the music, and her stocky body weaved and writhed in some private dance fantasy.

She was wearing a shot silk caftan which Zach had given Robyn the summer before last; it was maize yellow and amber, and one of her all-time favourite garments. It was too long for Cliantha, not her colour, and the hem was grubby.

Furious, Robyn made herself count to ten. Her hot anger

subsiding a little, she waited for a gap in the music, then said, 'Cliantha, what are you doing?'

Cliantha, still moving despite the absence of sound, froze in mid-writhe. Very slowly, she turned round. Her face, wearing a scowl, was heavily made up with a foundation that was a few shades too pale, so that there was a clear demarcation line between her jaw and her neck. Her eyes were circled in black kohl. She looked rather like a cross panda.

'Robyn,' she said, nodding, as if Robyn's sudden appearance was no more than she had expected. 'Robyn.'

'I didn't realize you were in Athens,' Robyn said.

'I didn't realize *you* were.'

'I came because –' Was it the right moment to reveal that Mr Efstathiadis had summoned her? Was this – Cliantha's presence in the flat – indeed the delicate matter that was not to discommode Robyn? But Cliantha was Zach's daughter, why shouldn't she live in the flat? 'Does anyone know you're here?' she said, aware she was sounding like some authority-wielding adult speaking to a naughty child, hardly appropriate when her stepdaughter was in her mid-thirties.

Cliantha was doing her infuriating nodding again. 'Yes, yes,' she said, 'I knew you . . .'

But at that moment the music began again – it sounded like exactly the same track – and Robyn missed the rest of the sentence. She was about to mouth, can we have that off? when her anger flared again. Striding across to the stereo, she stopped the CD and removed it from the player, switching the apparatus off.

Turning back to Cliantha, she said, 'Now, what were you saying?'

Cliantha had sat down on the arm of the long settee that filled one wall of the living room. Its cream leather was, Robyn noticed, filthy. Deliberately keeping Robyn waiting, Cliantha took a cigarette from an onyx box on the coffee table and lit it with the silver table lighter.

'I guessed you would come running when the solicitor wrote to you,' she said. The dark eyes, the thick kohl making them look almost black, were fixed on Robyn. 'Guessed you would want to come and check up on your property.' The tone was acid.

'*My* property?' Robyn was not sure what she was getting into.

'Yes. My father left everything to you, did he not? A flat, a house in England, a house in Crete.'

'The house in England was mine already,' Robyn said neutrally.

Cliantha shrugged, as if she couldn't be bothered with such hair-splitting. 'Well, just the same, you now have three houses. Are you not a fortunate woman? A – what is it? Ah, yes – a merry widow.'

It was not the moment to discuss with her stepdaughter her emotions at losing Zach, if, indeed, there ever would be such a moment. Robyn said calmly, 'The Rethymnon house is at my disposal, yes, and belongs to me. This flat, too, although I had understood that it was let.'

'And just where did you imagine *I* was going to live?' Cliantha shouted, fury spilling across the pale face in a hot blush.

'Well, I –' Robyn hadn't given the matter any thought. Zach had played his Cliantha cards very close to his chest, not sharing his anxieties with his wife, and Robyn had accepted this. With relief. If it had ever occurred to her to wonder where Cliantha was, she would assume she was still living with the boyfriend in the place outside Heraklion. Since Cliantha didn't appear to have notified her father to the contrary – she certainly hadn't notified Robyn – it was a perfectly reasonable assumption.

Zach must have met the young man, or at least have known who he was; he loathed him, and, during one of their infrequent meetings in the summer before the one when he'd had his first stroke, had ordered Cliantha not to see him any more, telling her the young man was a 'peasant', not worthy of someone from the Kazandreas family. The more he had railed at her, the more Cliantha had been determined to ignore him. Robyn, standing on the sidelines, could see exactly what was happening: Cliantha might be in her thirties, but she still hadn't outgrown the look-at-me, aren't-I-being-awful? tactics.

Better, by far, to have said, fine, Cliantha, go and live with him, here's a few thousand drachmas to buy yourself some home comforts. She would soon have got sick of love in a cottage. But Zach hadn't seen it that way. Zach had consistently risen to the bait.

'I imagined you were still living with Dimitri,' Robyn said now.

'*Dimitri?* Hah!' Cliantha sounded as if such a concept were inconceivable. 'He is a slob, that one! He behaved like a peasant!'

That was precisely your father's opinion, Robyn said silently. 'So you no longer live in the little house near Heraklion?'

'That place, it was bad even for *pigs.*'

'Ah. I see.' Robyn paused, collecting her thoughts. It looked as if, sick of slumming it, Cliantha had headed back for the comfortable life. Why hadn't she gone to live in the Rethymnon house? And how had she managed to get possession of this flat, when, Robyn was quite sure, there had been tenants in occupation?

'I live *here* now,' Cliantha stated. 'This is our home.'

Our. Letting that matter pass for the moment, Robyn said, 'And what of the tenants?'

'I told the solicitor to get them out. Their lease was up anyway, and I told him I had to have somewhere to live.'

Could she do that? Robyn wondered. Had the solicitor acted within the law? He *must* have done, he of all people!

Solicitors didn't do otherwise, even with an importuning, homeless daughter demanding possession of her late father's property. And if the lease was indeed up . . .

'You could have moved into the Rethymnon house,' Robyn pointed out. 'Nobody's living there at the moment.'

'I needed to be *here*, in Athens!' Cliantha threw out her arms, as if to embrace the whole city, from Acropolis to Lycabettus. The panda eyes returned to Robyn, and she added, 'Here is where Andy is.'

Ah. *Cherchez l'homme*, Robyn thought. 'And you and Andy are living here together?'

'Yes.' Defiantly. 'Here is where Andy works.'

That was something. At least this one had a city job; Dimitri had been a farmer. An ignorant swineherd, Zach had said, but that might have been paternal prejudice.

Robyn realised, with devastating suddenness, how tired she was. Moving across to one of the pair of armchairs that matched the sofa, she sank into it. She would have loved to take her shoes off – her feet always swelled when she flew – but there was a distinct possibility that she would soon have to force them on again. Cliantha was hardly being welcoming, and she wasn't sure she wanted to stay overnight in the flat, with Cliantha and this Andy no doubt performing at top volume in the next room.

She looked up, to find Cliantha watching her. 'I'd like a drink,' she said firmly. 'Would you please fetch me a large gin? I think we left some tonics in the cupboard, if they haven't all been used' – this neutrally, although she didn't feel like being neutral – 'and I imagine you've got some ice?'

Cliantha looked as if she were about to refuse. But, the ancient habits of Greek hospitality apparently proving stronger than her resentment and dislike of her stepmother, abruptly she turned on her heel and flounced off to the kitchen.

Robyn heard the sounds of the fridge door opening, of

ice rattling on glass. Then someone unlocked the front door and came into the hall, and Cliantha called out a greeting. The answering voice was interrupted as Cliantha said quickly, in Greek, 'Watch it, my stepmother's here.'

Robyn waited. Staring at the entrance to the living room, she saw Cliantha appear, a strange smile on her face.

She said, 'This is Andy.'

And stood aside to reveal behind her, dressed in jeans and a denim jacket, hair short and spiky, a young woman.

'Her name is really Antigone,' Cliantha purred, 'but she prefers Andy.' Then, in case Robyn had missed the message, missed the passion in *here is where Andy is* and the significance of the one bedroom in use, with its double bed, Cliantha said, 'Andy and I are living together. We are lovers.'

*

Robyn had drunk her gin, making polite conversation with Andy while Cliantha, smirking like the Cheshire cat, watched, her head turning from one to the other like a spectator at a tennis match.

Then Robyn had got up and, making her apologies, left them to it.

She found a small hotel a few streets from the Archaeological Museum and, in the morning, made an appointment and went to see Mr Efstathiadis.

She told him that she had visited the apartment, had spoken to her stepdaughter and, while she was sorry that the tenants had had to lose their home, felt sure that her late husband would have wished his daughter to live in the flat if that was what she wanted. She didn't think she was up to a prolonged wrangle with the clearly determined Cliantha. Especially when she couldn't really see any reason why Cliantha shouldn't live in the flat.

She had, however, relieved her stepdaughter of the silk caftan.

Mr Efstathiadis seemed relieved to have the matter settled amicably; perhaps he had been expecting a bit of family in-fighting and the appropriate shedding of blood. He could be forgiven for imagining the worst – there was surely plenty of potential drama in a father leaving all his property to a second wife, at the expense of the issue of the first marriage. Reassuring himself that Robyn appreciated the full situation – the tenants had been paying quite a high rent, and Cliantha was, naturally, living rent-free – he finally nodded and, ringing for his secretary, concluded the meeting by offering Robyn a coffee.

Ten minutes later, with Mr Efstathiadis's reassurances that he would keep the situation under observation – as if the flat and Cliantha were sick patients – ringing in her ears, and the taste of his coffee bitter in her mouth, she was out in the street again.

Her business in Athens was, it seemed, concluded. With no other course of action suggesting itself, she went out to the airport, managed to change her flight and, five hours later, was on her way back to England.

*

She reflected, on the flight home, that one of the greatest ironies about life with Zach had been this. That, having made a total fist of bringing up his own child, his relationship with whom was one of those that people must have had in mind when they coined the word 'dysfunctional', he had nevertheless seen fit to tell Robyn how to go about raising her own children.

Not only Jerome who, being Zach's son as well as Robyn's, Zach had every right to be involved in. No. What had scorched across Robyn like an unassuageable, perpetual irritant had been Zach's pontificating about Tim, Stevie and Will. 'Do not let him do this', 'The boy should be ordered to do that', 'Are you aware that the boy has done this?', 'You are wrong in allowing them to do that'. The judgements, carved in stone, issued from Zach as if he alone knew how to raise sound children. And how she had hated being caught in the terrible conflict of emotions, loving her sons and hence indulgent with them, resenting Zach's narrow-minded view of childrearing, yet, loving him too, aching for him because he was showing himself up to be autocratic and unreasonable.

Only once had she almost said what simmered so close beneath the surface. Will – of her three older sons, the most reasonable, the most amenable – had failed one night to telephone to say he was going to be late home, and Robyn had become slightly anxious. Zach, observing her distress, had embarked on a long lecture on the duty children owed to their parents, a duty of consideration and loving respect. Since this had been shortly after Cliantha had chucked in her fourth attempt to get some qualifications, shouting at Zach – whose idea it had been that she go to college – that he was an interfering bully and should leave her to get on with her own life in her own way, Robyn had considered the lecture a little inappropriate.

She wouldn't have minded, had Zach restrained himself to lecturing *her*. But, when Will finally came home, full of apologies for having forgotten to phone and hugging his mother to make up for worrying her, Zach had begun on him.

She listened for as long as she could bear. Then, her face aching with the effort to smile, to look as if this wasn't upsetting her as much as it was, she said, 'I think that's enough now, Zach. Give it a rest!'

He had looked in turn angry, resentful and hurt. Had left the room, muttering about not being wanted and *people* – by which he meant her – throwing it back in his face when he tried to help.

Sad, heartsore, she had sat with Will's arms round her till she – and he – felt better.

Sitting in her aircraft seat re-living the scene, she recalled her list of plus points about living on her own.

Eight, nine, ten, eleven and twelve must surely all be, I no longer have a well-intentioned but ill-advised second husband telling me how to bring up my children.

CHAPTER NINE

Deborah missed Robyn rather more than she had anticipated. Without her presence on the other side of the Great Divide, Haydon Hall seemed suddenly an echoing, slightly awe-inspiring place. There wasn't a lot of logic about Deborah's reaction, since, although she and Robyn had slipped into the habit of watching television together once or twice a week – usually heralded by Robyn tapping on the connecting door and saying, 'I'm just getting the ice out of the fridge, if you feel like a drink' – most of the time neither was actually aware of the other's presence.

Deborah was even spared the necessity of presenting her rent in person; she had arranged for it to be paid into Robyn's account by standing order on the first of every month. In view of their tentative friendship, it had been a good move, sparing both of them the small awkwardness.

It was, Deborah thought as she tried to make herself relax and fall asleep the night after Robyn's departure, as if merely knowing Robyn was there, in the other part of the house, was sufficient to reassure. And, she had to admit, she needed reassurance. Still did. Probably always would.

Giving up on sleep, she switched the bedside light back on, irritably reached for her glasses and re-opened *Mansfield Park*.

*

At half-past midnight, the resounding chimes of Haydon Hall's front door bell rang out through the silent house.

Stiff with alarm, Deborah sat bolt-upright in bed. *Mansfield Park* slipped, unnoticed, to the floor.

She could both feel and hear her heart thumping, a worryingly loud sensation simultaneously in ears and chest. It was quite painful. What to do? Go through and see who it was? It could be a perfectly legitimate caller – one of Robyn's sons, for example, unexpectedly stranded in Tunbridge Wells and without a key . . .

It didn't sound very convincing.

The bell rang out again.

Deborah got out of bed, put on slippers and dressing gown, and walked stealthily along to the Great Divide, through it, along the landing and down the stairs into Robyn's hall. She switched on the light. By the door was a brass tubular container full of umbrellas and walking sticks; arming herself with a stout blackthorn walking stick, Deborah took up position just behind the door.

The bell rang again. This time, as if the caller sensed that somebody was listening, a thin female voice cried out, 'Oh, *please*! I *know* someone's there, I saw the light go on!' There was a sob in the voice, and an edge of panic that was all too readily detectable to Deborah.

Taking a tight grip on her stick – which was already beginning to appear superfluous – Deborah said firmly, 'I shall not open the door until you tell me who is there.'

As she said the words, she noticed a spy-hole in the stout wood of the door. Putting her eye to it, she saw, on the step, the vague outline of a young girl. Shoulders hunched, head down, she looked the picture of dejection.

'My name's Phoebe Parry,' said the girl. 'I'm a friend of Stevie's.'

Stevie. Yes, Robyn had a son named Stevie. 'Yes? And what do you want?' Deborah said.

There was a muffled sob. 'I want to come *in*!'

Deborah didn't know what to do. Had Robyn invited this

girl to stay and forgotten all about it? Was Deborah risking her contempt and disapproval by refusing entry? Or was this just an elaborate ruse? Did this seemingly despairing girl have a posse of well-armed burglars waiting out of sight wearing stockings over their heads?

With sudden clarity, Deborah thought, this is quite *absurd*, and, struggling with locks and bolts, opened the door.

The girl looked up, the tear-stained face, caught in a beam of light from the hall, suddenly alive with joy. 'Oh! Oh, *thank* you!' she breathed, clasping her hands together in front of her breasts in a quaintly old-fashioned gesture. 'May I – would it be all right . . .' Trailing off, she indicated a suitcase at her feet.

'Yes, okay, bring it in.' Deborah stood back to allow the girl entry.

'Oh, and there's a taxi . . .'

'What?'

'I had to have a taxi, from the station.' She leaned forward confidingly. 'I couldn't *walk*, you see.'

'Yes, quite. What about the taxi?'

The girl whispered, 'I haven't paid him. Not enough money.'

Deborah baulked at the idea of going out in her dressing gown to pay off some taxi that might or might not be at the end of the drive. Wouldn't her absence on such an errand give the gang of cut-throats in stocking masks the perfect opportunity to tiptoe inside?

'I'll give you some money,' she said firmly. 'Wait there.' She closed the front door, re-locked the deadlock – the girl could admit her silent accomplices while Deborah was gone – and, pocketing the key, hurried back upstairs to fetch her purse.

When she got back, the girl didn't appear to have moved. Deborah was just asking how much the fare was when the door bell rang again.

This time, both Deborah and the girl froze.

Deborah, recovering first, peered through the spy-hole. 'It's the cab driver,' she said. 'At least, I think it is. Short and quite tubby, bald head and a dark anorak?'

The girl, wide-eyed, said pathetically, 'Oh, dear, I didn't notice! I was too worried!'

Deborah said loudly through the door, 'Are you the taxi driver?'

'No,' came the lugubrious reply, 'I'm Father Christmas, only I'm early.'

Deborah put the chain on and opened the door. 'How much?'

'Tenner'll do you.'

'Ten pounds?' It seemed extreme, for a journey up from the station. 'Where have you come from?'

'Central station. It's after midnight, see.'

Deborah didn't see at all. But paying off the cab driver was the only way she was going to be able to turn her attention to the stranger behind her in Robyn's hall. She pushed a ten pound note through the door, and a hand took it. Even before the taxi driver had stomped off down the drive, she had closed, locked and bolted the door.

'Now,' she said, turning to the girl, 'who did you say you are?'

'Phoebe. Phoebe Parry.' The girl's face, more clearly visible now that she was standing under the light, was very pale. Slightly greenish, Deborah observed.

'And you have just arrived, by train?'

'I got in ages ago. I've been sitting outside the station, trying to pluck up courage to come, only a policeman asked me what I was doing, and – oh!' Fresh tears sprang from the wide grey eyes. 'Oh, he thought I was – you know! A – *you* know!'

'Did he?' It hadn't occurred to innocent Deborah that there would be prostitutes in Tunbridge Wells. 'Well, I'm sure he – what's the matter?'

The girl had put a long white hand to her mouth. She was making strange gulping noises. She muttered something, but the muffling hand made it incomprehensible.

Just as Deborah realised that the girl was going to be sick, she was. With a sort of hiccupping retch, a pool of vomit shot out of her mouth and, describing a perfect arc, landed with a splat on the parquet floor.

Deborah said, 'Oh, dear.'

The girl – Phoebe – was crying in earnest now, all attempt at self-control gone. 'Oh, I'm sorry, sorry, sorry, *sorry*!' she wailed. 'I've got you up in the middle of the night, made you pay off my cab, and you've only got my word for it that I even *know* your son! Oh, it's just awful, *awful*!'

Deborah, who knew all the signs of imminent hysteria, took hold of the girl's thin arm. 'Now, then, Phoebe,' she said kindly but authoritatively, 'I don't think now is the moment to discuss all this. I'm not actually Stevie's mother, she's away. But, if you felt she would welcome you, then I dare say you're right.' She was surprised – and quite pleased – at how calm she sounded. How well she was dealing with this alarming crisis. 'The best thing, for now, is for me to put you to bed, and we'll talk over what we should do in the morning.'

Phoebe's huge eyes fixed on to hers. 'Oh, *could* I? Could I be put to bed?' She sounded like a child of eight, but it was probably only a product of her distress.

'Yes. Come along.' Deborah picked up the suitcase – which was awfully heavy – and, taking Phoebe by her chilly, clammy hand, led her upstairs. She found clean bedlinen while Phoebe undressed, and made up one of the spare beds while Phoebe did her teeth. Then she helped the girl into bed and tucked the duvet up round her shoulders.

'Do you want a bucket?' she asked.

'A bucket? Oh, no, I won't be sick again. I never am, not more than once.'

'I see.' Some sort of nervous reaction, probably. Deborah knew all about those, too. 'Well, then, Phoebe, you try to get some sleep, and I'll see you in the morning. I live in the flat next door, but I'll leave the connecting door open, so I'll be able to hear you if you call.' And, for that matter, Deborah added silently, if you get up and start bagging up the silver. Deborah was a chronically light sleeper.

'You're terribly kind,' Phoebe breathed, 'and you're not even Stevie's mother!'

'Quite.' Phoebe, Deborah was sure, meant no disparagement. 'Now, settle down, and I'll see you in the morning.'

'Night-night,' Phoebe said, eyelids drooping and a soft smile on the lovely mouth. 'Sleep tight.'

'Goodnight.'

*

Back in her flat at last – it had taken half an hour or more to clean up the sick, and the hall still smelled ghastly – Deborah lay awake for a long time.

Had she done the right thing? Could she possibly telephone Robyn in the morning, for guidance? Robyn hadn't actually *left* her a number, had merely said casually, 'If the house burns down or anything, the flat's number's in the book.' What book, and where Deborah might find it, she had not explained.

A bit of detective work would surely bring it to light! If not, Deborah could call one of Robyn's sons – this Stevie, perhaps – and do a little check on Phoebe Parry.

Suddenly she had a brainwave. Frances! She'd ring Frances! Her surname, Deborah knew, was Swift – Robyn had introduced them a few days ago, when Frances had just been leaving as Deborah returned from work, and Deborah had been impressed by Robyn's mother's grace. Yes! That was the thing to do! If Frances Swift's number wasn't readily apparent, Deborah would look her up in the phone book.

With a sensible, workable plan decided upon, Deborah turned over and went to sleep.

*

She was awake early. If she was going to have time to get in touch with Robyn's mother, outline the situation and get some advice, *and* get to work by nine o'clock, it was just as well.

She looked in on Phoebe, who was still fast asleep, a blissful expression on her face. Quickly she showered, dressed and ate breakfast, taking her second cup of tea to the telephone. It was now eight o'clock; hoping it wasn't too early – although it was just too bad if it was – she looked up Swift in the phone book, found the likeliest one (Frances, she knew, lived in the town), and dialled the number.

It was answered on the third ring. 'John Swift.'

Deborah, having overlooked the possibility of a husband and father, was temporarily taken aback. Recovering, she said, 'This is Deborah Warne, your daughter's new tenant at Haydon Hall.'

'Oh, yes?' He sounded quite friendly.

'I met your wife last week, and I wondered if I might have a word with her? I'm sorry it's so early, but I wanted to speak to her before I go to work.'

'Don't worry,' John Swift reassured her, 'my wife is an early riser. She's making scones at the moment – I'll call her.'

Deborah, trying to take in the concept of someone baking scones at eight in the morning, heard Frances Swift's voice come on the line. 'Good morning, Deborah, how can we help?'

The relief was enormous; Deborah hadn't realised how much the matter was worrying her. She explained, as succinctly as she could, and Frances made sympathetic noises. 'So, you see,' she concluded, 'the problem really is

124

that I have to leave for work soon, and I just don't know if it's all right to leave this girl in Robyn's house. I wondered if you –'

'I'll come over,' Frances said. 'Of course I will! My husband used to be a solicitor,' she added reassuringly, although Deborah didn't see the relevance. 'Give me a quarter of an hour to get my scones out of the oven and drive over.'

'Oh, I *would* be grateful,' Deborah said, 'I really –'

Frances Swift's bright 'Byeee!' cut her off.

*

Frances pulled up outside exactly sixteen minutes later. Deborah, standing in the open doorway, watched her climb out of the car; her grey hair looked as immaculate as if she had just left the hairdresser, and she was wearing black jersey trousers with tapering legs and a scarlet and mauve swirly shawl thing whose end she flung dramatically over one shoulder as she came hurrying across the drive.

She dresses like *this*, Deborah thought, to make *scones*?

'My dear, good morning.' Frances kissed her, and Deborah was engulfed in a glorious cloud of expensive-smelling perfume. 'I am *so* sorry you have had this wretched bother – did you manage to get a wink?'

'I slept a little,' Deborah said, following Frances into the hall.

'Did you? Well done, you! I'm sure I should not have done, with a total stranger only yards away.'

'Well, she's a very small and timid stranger,' Deborah said.

Frances laughed, a sound like singing. 'Not a mad axe-wielder?'

'I doubt it.'

'Better let me have a look, dear.'

'This way.'

Deborah led the way up to the spare room where she had put Phoebe. Opening the door, she and Frances peered in.

Phoebe's eyelids flickered, and her eyes opened. 'Oh, hello!' she said sweetly. 'Oh! It's Mrs Swift, isn't it?'

Frances was staring at her intently. 'It is. Do I know you, dear?'

'Yes! Stevie brought me to a party at your house, not last Christmas but the one before that. We had a lovely drink that your husband said was called a wassail cup, it was sort of hot, spicy wine, and you told him it had too much brandy in it.'

Frances leaned close to Deborah. 'Ten out of ten for accuracy so far,' she murmured. 'John had the gall to seem surprised when all the young got pissed. Phoebe,' she said to the girl, staring at her, 'yes, indeed, I remember now. And how is Stephen? Not with you?'

Phoebe's face clouded. 'No. He doesn't know I've come. In fact, we haven't seen each other for ages, not since . . .' The eyes did their tear-welling trick again, and Frances gave a distinct sniff. Disapproval? Indication that she was not to be so readily taken in? Deborah didn't know.

'Why, then, have you come?' Frances said. 'Is my daughter expecting you?'

Phoebe shook her head. 'No. I came because – because – oh, don't throw me out! Please, don't, don't, *don't*!'

Frances said, with what Deborah thought was admirable forthrightness, 'There is no question of throwing you anywhere, Phoebe. Besides the fact that it is not how the civilised behave, this is my daughter's house, and I do not presume to say who may or may not reside beneath her roof.' Golly! Deborah thought. 'All I am asking you is why you have come. That's not unreasonable, now, is it?'

Phoebe, responding to the kind tone, sniffed and said no it wasn't. Then, making a huge effort, she raised her head and straightened her shoulders – not easy, when in bed – and said, 'I have come because I've run out of choices. I haven't got a job, and I've no money to pay my rent – I was in a flat with three other girls, you see, we'd been sharing since university. I can't go home, because Mummy and Daddy wouldn't understand.' Her lower lip trembled ominously. 'So – so, you see, Robyn – Mrs Kazandreas, isn't it? Stevie said she remarried and had his half-brother, so she's not Kingswood like him – Robyn is my last hope.' She was crying again, face crumpled, desperation in her eyes. The long pale fingers were pulling at the duvet cover, as if she would like to have stuffed the corner into her mouth and sucked on it like a small child on a security blanket.

Frances sat on the edge of the bed and took one of Phoebe's restless hands. 'Now, then, that's enough crying,' she said, patting the hand. 'Last hope for what? And why, when you do not seem to have met my daughter, are you expecting her to help you?'

'Because she's Stevie's mother!' Phoebe exclaimed, as if any idiot could have seen that.

'And the relevance of that?' Frances prompted.

Enlightenment flooded Phoebe's face. 'Oh, I didn't say, did I?' She smiled, and the smile turned into a delightful laugh. Really, Deborah thought detachedly, she is a most pretty girl.

'Didn't say what?' Frances's tone was worryingly ominous.

Phoebe's happy smile flitted to Deborah and back to Frances. 'I'm pregnant,' she said. And, with a touchingly joyful pride, as if she was certain they would share her delight, 'I'm going to have Stevie's baby.'

CHAPTER TEN

◈

Robyn's flight got her into Gatwick at seven in the evening, local time, which was in fact nine o'clock Greek time. It had been a long and fairly stressful day, and she was exhausted.

There was, of course, nobody to meet her. Her energy failing her at the thought of making the tedious journey home on the train, she went outside and found a taxi. Telling herself that it was £30 well spent, she sat back in her seat and closed her eyes.

*

Her mother's car was parked in the front drive of Haydon Hall. And, hard on the heels of this warning sign, she noticed that the lights on her side of the house were on.

Alarm bells sounding in her mind, she paid off the taxi and hurried inside.

'. . . think you should try to eat something less rich,' her mother's clear tones rang out from the direction of the kitchen.

'I've got some eggs, and a packet of Ryvita,' said Deborah. 'Or toast? What about boiled eggs with soldiers?'

'Marmite soldiers!' cried Frances. 'The very thing!'

A voice which Robyn did not recognise responded. 'Oh, you're both being *sweet* to me! Lovely, nursery food – can we have blancmange, too? I really feel like blancmange!'

There was the sound of a cupboard opening; the pantry,

Robyn decided. Frances said, 'There's a packet of blanc-mange powders here, assorted flavours. Have we enough milk, Deborah?'

'Plenty.'

Frances was in the middle of offering the unknown guest a choice of chocolate, vanilla, strawberry or raspberry blanc-mange when Robyn walked into the kitchen and dumped her fat holdall on the floor.

Three heads spun round, three pairs of eyes stared at her. The stranger – a small, delicate, pale girl, dressed, Robyn noticed, in what looked like Stevie's old dressing gown – said, 'Oh, gosh. Oh, it's Mrs Kazandreas, isn't it?'

Frances said, 'Robyn, darling, I think you –'

And, at the same time, Deborah said, 'Robyn! We weren't expecting you! I thought you said –'

Interrupting them both, Robyn said, 'What's going on? And who's this?'

She hadn't meant to sound so savage. But she was tired, fed up, worried about the situation she had left behind in Athens, very hungry and desperate for a large gin.

The strange girl, of course, didn't know all this. Had no idea that an angry bellow wasn't Robyn's normal form of communication. Opening her mouth like a distressed baby, she wailed, 'Oh, I just *knew* it wouldn't be any good!', dropped her head on to her folded arms on top of the table, and burst into loud tears.

Quite distinctly, Deborah said, '*Christ*.'

Robyn had never heard Deborah curse, even, let alone blaspheme. Turning to her mother, she said, 'Mum, what *is* going on?'

Frances said, 'Sorry, darling, but we're rather at the end of our collective tether. Deborah and I have had a trying evening, and Deborah, poor girl, was up most of the night. We're both, I fear, a little fraught.' She had to raise her voice over the escalating sounds of the girl's distress.

'Can't you shut her up?' Robyn yelled, at which the girl's wailing went up yet another decibel.

Deborah, surprisingly, suddenly took a firm grasp of Robyn's shoulder, marched her out of the kitchen and back to the hall; faintly Robyn heard her mother say, 'Oh, *good* idea!', and looking over her shoulder, saw her sweep down to embrace the girl.

Quickly recovering from her amazement, Robyn rounded on Deborah. 'What the hell are you doing?' she demanded.

Deborah flinched visibly, but said, 'That's Phoebe Parry. She's a friend of your son Stevie, and she arrived in the middle of the night, thinking you would take her in. I gave her a bed, and this morning I called your mother, who in fact did recognise her, so we believed her story. Accepted her bona fides, as it were.' She tried a half-hearted smile. 'We've been trying to calm her all evening – she's got this idea we're going to chuck her out, you see, and she's too far gone to listen to reason, and –'

'Why,' Robyn said clearly, 'should she imagine I would take her in, and what's it got to do with Stevie?'

'Ah.' Deborah's clear skin flushed. 'Er – actually, she's a girlfriend of his. Or, rather, an ex-girlfriend, I think. But – er – oh, dear, this *is* awkward. It seems they must have been – er – intimate, at least, they must have been it once.'

Robyn, her mind racing, was beginning to see where Deborah's embarrassed, stumbling explanation was leading. 'She's not pregnant, is she?' she demanded.

Deborah looked fleetingly relieved. 'Yes. I'm afraid she is.'

Robyn sank down on the camphorwood chest by the telephone and said, 'Oh, *shit*.'

*

Deborah suggested that Robyn's best immediate course of action was to return to the kitchen, reassure Phoebe that there was no question of her not being welcome – I'll need to grit my teeth over that bit, Robyn thought wryly – and go on to say that she was very tired and was going to have a bath and go to bed, and would see them all in the morning.

'Your mother and I seem to have evolved a method of coping with her,' Deborah finished earnestly.

'By treating her like a five-year-old?'

Deborah smiled briefly. 'Pretty much that, yes.'

'Blancmange and Marmite soldiers,' Robyn scoffed. 'No doubt one or other of you – or even both – will subsequently take her up to bed, read her a story and tuck her in with Teddy.'

Deborah said, with dignity, 'If that's what she seems to need, then, yes.'

Robyn studied her. She had the distinct feeling that she had just been given a mild reproof. 'Okay,' she said. 'I suppose you and Mum are better qualified than I am to say what she needs.'

Suddenly Deborah said, 'I can hardly believe it! I know it's a hoary old cliché, but she's scarcely more than a child herself!'

'I don't think I even want to *start* dwelling on that right now.' Robyn got tiredly to her feet. 'Come on, let's get this welcoming address over and done with, then I can go to bed.'

★

Having thought that the sum of her anxieties would make her too tense to relax, Robyn surprised herself by falling asleep almost as soon as she settled into bed, and staying asleep until her alarm woke her at eight.

She lay looking at the November sunshine shining through the branches of the birch tree outside her window. Then, telling herself that problems didn't conveniently go away if you tried to ignore them, she got out of bed and went to have a shower.

There was nobody in the kitchen; Deborah must be in her flat. Robyn put the kettle on and made two cups of tea. Putting milk and sugar with them on a tray, and picking up a half-empty packet of digestive biscuits – she'd always found when she was pregnant that a biscuit went down well with early-morning tea – she went upstairs to talk to Phoebe.

Deborah had put her in Stevie's old room, which must have been a coincidence, since Deborah couldn't have known whose it was. Robyn stood in the doorway, looking down at the young woman who, apparently, was carrying Robyn's grandchild.

Fighting the strong reaction – I'm not *ready* to be a grandmother! – Robyn went on into the room and said gently, 'Phoebe? Are you awake?'

As she put the tray down, she heard Phoebe stir. Turning, she saw that the girl had her eyes open. 'Oh! Have you brought me tea? Aren't you kind?' Phoebe said.

'Milk and sugar?'

'Milk, no sugar.'

'Biscuit? I used to find they settled a delicate tummy.'

Phoebe's face clouded. 'They've told you, then.'

'Yes.' Robyn proffered the packet of biscuits, and Phoebe took one.

'Thanks. Actually, I'm not often sick in the mornings, not first thing, anyway.'

'How far gone are you?' Better, Robyn thought, to take the fences head-on.

'Four months – a bit over, really,' Phoebe said, wiping digestive crumbs off her chest.

'And what does Stevie think about it?' Watching the girl's face, Robyn noticed a sudden furtive expression, quickly replaced by a nervous smile. She imagined she probably knew its significance. 'You haven't told him, have you?'

Phoebe whispered, 'No.'

'Well, don't you think you –'

'Please!' Phoebe sounded quite desperate. 'Oh, please, won't you let me tell you how it happened? I want you to understand, you see. I couldn't bear it if you didn't!'

Robyn studied her. Either Phoebe was genuinely eager to gain Robyn's approbation – which she would be, wouldn't she, if she was hoping that Robyn would give her a place to stay – or else she was a damned good actress. 'Go on, then.' She sat down on the end of the bed. 'I'm all ears.'

Phoebe propped herself up on her pillows and settled back, cradling her tea mug in her thin hands. 'Well, you probably don't remember, but Stevie and I went out together a couple of years ago at uni. Actually it was for quite a long time. We came to visit you all here one Christmas, well, New Year, actually, but you and your husband were away. We went to a party at your mother's house – she remembered me, when we met yesterday.'

'Yes, she said.'

'Well, things sort of fell apart, after a while. We were both working hard' – that didn't sound like Stevie – 'and maintaining a full relationship was becoming difficult under less-than-perfect conditions.' God, listen to her! Robyn thought, biting down her irritation. You'd think she was some weary wife with a dead marriage, too many children and too little money. 'Anyway, Stevie and I broke up, although we stayed friends. I started going out with someone else – a boy from Peru, actually, doing post-grad work – and after a bit, Stevie found someone else, too.'

She paused to sip at her tea. Robyn offered her the biscuits again, and she took another. 'Anyway, we hadn't seen each other for ages when we met up at a party, back in the summer. It was somebody's birthday, and we all had quite a lot to drink.' She gave a rather unconvincing giggle. 'Stevie and I started dancing, and it was such a great party, and neither

133

of us was with anyone – Antonio, that's the boy from Peru, had gone home, and Stevie's girlfriend had gone to London for an interview – and, what with the drinking, and the lovely, summery night, well . . . he came back to my room with me and we slept together.'

And, Robyn supplied silently, it didn't occur to either of you to use a condom. No doubt you were both too drunk. Or you believed, in the time-honoured but totally erroneous way of the young, that just once wouldn't make you pregnant.

Only it did.

'I see,' she said eventually. 'So, a couple of months on, you realised you were pregnant, yes? Presumably you've had a pregnancy test?'

Phoebe nodded vigorously, as if keen to show that she wasn't always so careless of her own well-being. 'Oh, yes. I did a home one, and then went to my doctor.'

'You're having proper antenatal care?' Robyn realised that she really should have asked that question first. 'Everything's okay?'

'Everything's fine,' Phoebe said, adding, with a faintly smug smile, 'My doctor says I'm disgustingly healthy!'

'I'm glad to hear it,' Robyn murmured. Then, while Phoebe was still looking self-congratulatory, 'Why haven't you told Stevie?'

Phoebe's smile vanished. 'Oh. Oh, dear, it's not easy to say.'

'Try,' Robyn said relentlessly.

Phoebe shot her a glance. 'Oh. All right. Well, it's really that – oh, I don't want him to come back to me purely because I'm pregnant. I mean, if he didn't want to continue our relationship when I *wasn't* pregnant, I can't see that it stands much of a chance of working if we get back together just because I *am*.' She frowned intensely at Robyn. 'Do you see what I'm saying?'

All too clearly, Robyn thought. She said, 'Yes, indeed I do. Isn't it a pity you –' A pity you didn't think of that at the time, she'd been going to say. But then, she reflected, whoever does stop to think, when passion flares up so hotly? Thinking back to her early days with Zach – oh, Zach! – she had to admit that she'd rarely stopped to think of *anything* when the urge was on to leap into bed with him.

And that, exactly like this vague group, the young, that she had just been mentally chiding, she and Zach hadn't been terribly good at taking precautions. Robyn had got pregnant, just like Phoebe.

She didn't have any moral high ground to stand on. None whatsoever.

'Isn't what a pity?' Phoebe was prompting.

Robyn looked at her. A minute amount of fellow-feeling stole into her, and she found herself smiling. Instantly Phoebe beamed back. 'Nothing, it doesn't matter,' Robyn said. 'So, are you going to wait and see if Stevie makes contact, and, on the basis that if he does so he must want to resume your relationship, tell him then?'

Phoebe's mouth pursed a little. 'I don't *know*,' she said with a dramatic sigh.

'But surely –'

'I'm not actually sure I want to marry Stevie anyway,' Phoebe burst out. 'Oh, I'm sorry, he's your son, of course you think he's perfect, but –'

'I don't think anything of the sort!' Robyn protested.

'– But I don't know if it'd work any better this time than it did before,' Phoebe plunged on, as if she hadn't registered the interruption. She met Robyn's eyes. 'I mean, I'm sorry, and all that, but he's not actually very good husband material. Is he?'

Robyn felt the instant, angry reaction burn through her. Not good husband material? How dare she! Then she thought: but *is* he? Have I ever looked at him in that way?

He's just Stevie, who enjoys life, is popular, has always had lots of phone-calls from both chaps and girls, who sticks by his mates and whose mates stick by him.

She thought about it more deeply. Of all her three older boys, Stevie was most like Paddy. Paddy hadn't really been suited to the role of husband – what was Phoebe's phrase? 'Not very good husband material'. Ha! Maybe she'd just gone and hit the nail on the head.

'You're smiling,' Phoebe observed. 'Does that mean you've forgiven me?'

'For what? For your character reference for my son, or for turning up here on my doorstep pregnant with his child?' She spoke gently, so that Phoebe would not feel any sting in the words.

Phoebe looked directly at her. 'For everything,' she said simply. For the first time, Robyn sensed that she was seeing the real person behind the various subterfuges. 'Will you let me stay here, at least till the baby's born? I'll pay you rent. I'm planning on finding part-time work, and I'm going to see about getting help from social security, though I don't think I'm eligible for anything till the baby's born.'

Robyn wasn't really listening. 'I'll let you stay, if you're sure that's what you want.' She could hardly believe she was saying it. But then, what else could she do? 'I mean, if you're sure there's nowhere else that would be better for you. Your parents, for example – do they know?'

Phoebe shook her head. 'No. Oh, Robyn, there's just no way I can go to them! Mummy's delicate, you see, and she had an awful time with me, she says she's never been the same since, and I just *couldn't* go home and make her see me going through the same thing! And Daddy's on the PCC, he's terribly, terribly proper, he thinks girls who get into trouble should go to the workhouse!' Abruptly she began to cry.

Robyn put both their tea mugs on the tray and then sat

down next to Phoebe, putting her arm round the shaking shoulders. 'Now, then, don't upset yourself,' she said kindly, 'got a tissue? No? Here, I've got a clean one in my pocket. Blow!'

Phoebe obeyed, blowing her nose with a loud trumpeting noise, which made them both laugh. 'Oh, God! Am I getting hysterical?' She gave Robyn a watery smile.

'No,' Robyn said firmly. 'And you're not going to. It's bad for baby, as my health visitor used to say to me whenever I wanted some minor personal indulgence like a strong drink or a hot curry.' She still had her arm round Phoebe, and gave her a squeeze. 'Look, Phoebe, I think it's probably a good idea for you to stay here for a while, to give you time in a secure place to think about the future.' She hesitated. Had she the right to suggest it? Plunging on anyway, she said, 'Did you talk to anybody about other possibilities?'

Phoebe turned briefly to look at her. 'An abortion, you mean?'

'A termination, yes.'

'It's still an abortion, no matter what you call it,' Phoebe said, which seemed to sum up her attitude. 'And yes, my doctor went through it with me. I said no then, and I still say no now. Anyway, it's too late.'

'Fine,' said Robyn. Then, filling the rather awkward silence, 'Let's say I'll put you up, for a fair rent, until the baby's born. I can help with things like taking you for appointments, and you'll have a proper home to live in rather than making do in some place by yourself.' Robyn did not think Phoebe would be capable of looking after herself on her own, but refrained from saying so. 'But I must make it clear that it's only to be a stop-gap,' she went on. 'You have some decisions to make, Phoebe, and quite a few revelations – you'll have to tell both Stevie and your parents sooner or later – and only you can make them.'

Phoebe seemed to relax. 'I know.' She reached up and

took Robyn's hand, squeezing it. 'Thank you. I had a feeling you wouldn't turn me away. You're very like Stevie, or, I suppose, he's very like you.'

And that makes me bad husband material, too, Robyn thought, or the female equivalent? 'Thanks,' she murmured.

'Strong, I meant,' Phoebe said, apparently realising she'd made a slight error. 'Knowing what to do. Decisive.'

'Ah.' Okay, Robyn thought, that'll do. 'Phoebe, where exactly do your parents think you are at this moment?'

'London. I was sharing a flat with three other girls I knew at university. I couldn't stay on there, I can't afford it now.' She gave a great, gusty, self-pitying sigh, which made Robyn change her mind about asking for any more details.

'So, if you ring them occasionally, just to say hello,' she said, 'then presumably they'll think you're ringing from London?'

'Yes. Why?'

Wasn't it obvious? 'Because,' she said patiently, 'if you suddenly break contact and they don't know where you are or *how* you are, they'll worry.' And that was putting it mildly.

'Oh, I *see*.' She looked at Robyn again. 'Is that a condition of my staying?'

'If you like, yes.'

'Then I will.' The tone was reluctant; clearly, this was not a consideration Phoebe would have thought of for herself.

And thereby, Robyn thought, hangs a tale. But she had enough on her plate already without delving into this strange girl's relationship with the delicate mother and the authoritarian father on the parochial church council. Standing up, collecting the biscuits and picking up the tray, she said, 'Right, I've got things to do. I'll be going into town later, if you want anything?'

Phoebe said, 'Could I come with you?'

It was a moment to be forthright; Robyn's trips to town were, and always had been, solitary; she hated having someone at her shoulder while she browsed and shopped. Zach had tried to go with her a few times; eventually, when discreet hints had failed to do the trick, she'd had to resort to slipping out of the house without telling him. Once she'd seen him standing at the end of the precinct looking for her, and she'd hidden in Boots. It had hurt – how pathetic, that he'd found her gone and followed her! – but it was, she had known, quite essential for her to have at least that time on her own.

'I'll show you the way – it's near enough to walk in,' she said now to Phoebe. 'Then we can split up. I'll give you a key, and you can make your own way back when you're ready.'

'Oh.'

Robyn's heart softened momentarily at the forlorn tone Phoebe had managed to get into the one brief syllable.

Only momentarily. She was, she told herself as she quietly closed Phoebe's door behind her, doing quite enough already. And, with this new, additional pressure, it was all the more vital that she retain at least some part of her rapidly eroding privacy.

Deborah caught her up on the landing. 'How is she?'

'Fine.'

'Is she going to stay?'

'Yes.'

'Don't you want to talk about it?'

'No.'

Deborah smothered a laugh.

'I'm glad you find it funny!' Robyn hissed.

'Oh, not funny.' Deborah followed her down the stairs. 'It's just you.'

'Me. Fine.'

Deborah took hold of her arm, and the empty tea cups slid alarmingly across the tray. 'Oh, sorry. It's okay, no harm done. Robyn, I didn't mean to offend you, but –'

'You didn't.'

'– But,' Deborah was laughing again, 'it's the way you shout at people and then do really kind things for them.'

'I don't shout!'

'I'm afraid you do, dear Robyn.'

Robyn turned and stared at Deborah. Surprised both at what she had said and the fact that she had said it – reserved, private Deborah, making a remark both personal and perceptive! – she found that she was pleased. Warmed, that, in this suddenly difficult time when people with problems and attitudes were leaping at her from all directions, she seemed to have found a friend. An ally, even, who approved of what she was doing and didn't mind saying so.

'Thank you, Deborah,' she said.

'You're welcome, Robyn.' There was still amusement in Deborah's eyes.

'Shouldn't you be going to work?' They were standing in the hall.

Deborah looked at her watch. 'Goodness, yes. I must be off – see you tonight.'

'Come down for a drink,' Robyn called after her. 'Sixish.'

Deborah waved a hand in acknowledgement as she hurried out.

Walking along to the kitchen, Robyn discovered she was actually looking forward to six o'clock, and not purely because of the prospect of alcohol.

CHAPTER ELEVEN

Malcolm Teague, known to his friends as Malc and to his enemies as Wanker, cursed as, coming to the outskirts of town, he encountered the tail-end of a traffic jam. There were blue lights flashing ahead, and a recovery truck was easing its way through the bunched-up cars and lorries.

Too late to avoid the jam – he'd passed the last side road half a mile back, and now there was no room to turn round – he sat inching forward.

He turned on the radio, and pushed a tape into the cassette player. Humming along with 'Hits of the Sixties' – really, you couldn't beat Tom Jones, they broke the mould when they made him, and he was still going strong, raunchy old devil – he glanced at himself in the rear-view mirror. Now might be a good time to practise his eyebrow-raising trick . . . Concentrating fiercely, he knotted the muscles over his right eye while lifting the left eyebrow . . . great! That was bloody nearly it, that time!

The car behind hooted, and Malc hurried to catch up with the queue – it had moved on all of five yards.

Then it began to rain.

Malc watched a woman run out of the road that led up to Sainsbury's, hurrying off towards the bus stop, trying to hold an empty plastic bag over her head with one hand while carrying all her shopping in the other. A sudden surge in the traffic coincided with her reaching the pavement; a transit van with ladders on its roof accelerated and its near-side wheels splashed the contents of a large puddle all over the woman.

Malc was going to laugh, but happened to notice – probably because she was raising the hem of her skirt to inspect the damage – that the woman had bloody good legs.

Malc was the sort of man who, imagining he was doing a woman a favour, would look across a crowded bar or a buzzing dinner table and say, loudly and seriously, 'Great breasts!'

He pulled up beside her, carefully so as not to splash her again, and pressed the switch that let down the window. 'I saw that,' he called out, with genuine sympathy – poor woman, she was soaked. 'Rotten sod did it on purpose!'

The woman turned a dripping face towards him. The rain, he noticed, was rapidly turning to sleet. 'Yes, I know. Oh, dear, I'm drenched!'

Her face was pretty, too. And the rest of her figure was as good as her legs – he liked his women on the thin side. He made up his mind. 'Look, I don't usually do this, but I seem to be going your way, and the weather's getting worse – can I offer you a lift?'

She looked doubtful. 'Oh, I'm not sure – I was going to get the bus.'

'The bus has gone,' he lied.

A sudden flurry of wind flung a handful of freezing raindrops into her face. He sensed she was weakening. 'I'm a local boy,' he said, grinning. 'Rugby-club member, pillar of the community.'

'I would have thought that the two did not necessarily go together.' She was smiling, too.

The car behind was hooting again. 'Well, I'll have to go,' Malc said, making a show of starting to put the window up again, 'the bloke behind'll have kittens in a minute.'

Abruptly the woman wrested open the passenger door, flung in her sodden shopping and sank into the seat beside him. 'Could you drop me at the top of the town?' she said breathlessly. 'I'm meeting my friend at the multi-storey, she's got her car.'

Malc studied her. She looked nice, even with her hair plastered to her head. 'Gladly,' he said. He held out his hand – awkwardly, since he was trying to move off smoothly at the same time – and said, 'Malc Teague.'

The woman took his hand. 'Deborah Warne.'

★

Robyn had decided that the best course of action was to prioritize – to use the unattractive modern word – her various concerns. Or, as Paddy used to say, create a critical path. She smiled as she began on her list; the trouble with Paddy's critical path had been that things like, 'take my sons swimming', 'give up a Saturday rugby game so we can go out for the day', and, 'try to *think* what Robyn/Mum/Dad/the boys would really like for their birthdays instead of rushing to the shops at the last minute and buying something stupid and unsuitable', came so far down the path that he never reached them.

Top of Robyn's own list was the Athens flat. She phoned her father, who, predictably, was off to play golf, and arranged to meet him in the bar of his favourite pub at twelve-thirty. 'If I win,' he promised, 'I'll treat you to a baked potato.'

'Steady on, Dad,' she said, grinning. 'Anyway, since I need to ask your professional advice, I'd better do the treating.'

'Professional advice?' Instantly his tone sharpened.

'Yes. Nothing desperate. See you later.'

He *had* won; she could tell by his expression. Over a pint (his) and a half (hers) of Level Best, he gave her a brief run-down of the finer points of his game, then said, 'Now, what's this advice you want?'

She told him about Cliantha's occupation of the flat, trying to remember all that the Greek solicitor had told her and trying not to let her disapproval of Zach's daughter show in her face or her voice.

Unsuccessfully: John Swift said, 'Why don't you like her?'

Robyn smiled faintly. 'I suppose the honest answer is because she makes absolutely certain I don't. That nobody does, outside a band of cronies. She always antagonised her father – Zach didn't have a *clue* how to deal with her. It all just kept on escalating – she'd do something awful, he'd react, she'd respond with something even worse, and he'd blow his top.'

'Hm.' John took a long draught of beer. 'Delicious, this. Lovely and bright. So, do you think she's moved into the flat to start the same shenanigans with you?'

'I dare say.' She toyed with her glass. 'Well, almost certainly. She's moved in with a person called Andy, whom she made quite sure I knew was her lover, and this Andy's a woman.'

'I see.' Her father took it admirably in his stride; perhaps Tunbridge Wells was full of closet lesbians, all of whom had had cause to consult Swift and Robinson, Solicitors, and nobody had told Robyn.

'I thought you'd be amazed and highly disapproving,' she said.

'Really? Why?'

'Oh – most men seem to look on lesbian liaisons as slightly worse than bestiality.'

Her father laughed. 'Perhaps they are perceived as a threat to the male ego.'

'You could be right.' She remembered the infamous remark of one of Paddy's friends, rejected by a girl he fancied to distraction, who'd claimed, 'It's got to be 'cos she's a dyke, it's the only explanation'.

She said, 'Dad, my instinct is to ignore Cliantha and her

little love-nest. I don't need a flat in Athens, and it doesn't really bother me if I never set foot there again. I've seen the Acropolis and the museum, and the pollution's appalling.'

'Zach left the flat to you,' her father pointed out. 'Cliantha is, technically, living there without authority. And what about the tenants?'

'She said their lease had expired.'

'And the Greek chap okayed that?'

She shrugged. 'Apparently.'

He went 'Hmm' a few times, frowning in concentration. Then he said, 'Of course, I'm not familiar with Greek law as it applies to the letting and the ownership of property, but if you're sure you want this girl to have the flat, you could probably make it over to her.' His frown increased. 'Strange, that Zach didn't make provision for his daughter in his will. Most irregular, I'd have thought. I'm surprised she didn't get a lawyer to challenge.'

'He left her money,' Robin said. 'And some stuff of her mother's that was still in the Rethymnon house.'

'Hm. But why did he not leave her the flat? Surely that would have been fair – the house in Crete for you and, eventually, Jerome, and the flat for her?'

Robyn had her own ideas about that. 'I think he probably intended to, you know, Dad. But when he died, they were on non-speaking terms – she'd thrown a wobbly down the phone, although I don't know what it was about, and he was simply furious with her. Anyway, I think maybe he always hoped that one day she'd be more reasonable – more lovable – and he could allow himself to treat her better. Treat her, I sense, as he really wanted to.'

'Could the row have been over this Andy woman?' John suggested.

Robin thought about it. Then said slowly, 'Yes. Of course. Well done, Dad – I'm surprised it didn't occur to me.' She laughed shortly. 'The one thing most certain to make Zach apoplectic would be to know a child of his was homosexual. Despite the ancient Greeks and all that, he was . . .'

Suddenly the implications of what she had just said struck her, with the weight of a flat iron. Horrified, she turned to her father. 'Oh, Dad, you don't think that's what gave him the stroke, do you?'

John Swift was frowning. 'It was, I'm afraid, just what I *was* thinking. But, Robyn, love, we mustn't get carried away – Zach had his first stroke in the summer, didn't he? While you were away?'

'Yes. August.'

'And was he in touch with his daughter – what was it again? Cliantha? – with Cliantha then?'

Robyn tried to remember. Lazy, sunny days, Jerome and his friend Charlie off on their own pursuits, she and Zach with nothing very demanding to do . . . Zach had been out quite a lot, but then he always was when they were in Rethymnon; he liked to keep up with his family and, with Robyn's Greek just not up to following fast conversations, it made sense for him to visit on his own.

Had he been seeing – trying to see – Cliantha? Had he gone to Dimitri's house and been told, in no uncertain terms, where she had gone and with whom?

She made herself concentrate, trying to remember . . . How had he seemed? Happy? Preoccupied?

In a flash of memory she saw him, the day before he was taken ill. He'd been out – he'd said he was going to see his mother – and, when he came in, had rejected her suggestion that they go out to a restaurant for supper, patting her arm absently and saying he was rather tired. He'd said the same the following day. Had slept all afternoon. Then he'd had the first stroke.

She saw his face in her mind. He looked . . . drained.

What if it hadn't been his mother he'd visited? What if it had been Cliantha?

Oh, no. Don't think of that. Don't think of it, because of what came next.

Back home in England, when she was trying to cheer him up, persuade him he wasn't really that ill, she'd suggested they ask Cliantha to come and stay. She had imagined that his subsequent distressed reaction had been because he thought Robyn guessed he hadn't long to live: but what if, acting on her idea, he'd phoned Cliantha? And she'd informed him that, far from abandoning her female lover, she was now living with her? And *that* was what had been so upsetting?

Oh, it all added up. Zach had spent hours, *hours*, on the phone – she'd never known such a large bill as the one for that quarter! And there had been that formidable row, which, although she'd only overheard his end of it, had sounded pretty serious. Had he been trying to talk Cliantha out of her latest, and, from his point of view, her worst folly? And, receiving nothing but abuse and rejection from her, had the resulting stress and heartache precipitated his final stroke?

Unable to bear it, she dropped her face into her hands.

After a moment, she felt her father's hand on her shoulder. 'Brace up, Robyn,' he murmured. 'Do you want me to order you a brandy?'

She raised her head. 'No, Dad. Thanks. I'm okay.'

He went on studying her. 'Sure?'

She managed a quick smile. 'Sure. It's a bit shocking, coming face-to-face with a realization like this.'

'You don't think you're over-reacting? Making a certainty out of what is actually only a possibility?'

'Perhaps. I don't know. It all seems to fit together with distressing snugness, though.'

'Hm. Well, if you're right, and this last antic of Cliantha's was in fact what brought about Zach's stroke, then are you sure you want to be quite so generous? Would it not be better to think about it for a while, consult the Greek lawyer again, and not do anything rash until you've done so?'

It was, she reflected, so typical of dear old Dad to advise not doing anything rash. But, in this instance, he was right. 'Yes. Probably.'

He touched her hand. 'I always used to advise my clients not to make decisions of any kind, especially momentous and costly ones, when they were in an emotional state,' he said.

She glanced at him. 'Sound advice,' she remarked. 'Which I shall follow.'

They sat in silence for a while. Then he said, 'Your mother tells me you have a new tenant at Haydon Hall, too. Some girl who's got herself into trouble.'

'Who Stevie has got into trouble, if we're going to insist on using the quaint old phraseology.'

'Ah. Quite. And what are your arrangements with her?'

Robyn tried to think how to word it so as to make it sound as if she'd been businesslike and sensible over the matter. Which was in fact quite difficult, since she'd acted fairly impulsively and let her heart pretty much lead her head. 'Her name's Phoebe, Phoebe Parry, and she was at university with Stevie, where she got a two-one in English. She's promising to look for a job, and will be paying me rent. I've said she can stay till the baby's born.'

'And then what?'

'Then she'll have to leave and find herself somewhere of her own.'

'Hm. It may not be as easy as all that to get her out. Has she got a lease?'

'No, it's all pretty informal.'

'Not a good idea. Better to get something in writing. I could suggest a form of words, if you wish.'

Suddenly it was all too much. 'Yes, Dad, okay. If you think it's necessary. Thanks,' she added, 'I do appreciate it, really.'

'I do think it's necessary. People so often fall into the

trap of believing arrangements between friends are in some way . . .'

But she had stopped listening. She was thinking about Zach.

Evenings at Haydon Hall fell into a set and, for all three women, an enjoyable routine. When each had finished her supper, they would convene in Robyn's sitting room, where they would watch an evening's democratically decided television. Phoebe had started to knit some soft and fluffy white garment, Deborah usually brought *The Times* crossword, Robyn would sit with idle hands dozing in front of whatever the television was quacking out.

This evening, more tired than usual, she was only vaguely aware of the conversation between Deborah and Phoebe. It was, in any case, fading in and out of the sound of Jill Dando extolling the attractions of some place in Turkey. I am, Robyn reflected, worn out. Early night for me.

She yawned. And, suddenly noticing what the other two were talking about, homed in on Deborah.

'Of course, it wasn't a very sensible thing to do,' she was saying, smiling rather coyly, 'but the weather was dreadful, and, really, the traffic was moving so slowly that I could have jumped out if I'd had to.'

The lift. Robyn remembered Deborah saying something about a kind stranger giving her a lift from the bottom end of town.

'You might have had to sacrifice your shopping,' Phoebe said. 'There could have been some bloke at home now, tucking into that chicken Kiev thing you bought – was it really good? I might try it another day – and putting all your other nice feminine purchases away in his cupboards.'

Some bloke. Deborah hadn't said anything to Robyn about it having been a man whose car she'd got into.

'One shouldn't take risks, I know that perfectly well,'

Deborah said sententiously. 'Wasn't it what all our mothers used to tell us, never to accept lifts from strangers?'

'Yes, mine used to say exactly that,' Phoebe agreed. 'But, statistically, you're actually safer with a stranger. The great majority of rapists are known to the victim.'

There was a sudden and, to Robyn, dreadful silence. Phoebe, who didn't seem to have noticed, reached down for a dropped knitting needle and said something about needing some more wool.

Robyn stared at Deborah. Her face had gone deathly pale, and the soft brown eyes appeared to be straining out of their sockets. At the same moment as Robyn said softly, 'Deborah? All right?', Deborah abruptly stood up and hurried out of the room.

Robyn got up to follow her. Phoebe – surely one of the world's most unobservant people – said, 'Oh, Robyn, while you're on your feet, can you pass me the remote control? I want to put the telly on to BBC1.'

Robyn tossed the remote into her lap. Then she went out, closing the door behind her.

The cloakroom door was shut, but she could still hear the sounds of Deborah being sick.

She sat down on the camphorwood chest and waited.

There was the sound of the loo flushing, then of water running in the basin. Then, after quite a long time, Deborah came out.

Seeing Robyn, she jumped visibly.

'Sorry,' Robyn said. 'I don't wish to intrude, Deborah, but can I help?'

Deborah looked at her for a moment. Then she began to cry.

Robyn led her through to the kitchen, sat her down at the table, and flicked on the switch of the kettle. 'We'll have that wonderful English panacea, a nice cup of tea,' she said easily, 'and soon you'll feel better.' Don't ask, she told herself. Don't say, gosh, Deborah, whatever is the matter? 'Biscuit?' She waved the tin towards Deborah, who shook her head.

'Where – what did Phoebe – did she say anything?' Deborah asked presently, her voice low and furtive as if her abrupt departure from the living room were cause for shame.

'Debs, my love, she didn't even *notice*.' Debs, Robyn observed. Why should I suddenly call her by a short form of her name? An informal, friendly form?

Deborah was nodding. 'Oh, thank goodness.' She managed a faint smile. 'I'm sorry, Robyn. Sorry to be so silly and dramatic.'

The kettle boiled, and Robyn made two mugs of tea. 'Dramatic, I grant you,' she said, giving one to Deborah. 'Silly I can't comment on.'

'Because you don't know what made me react like that,' Deborah finished for her. 'Oh, Robyn, Robyn.'

She lapsed into silence, stirring her tea. Which was, Robyn thought, pretty unnecessary since there wasn't any sugar in it.

Eventually Deborah said, 'Robyn, can I talk to you?'

'Of course! But,' – and it seemed important to say this – 'there's no obligation.' Impulsively she reached out and touched Deborah's hand. 'You can be sick in my loo without the need to explain, you know. Any old time you like.'

Again, the watery smile. Then: 'But I think I do need. To explain, that is. Not for your sake, for mine.'

'Okay. Then fire away.'

And, while Phoebe sat watching *EastEnders*, oblivious to the torrid real-life drama being related in a kitchen not ten yards away, Deborah told Robyn the full story of her terrible, destructive marriage to Br—.

Robyn has not been asleep. She has been lying with her eyes closed, fiercely concentrating on what she can possibly say to make Deborah reconsider this idea of getting married again.

She raises herself to a sitting position, leaning briefly against Deborah to announce that she's back in the land of the living.

'Debs?'

Deborah affects surprise. 'Robyn! Oh, *there* you are.'

'Debs, the trouble with men,' Robyn begins. 'No, the trouble with *living* with men, is that they need so much of the available space.' Remembering Paddy, remembering Zach, she elaborates: 'They're untidy, for one thing. They don't see anything wrong with littering the dining table or the floor of the living room with some project they just *have* to get on with. And, when you ask quite reasonably how long they're going to be because you want to lay the table or hoover the carpet, they look at you as if you're stupid not to see the importance of what they're doing, and they say, "don't *nag*".'

She is cross. Suddenly, hotly cross. It was grossly unfair of both her husbands and all four of her sons to accuse her, as all of them did, of nagging. I am not and never have been a nag, she tells herself. Why is it that a man telling a woman to do something is being logical, constructive and sensible, whereas a woman suggesting the same thing to a man is nagging?

It's the male ego, she thinks. That male need to be king of his own castle. Boss. Captain. Commander. Manager. Director. The very words have a masculine ring! And why is it that men get so edgy when a woman does a task that *they* usually do? God, how it used to irritate, having Zach stand right behind her when she changed a plug or unblocked the sink, frowning, getting in her way, saying unnecessarily, 'Don't forget that the screws must be very tight', and 'I do not think you are going to be able to shift the blockage'. As if he had been any good at such tasks! He just couldn't bear her to be able to do them better.

Huh!

Deborah has been contemplating Robyn's last remark.

'The trouble with living on your own in a large house,' she says now, 'is that you'll get it all tidy and the way you want it, then you'll discover you miss the very people who used to mess it up.'

'I won't. I *don't!*'

Deborah shrugs eloquently.

'Debs, I really don't! I love it when one of the boys comes to visit, but I'm just as happy when I'm on my own!'

'But you're not on your own,' Deborah points out. 'You never have been. Since Zach died, you've always had at least one other person in the house.'

Robyn goes, 'Huh' again, in a different tone. One of rueful regret; Deborah has touched on a tender spot.

'Sorry. Didn't mean to bring that up.'

'No, it's okay,' Robyn assures her. 'I was thinking about it anyway.'

'I'm sure you were,' murmurs understanding, sympathetic Deborah.

Ah, Debs, thinks Robyn. Dear old Debs. What a strong, dependable person she has become. Living her own life, with no man – no husband – to order her about and undermine her has allowed Deborah to blossom. And her confidence has been further restored by her job. Maria Fletcher, astute, high-powered, and not a woman to sit back and let talent go unused, recognised Deborah's quiet efficiency within a week, and swiftly increased both the quantity and the quality of her workload. Deborah's willingness and ability to cope with whatever was thrown at her convinced Maria Fletcher that she was worth a salary increase. Quite a large one. Deborah has opened a savings account and is considering buying a PEP.

And, despite happiness, security, and the new serenity which has removed the taut lines from her lovely face, Deborah, it seems, is *still* tempted to chuck the whole kit and caboodle away and get married again!

Debs, Debs, *don't.*

As if Deborah has heard the unspoken plea, she turns to Robyn. 'It's not really a joke, is it?' she asks.

'A joke? What?'

'Your one-woman attempt on the Everest of my thinking about marrying again. Your determination to point out to me every bad aspect of living with a man.'

'I haven't even begun yet,' Robyn says lightly. 'Haven't started on the socks rolled up into relentless clumps that come out of the wash like cricket balls. On the way the loo seat is always left up and, if it's down, then there'll invariably be a nice pattern of skid-marks in the pan. On the snoring and the farting, and –'

'Women fart and snore, too,' Deborah points out mildly.

'Okay, but they have more discretion.'

'You're making it sound like a joke now,' Deborah says seriously. 'But it really is more than that. Isn't it?'

Robyn turns to look at her. Deborah's brown eyes meet hers intently. 'It's more than that,' Robyn agrees.

'You really think I should stay with you at Haydon Hall and forget any idea I might have of marriage. Don't you?'

Robyn resists the temptation to look away. 'Yes,' she says. 'That's exactly what I think.'

Deborah makes a small sound of impatience. 'Robyn, *you* won't want to live like this for ever! Really, you won't! You'll meet someone, and –'

'I *won't*.' In her own ears, Robyn's remark sounds like that of a tetchy child being told it will soon learn to adore school. 'Debs, I've done it, twice. Believe me, I've had it with marriage!'

Deborah is silent for a moment. Then says, 'Robyn, have you ever read *Gone with the Wind*?'

'Of course. Heaps of times. The first time, one of my school mates was reading it at the same time, only she was a bit ahead of me.' She smiles suddenly at the memory. 'This friend came dashing into class one morning and said, "oh, Robyn, have you got to the bit where Bonnie dies?" And I said, "no".'

Deborah thinks for a second, then, understanding, laughs. 'I was thinking of another bit.'

'Go on.'

'When Rhett Butler was trying to persuade Scarlett to marry him, she said roughly what you just did. She'd been married, thank you very much, twice, and didn't want to be it again.'

'Sensible woman,' Robyn mutters.

'And then,' – wisely, Deborah takes no notice – 'Rhett tells her she's had bad luck with her two previous husbands, one being a boy and one an old man, and –'

'Zach wasn't an old man!' Robyn protests. 'At least, he wasn't when I married him! He was terrific, full of energy!'

'Yes, I'm sure,' Deborah says consolingly. 'I didn't mean the comparison to be that thorough. I was merely making the point that, just possibly,' – here she pauses, as if gathering herself to make a remark which Robyn may not like – 'you're so anti-marriage because neither of your two husbands was entirely right for you.'

'They were!' Robyn's protest is instant. Instinctive? 'Paddy and I divorced, yes, okay, but we had some fun in the good old days! We were good mates, we made each other laugh!' That doesn't sound very convincing. She dashes on to Zach. 'And Zach and I were terrifically happy; he was generous, we had a great life flitting off to Greece when we felt like it, and there were always lots of parties, friends. Presents.'

That doesn't convince, either.

'I loved Zach!' she bursts out. 'Really, I did!'

She feels stupidly near to tears. Deborah, sensing the emotion, puts out a hand, takes one of Robyn's. 'I didn't mean to upset you.'

'You haven't.' Robyn sniffs. A tear goes splat! on to their linked hands.

'Okay,' Deborah says. 'Robyn, it's your business, and I'm very sorry if I seemed to be straying into forbidden territory. I was just trying to put the pro-marriage case. Being a devil's advocate,' she adds, although Robyn doesn't take this in.

Robyn's turbulent reaction is subsiding. She is not cross with Deborah – it is very difficult to be cross with Deborah unless your name is Br—, who didn't find it a problem – but, instead, understands what she was trying to do.

She *would* suggest something like that, Robyn thinks, because she has to find some very daunting ammunition if she's to counter all the stuff I'm spouting in favour of *not* marrying.

That's all it is.

Silence descends on the warm cliff-top.

And, like a dark intruder, the thought sneaks into the edges of Robyn's mind: what if she's right?

What if, Paddy and Zach and the fun and the presents notwithstanding, I *have* never been married to the right man?

It doesn't bear thinking about.

So why can't she banish the idea from her mind?

CHAPTER TWELVE

Robyn had mixed feelings about Christmas. Her experience of it had differed so greatly in the various phases of her life that it was quite difficult to have one view that covered all of her forty-nine celebrations. Childhood Christmasses had been universally wonderful; Frances and John had retained enough of the child within them to give their only daughter a magical time. The solemn placing of the Advent candle on the windowsill on the first day of December was the signal for the season to begin, and there would be whisperings and furtive expeditions to the shops throughout the next three weeks. On Christmas Eve, there would be a small party, and Robyn would go to bed determined to stay awake to hear reindeer hooves on the roof. One year when there was snow, John had gone outside and put pretend boot and hoof prints in the garden, and Robyn had felt sick with the thrill of discovery. Her presents had always been satisfactory: dolls, books, one year a rocking horse, another, a pink angora jumper and bronze leather pumps. Then, as if all that were not enough, the three of them always went to some London production, at first the pantomime, later, ballet and even a musical.

Paddy had been good at Christmas, too, although in his case it was just his natural talent for throwing a good party coming into its own. Robyn remembered, with mixed emotions, the year after Tim was born, when the party was so good that half the guests had to sleep on the living room floor. Fortunately, she'd filled every cupboard with seasonal food, and they had one of the best Christmasses ever.

Zach had not hurled himself into the celebrations with quite the same vigour, although that might have been because he was foreign and didn't appreciate the importance of every single tradition, from too many mince pies and too much cold turkey through silly cracker jokes to the Queen's Speech; regarding the latter, he once said to Robyn, 'I do not understand why you insisted on watching this woman if you are going to make remarks throughout so that you cannot hear.' Robyn, trying not to laugh with her convulsed older sons, had been at a total loss to explain.

This year, this first Christmas without Zach and, now, without Jerome, was going to be strange, whatever happened. Robyn was used to the elder boys absenting themselves for at least part of the festive season to go and stay with Paddy, but having a son not there at all was something else entirely.

As the cast of characters for the event gradually announced itself, Robyn increasingly felt she was voyaging into uncharted territory. Deborah, when asked, said she didn't want to invite anyone, although she did stay out late after work one night; she said to Robyn that 'a friend' had invited her to go for a drink. Tim was coming down – that was excellent. Stevie was not – one of his colleagues was going to Austria with a group, and some last-minute hitch meant there was a place in the party for Stevie. He didn't say whether the colleague was male or female; Robyn, sorry that he wouldn't be with her yet, at the same time, relieved because of the presence of the still-indecisive Phoebe, didn't think to ask until after she'd put the phone down.

Will was coming.

Two out of four sons. Fifty per cent. Not bad.

In the event, the six of them – Tim brought a Japanese girl called Kazuko, who proved to have a talent for making paper hats out of old bits of *The Times* – had a magnificent three days. Robyn, slightly anxious about how she would explain Phoebe without mentioning Stevie – what if one of the boys recognized her? – need not have worried, since, after quick assessing glances which, presumably, were enough to make both sons conclude that Phoebe wasn't their sort, they treated her like some jolly cousin whom they hadn't seen for a while and were quite pleased to see again. Phoebe appeared to enjoy having two men around; she had, Robyn observed, got her flair for getting other people to do things for her down to a fine art.

Deborah, bless her, noticing how hard Robyn was working to look after a household of six, not only mucked in and volunteered to mastermind the food, but also galvanised Tim and Will into taking over the tending of the fire and, amazingly, the hoovering. Standing in the kitchen doorway – Deborah was making chocolate truffles – and watching Tim come backwards down the stairs, the vacuum cleaner's nozzle sucking dirt from the most difficult bit in the right-angle of the treads, Robyn said, 'Debs, how did you manage it? I wasn't even aware he knew we *had* a hoover.'

Deborah smiled. 'I told him a white lie. I said you'd wrenched your back again, and, anyway, since he and his brother put down most of the muck, wasn't it only fair that one of them removed it?'

Robyn went up to stand behind her and, putting her arms round the aproned waist, kissed the glossy hair. 'Thanks, Debs. I always knew it was a good idea having a lodger.' She put a finger in the truffle mixture. 'Mmm, that's delicious. Can I taste brandy?'

Deborah smacked her hand lightly with the wooden spoon. 'Flattery will get you nowhere. I recognise cupboard love when I see it.'

Christmas morning passed in a long present-opening session, followed by an even longer lunch. Then they watched a film on television, then they had another drink. By ten-thirty, tired out from food, drink and laughter – they'd been playing charades, unexpectedly funny when one of the players was Japanese and, despite their best efforts to explain, didn't entirely comprehend the game – Robyn announced she was going to bed.

She put her *Times* paper hat on top of the chest of drawers, then got undressed and into bed, snuggling down under the duvet and reaching for the new Penelope Lively that Will had given her. She was, she thought as the peace of her room fell around her, entirely happy.

★

In the middle of January, at the end of a miserably bleak day when Robyn's efforts to re-ignite her singing career had suffered another setback and Deborah had come home early from work and gone to bed with a cold that had turned to 'flu, there was an unexpected ring at the front door.

Robyn, reluctantly leaving the warmth of the living room for the draughty hall, called upstairs to Phoebe, 'I'll get it.'

She peered through the spy-hole.

On the step, clutching a thin jacket round her like a security blanket, stood Cliantha. At her shoulder was the bulkier figure of Andy.

Oh, *Christ*.

Robyn opened the door. 'Cliantha. How nice.' Even to her own ears, her voice had not a flicker of sincerity to it.

The corner of Cliantha's mouth twitched down briefly, then up, a mannerism so exactly like her father's that, for a second, Robyn felt as if Zach were standing behind her. 'And Andy,' she said, a shade more warmly. 'Come in, come in.'

She stood back, and Cliantha strolled into the house. Andy, following, was carrying two large holdalls. Robyn closed the door, leaning against it for a moment and counting to five. There wasn't really time for ten.

'So this is Haydon Hall,' Cliantha said, turning in a slow circle and staring around her. 'My father always had a taste for elegance.'

Maybe it wasn't the moment, but Robyn didn't intend to let that stop her. 'As I have told you before, Cliantha, this is my house. It was my home before I knew your father.'

Cliantha said, with devastating accuracy, 'He lived here. He certainly found it part of the appeal of moving to England.'

Fifteen all, Robyn thought. 'What can I do for you?' she asked frostily. 'I didn't know you and your friend were in England.'

'You can talk to her, you know.' Cliantha was inspecting a statuette of the Cretan snake goddess that stood on a shelf. 'She speaks quite good English.'

Robyn ignored that. 'Cliantha? I asked you a question.'

Cliantha spun round to face her. 'The Athens flat, it's a terrible place! I no longer want to live there. I have nowhere to go, so I have come here to find work.'

Dear God. Surely she wasn't proposing to move in? To take up Robyn's long-ago invitation for her to come and live at Haydon Hall? Oh, but that was *then*, when Zach was alive, when Robyn had still believed she could demolish the rigid and prickly fences that separated him from his unsatisfactory and difficult daughter.

The prospect of having Cliantha and her lover living at Haydon Hall *now* was quite dreadful.

Robyn rounded up her thoughts. One thing at a time. 'What do you mean, the flat is terrible?' she asked. 'You seemed happy enough to live there when I saw you in November.'

Cliantha made an impatient gesture which seemed to indicate she wasn't going to reply. Andy, speaking for the first time, said, 'The other flat people. They say we not good. They not like us.'

'Ah.' Robyn was beginning to understand.

'They tell Cliantha, no music, no friends. Too much!' She flung out her hands dramatically, knocking a vase of dried flowers off the top of the camphorwood chest. She was, Robyn had observed, quite a large young woman.

'So you decided to move to somewhere more tolerant?' Robyn suggested, bending to pick up the flowers and pushing them back all anyhow into the oasis. 'And you've come here?'

'You will not turn us away,' Cliantha declared. 'I am your stepdaughter. Your husband's child.'

'Indeed you are,' Robyn muttered. Then, more audibly, 'It's not quite as simple as you imagine, I'm afraid. The house is already full.' It was a lie, but she was damned if she was going to let Cliantha push her around.

Cliantha was staring at her disbelievingly. 'Full?' she repeated, in the manner of Edith Evans saying, 'A *handbag*?'

'Yes.' Robyn met her challenging eyes. 'I have turned two of the bedrooms into a self-contained apartment, for which I have a tenant. And I also have a guest, a friend who is staying with me for the foreseeable future.'

Andy had gone to the foot of the stairs and was staring up towards the landing. 'There are many doors,' she called. 'Many rooms.'

'Many rooms there may be,' Robyn said firmly. 'All, unfortunately, are being used.'

Abruptly Cliantha changed her tactics from direct frontal assault to diplomacy. 'If the situation was reversed and a child of yours was seeking a place to stay in *my* country,' she announced grandly, 'that child would not be turned out into the street.'

She came close to Robyn, raising her head to stare up into

Robyn's face. 'May we not stay for a few days, until we can look for somewhere of our own?' she wheedled.

Robyn thought rapidly. There *was* a spare room, of course there was; she had turned it into her sewing room, and she had installed a new stereo; she'd put all her music stuff up there, too, so that she could sing well away from the others. She *could* put Cliantha up.

'You can stay for a few days, yes,' she said eventually. 'I can't offer you more.' Which famous general had said, never explain? 'I'm sorry.'

Cliantha was giving her a strange look. Half resentful, half – surely this couldn't be right? – grudgingly admiring.

Perhaps she wasn't used to people not instantly acceding to her requests. Perhaps it was such a novelty that she had to make some response in acknowledgement.

'Up here.' Robyn marched towards the foot of the stairs, and Andy, after a glance at Cliantha, stepped aside. 'It's a small room,' she added, 'and two of you in there will be very cramped.' She wasn't going to be hostess-like and apologise for that. 'There's a small single bed and a put-u-up,' – she was maliciously pleased that the girls were going to find it difficult to share a bed – 'and a wash basin.'

They had reached the landing, and she opened the bedroom door. 'It's my music room,' she said, removing a stack of scores from the top of the chest of drawers. Music room sounded more impressive than sewing room.

Andy was touching the ancient Singer sewing machine on the dressing table. She said something in Greek to Cliantha, something about this being a weird sort of musical instrument, and Cliantha, with a nervous laugh and a rapid glance at Robyn, said, also in Greek, watch out, I think she can understand.

Robyn put her full brain power to seeking out and rounding up her rusty Greek. Then, sure of the words if not entirely confident about the accent, she addressed the girls in their own tongue. 'I do understand. Welcome to my house.'

They both had the grace to look ashamed. Only slightly ashamed, but it was better than nothing.

Deborah was too ill to be bothered with Robyn's problems, and Phoebe didn't seem to take in what was happening. Increasingly self-absorbed as her pregnancy advanced – and she had been pretty self-absorbed to start with – she greeted Robyn's announcement that two Greek women, one of them her stepdaughter, would be staying for a while with an absent-minded 'Oh, right.'

Robyn's anger had, therefore, no outlet. I had no choice but to let them stay! she fumed silently as she went out a couple of days later to do a mammoth shop – Andy ate like a carthorse, and Cliantha had revealed herself to be 'picky'; let her be! – she's Zach's bloody daughter, I couldn't have shut the door in her face! And, having allowed her over the doorstep, could I honestly have said, *you* can come in, but I'm not having your dyke pal?

Still angry, still muttering under her breath, she shot her trolley round the supermarket as if it were a battering ram. Bread, potatoes – bags of potatoes, they're the basis for lots of cheap meals and I'm damned if I'm going to go pushing any boats out! – and anything that's on special offer. And – reaching the wine and spirits aisle – a bottle of Bushmills for me, for being so tolerant.

The queues were all long. It was, she realised belatedly, quite the wrong time to have come shopping.

Under his breath she said, '*Fuck.*'

Not far enough under her breath; the man in front of her, into whose leather-jacketed back she had just impatiently pushed her trolley, turned round and said politely, 'Your irritation suggests you may be in a hurry. Would you like to go in front of me?'

She felt about a foot high, and it wasn't only because he

was so much taller than she was. She looked up at him, feeling a shudder of embarrassment. 'No. Of course not, I've got enough to feed an army and you've only got a basket.' She added belatedly – he had a most attractive smile – 'Sorry.'

'Sorry?'

'I shoved my trolley into you.'

'Ah, yes.' He was still smiling.

'I've had a bad day,' she confessed.

'Have you?' In addition to the smile, he had a nice sympathetic voice.

'Mm. A houseful of seriously annoying people and a setback on the employment front.'

'Oh, dear.' He put his basket down on the shelf at the end of the conveyor belt, leaned a thigh against the side of the neighbouring till and folded his arms. The gesture was so like Les Dawson pretending to be a fat woman settling down for a good gossip – although this was where the similarity began and ended – that she started to laugh.

'Ah! You can smile!' he exclaimed. 'And how nice, to hear someone laugh when it's snowing outside!'

'Is it?' She hadn't noticed. 'Oh, *bugger*.'

'Bugger?' he asked. 'Why?'

First fuck, now bugger. Oh, dear. 'Because I've got to load this lot into my car, and then *un*load it at the other end, and there's nobody around to help.'

'What about the houseful of annoying people? Or is the unlikelihood of their coming out to help precisely why they're annoying?'

She looked at him with renewed interest. Tall, good-looking men who stood in the supermarket queue and said 'their coming' and not 'them coming' were, in Robyn's experience, few and far between. 'Precisely,' she said. 'And, in addition, one's pregnant and sits around all day on her backside like some sultan's favourite in a harem, and the other two are sleeping together and, since they do it in the daytime, make quite sure I know all about it.'

'I see.' He was listening intently, as – although Robyn hadn't noticed – were the two neighbouring cashiers and the people in the queue behind her. 'Rather disturbing, I imagine.' He was suppressing another smile.

'Mm. Especially when one's your late husband's daughter who you don't much like and the other's her girlfriend.'

His eyebrows shot up. 'What a bohemian household,' he observed.

His own groceries were being shunted along the conveyor belt now, and she reached past him for the Next Customer sign. He, she noticed, had bought fresh tagliatelli, pesto, a block of Parmesan, some wonderful-looking olive oil in a tall bottle full of peppercorns and a sprig of rosemary, some chianti, a Häagen-Dazs ice cream – the gorgeous Bailey's one – and a box of white chocolate mints. Piling up her own dull-looking purchases, she wished she was having dinner with *him*.

But then, undoubtedly, some other woman was going to have that treat. Some bloody *wife*. She picked up one of the special-offer five-kilo bags of potatoes and thumped it, with some venom, on to the conveyor belt.

Her back seemed to twang. An instant later, it began to hurt so badly that she gasped.

The man was packing up his shopping. He turned, saw her face and said, 'Are you all right?'

She was bent double, and the pain took her breath away. With some difficulty, she said, 'Yes. I always shop like this.'

Someone in a supermarket uniform was at her side, and she put one arm round Robyn, saying something about an ambulance. 'I don't want an ambulance,' Robyn said – she was feeling quite faint – 'I just need to stand somewhere quiet for a while . . . aaagh! It'll pass, I – aagh!'

Her shopping had gone through the reader; the cashier,

mouth open, was waiting to see what she should do next. The woman holding Robyn said, 'Have you got your purse? Only there's a bit of a queue, and –'

The tall man was quietly paying for Robyn's shopping. He wheeled her trolley to the side of the shop, where there was a chair, then came back for her. 'I could wait with her,' he offered, addressing the supermarket woman. 'I can see how busy you are.'

The woman glanced at Robyn, then back at the man. 'I still think I should call an ambulance for her,' she said. 'She's gone very white.'

Robyn wished they wouldn't talk about her as if back pain made you go deaf and stupid. 'I don't *want* an ambulance,' she repeated. 'I'll go and crouch over there by my shopping till I can move, then I'll be out of your way.'

She had, she thought, spoken with unnecessary sarcasm; the woman was trying to *help*, for God's sake! 'Look, I'm sorry, I –'

The man placed himself between her and the supermarket woman; she heard him say something about shock. The woman's face lightened into a smile; no doubt the tall man's charm was working on her, too. 'All right, if you're sure,' she was saying. She turned to Robyn, and, speaking slowly and carefully, said, 'This kind man, Mr –?'

'Preston. Rory Preston.'

'– is going to look after you. If you change your mind about the ambulance, let me know. Okay?'

Robyn started to nod, but it hurt, so instead she said, 'Okay.'

Rory Preston bent down so that he could look into her face. 'I've done a first-aid course,' he said.

'Oh, good,' she said with heavy irony. '*That's* all right, then. Maybe you'd like to open me up and operate.'

'We didn't do advanced spinal surgery, I'm afraid. But I was a star with the blow-up dolly.'

She laughed. 'Ouch! What dolly?'

'The one you practise mouth-to-mouth on. *You* know.'

'Oh, that dolly.' The pain was lessening. Tentatively she straightened up by a millimetre or two. That was all right, too.

'Getting better?' he asked, still peering at her.

'Yes. A bit.'

'Does this happen often?'

'Yes.' She unbent a further few degrees. Still all right. 'Never before in a supermarket queue, however.'

'Perhaps it was the way you tossed that bag of potatoes,' he suggested. 'Plenty of strength there, but you might do better to let your arms and shoulders do the work and not your back.'

Now fully upright, she shot him a glance. 'I'll try to remember that.' She put both hands on the handle of her trolley and did an experimental push. 'Oh.'

'Trouble?'

'Mm.'

He gently removed her hands and, placing his plastic bags in the trolley, pushed off in the direction of the doors. 'I'll do it for you,' he said. 'And I'll load your car.'

'You're very kind,' she said, wondering what the chances were of getting Phoebe to be so helpful at the other end.

'Will you be able to drive?'

'I'll manage.'

'And how about unloading?'

She was not, she decided, going to let an unknown man go home with her to unpack bags of potatoes, even assuming he was about to offer. She'd tell Andy that if she didn't help, then the food would stay in Robyn's boot and there wouldn't be any supper. That ought to do the trick. 'Again, I'll manage. Thanks.'

He put her bags into the back of the Peugeot and stood back. 'Sure you'll be okay?'

'Quite sure. You've been most kind.'

'Glad to help.' He was still standing there smiling at her.

She got into the car, put on her seatbelt and started the engine. He was still standing there. The only thing to do was say goodbye, so she wound down her window and said it.

It was only when she was pulling into the drive of Haydon Hall that she remembered she hadn't paid him back for her shopping.

CHAPTER THIRTEEN

❧

Deborah was actually quite glad that she had 'flu. As much as anyone ever is, anyway. She considered the thick, pounding head, the aching of all her limbs, the furnace temperature and the sudden, racking shivers a price that it was almost worth paying, for it meant that she could postpone making up her mind about Malcolm Teague.

She preferred Malcolm to Malc. Malc was so like talc, an un-macho, un-modern word. It made her think of Timothy White's the Chemists, and, heavens, they didn't even exist any more. She remembered going into one with Edith – Edith was a frequent patron of chemists' shops, always fussing over this or that minor ailment, always a sucker for some expensive patent cure-all. Deborah had a sudden vivid picture of her mother in a long skirt and a gingham bonnet, standing in some dusty Wild-West town, tumbleweed tumbling, cowpokes poking cows, queueing up beside a wagon and passing over hard-earned dollars for Dr Somebody's Marvellous Medicine . . .

She dragged her wavering mind back to the question of Malcolm. It wasn't like her to daydream – it must be the 'flu. Perhaps she was delirious. Like Beth in *Little Women* when she had scarlet fever and almost died . . . did die. No, that was later, in the next bit. *Good Wives*, was it? And what *did* she die of . . . ?

When Deborah woke up, she could tell by the dramatic reduction in daylight that it was much later. Another whole day in bed! She hoped Maria Fletcher had really meant it when she told Deborah to take the rest of the week off, not to come back till she was a hundred-and-ten per cent. That was one of Maria's favourite expressions. It made her quite exacting to work for.

Malcolm had phoned Deborah at work. She had worried about how he'd traced her, but, when she'd plucked up courage and asked, he had said, with a disarming laugh, 'Saw you in the street, didn't I? And I watched where you went.'

Deborah had tried to laugh, too, but not very successfully. She told herself not to get paranoid. To feel flattered that she had made such an impression on him in the short journey from the bottom of the town to the multistorey, that he'd just *had* to try to find her.

'I was wondering,' he'd said, when pleasantries about the weather had been exchanged, 'if you're free at lunchtime? I'm around Tunbridge Wells today, and I usually pop into a pub for lunch.'

'Oh!' The suggestion wasn't exactly unexpected – why else did a man phone a strange woman, except to make arrangements to see her? Well, actually quite a lot of men phoned strange women for entirely different reasons, such as . . . She'd pulled her thoughts back to the matter in hand. 'Oh, well, I'm afraid I can't, you see, there's a set of accounts we're working on, I promised I'd have it ready by this afternoon, and now there's been a hold-up – some of the figures I'd been given are in fact not right, and –'

'No problem,' Malc had interrupted her. 'How about after work? We could meet for a quickie?'

Her heart pounded with alarm. A quickie. No, idiot, he means a quick *drink*.

She had taken a deep breath. Held it. Heard herself say, quite calmly, 'That would be very nice. Perhaps I may be allowed to buy the drinks, to thank you for your kindness the other day.'

He'd laughed again. He had an attractive laugh. 'No need for that, it was my pleasure.' He named a pub and a time; both were convenient.

'I shan't be able to stay long!' she cried, panicking now. 'I promised I'd be home in good time!'

'No problem, Cinderella.' Warm, affectionate voice! 'See you at six-thirty.'

They'd got into the way of meeting for a quickie after work once or twice a week. Malcolm – he accepted her use of his full name with a rather dashing lift of the left eyebrow and a swift smile – was always waiting, and, after the first occasion, always had a gin and tonic on the bar for her. And, when the fluttering in her stomach settled down and allowed her to eat, a bag of Worcestershire-Sauce-flavoured crisps.

He seemed content – happy – to sit at a table by the fire and just talk. He talked quite a lot about himself: he was a sales rep for a cosmetics company, lived in a house in Southborough, had been married, it didn't work out, no children, still occasionally ran into his ex, 'and we manage to be pretty civil!'

But as well as talking, he asked questions, and, so it appeared to Deborah, *really* listened to her increasingly confident answers.

Oh, but it wasn't easy! Deborah had spent too many years with Edith ('*Hush*, Deborah! People won't want to hear what you or I have to say, we don't know anything!') and with Br— ('Shut up, Deborah darling, I'm trying to get this sorted') to have much faith that anything she said could possibly interest someone else. Especially when the someone was quite tall – taller than average, anyway – handsome in a rugged way, and treated her with consideration and, so she thought, kindness.

Just before Christmas, their usual after-work drink took on a new dimension. It could just have been the sentiments of the season, it could have been because everyone else was laughing and happy, everyone was exchanging presents. Everyone was kissing. Malcolm gave her a beautifully wrapped gift, which, when she opened it – and he insisted that she did there and then – proved to be a crystal perfume bottle with a gold top. She had bought him a book about wine – he said it was one of his hobbies – which, when it was his turn for present-opening, didn't look half as exciting.

But he seemed very pleased. Touched, even, that she'd remembered 'one of my special interests'.

He looked deep into her eyes for a few seconds. That fascinating left eyebrow twitched, almost as if he were asking her something. Then – for she was now frozen into position and couldn't move – he leaned forward and, oh, so gently, kissed her on the lips.

'Oh!' Involuntarily, her hand flew to her mouth. It was a long time since a man had kissed her. It was at the same time thrilling and frightening.

Malcolm, as if he read her reaction, instantly pulled away. 'I'm sorry, Deborah,' he murmured. But he didn't look very sorry.

She rallied. Smiled. Said, 'Don't be silly! Nothing to be sorry about!' Then – *very* bold – whispered, 'It was lovely.'

He was watching her. He said softly, 'Plenty more where that came from.'

Again, the fear and the thrill.

To save herself having to experience any more of that exotic cocktail of emotions, she got up and bought them another drink.

Since Christmas, it had become the norm for him to kiss her lightly when they met and when they said goodbye. Last week – just before she'd gone down with 'flu – his farewell kiss had been more intense. They'd been standing in the porch of the pub, and he had taken advantage of their tem-

173

porary privacy to do the job properly. Mouth pressed to hers, he put his arms round her and pulled her towards him, parting her lips with his tongue, sweeping it swiftly inside her mouth to seek her own.

For a moment she had responded. He was warm, solid, very male, and she had been celibate for a long time. Why should she not respond?

But then the pictures flooded her mind. Br—, grabbing her as she tried to flee upstairs and put a locked bedroom door between her and her furiously aroused husband. Br— with his long, strong arms whipping round her like a boa constrictor, squeezing, squeezing, while the swift breath she tried to draw was abruptly cut off by his thick tongue thrusting so far into her mouth that she gagged.

Such was Br—'s concept of *making love*.

Now, in a different man's embrace, she broke away. Found that she was shaking, and began to cry.

Malcolm said, 'Deborah? What's up?'

She shook her head wildly. 'Oh, sorry! *Sorry!* It's just – I'm –'

He took her arm and led her to the car. 'Come along. We'll talk as we drive.'

He didn't usually take her home; the pub was near enough to Haydon Hall for her to walk. 'Oh, but –'

'You're not walking tonight,' he said masterfully, 'not in that state.'

Sitting in the car, he took her hand. Held it in a loose, gentle grip. 'I suspected you'd had a tough time,' he said quietly. 'Sex, was it?'

She wasn't sure how she felt about him coming right out with it like that. Thought, perhaps it was a little crude. But then he was right! Oh, how right he was!

She made herself say, 'Yes. My late husband was –' She swallowed. 'He made me do things I didn't like.'

'Ah.' Silence. Then: 'What, bedroom things?'

'Yes.' He wasn't expecting details, was he?

There was another, longer silence. Perhaps he was. Then he said, 'How appalling. Some men are such brutes.' He sounded vaguely disappointed; how nice of him, to be sad, on her behalf, at the behaviour of his fellow men!

'I should be over it,' she said, trying to make her tone light. 'But, you see, Malcolm, you're the first man I've been out with since – since I was married.' She glanced at him. In the lights from the pub, she could see his profile. Stern, slightly frowning. Goodness, he really was taking this business of her dreadful experiences with Br— to heart! She was emboldened to add, 'You're the first man, since him, that I've kissed.'

He turned to her, and took her in his arms. Tenderly, he kissed her forehead. 'There. Another kiss for poor Cinderella.' He often called her that, because she always said she had to get home early. 'One day, Deborah – or should I say, one *night* – my Cinderella may find she wants to do more than kiss her prince.'

In the turmoil of her thoughts she didn't notice how hackneyed the cliché was. She gasped, 'Oh, *no!* Oh – I'm sorry, I didn't mean – Malcolm, oh, dear, I –'

He stroked her hair. 'There, there. My lovely Cinderella shall not have to do anything she's not ready for. But, Deborah,' – he disengaged his hand and reached to start the engine – 'don't stay in your nunnery for ever, will you?' He shot her a quick look, then turned his attention to backing out of the car park. 'It would be,' he said softly, 'such a waste.'

Drifting in and out of sleep, Deborah dreamed of Malcolm. He was dressed all in white, and rode a white horse; his brown hair was long and flowing, and he wore a circle of gold around his head. Oh, my dreams are so stereotypical, she thought in a conscious moment, look, there's Malcolm, my white knight! Where's your shining armour, dear Malcolm? And her sleeping mind produced it, gleaming so brightly that it dazzled.

And there, in her dreams, was Deborah, dressed in medieval costume, thick plait of hair swinging down her back, heavy girdle round her hips. The knight in white rode up to her, raised her effortlessly on to his horse, sat her astride it in front of him. Said, his warm breath in her ear, Sorry about the pommel, and she felt him thrust something hard and thick inside her. Then, with a laugh – and it was Malcolm's laugh – That's no pommel, Cinderella!

Shocked into wakefulness, she felt her body throbbing with an intense, powerful orgasm.

As the delight subsided, she lay back in a pool of her own sweat. And, with her body calm again, her mind rose up in horrified protest.

To dream that! About *Malcolm!* What did it mean? That she'd been fancying him all along and hadn't dared admit it to herself, because to do so would mean she'd have to do something about it? Have to persuade herself she was ready for another relationship – another *full* relationship – when she wasn't convinced she was anything of the sort? Oh, dear! Oh, *God!*

She could feel the unpleasant clamminess of cooling sweat on her nightie. On the bed, probably. It was making her shiver. Damn, she was going to have to do something about it. It wasn't going to aid her recovery to lie in a cold mess all night.

She got up – her legs were very shaky – and went along to her little bathroom. She was aware of muttered voices on the other side of the Great Divide; when she came out of the bathroom, sponged and in a clean nightie, Robyn was standing on the landing.

'Debs? I would have come along earlier, but I was afraid I'd wake you. How are you feeling?'

'Awful.' Debs put a steadying hand on the wall as she headed back to bed.

'Can I get you anything?'

'No, thanks.'

Robyn turned towards the connecting door. 'I'll leave you in peace, then, best if you can get back to sleep.'

'No!' She had made the protest before she'd even thought. 'Can you stay for a while? Talk?' She was aware of sounding desperate. 'It gets a bit lonely,' she said with a smile.

Robyn believed the excuse. 'Of course! I'd like that.'

Deborah settled herself in bed, and Robyn plumped the pillows and tucked her in. 'There! Snug again.'

'Yes. Thanks.' She stretched, and her feet found a cold bit of sheet. She shivered again. 'How are things in the land of the living?' she asked, to take her mind off how unwell she felt.

'Oh, fairly dire.' Robyn sat in the small armchair and put her feet up on an empty bit of bed. 'Cliantha and Andy keep to their room and play very loud rock music, which I'm sure you're only too aware of, and it took me ages to make them hear me knocking on the door earlier – I went shopping and tweaked my back again, and I wanted Andy to take the stuff inside for me. She's big enough to carry a sideboard, so I thought she was better equipped than me to cope with a few bags of shopping.'

'Poor you!' Deborah exclaimed. It was good to have someone else's troubles to think about. 'You've got a lot on your plate, Robyn. And precious little help. Unless Phoebe has rallied round and cooked up a batch of evening meals?'

'In your dreams.'

Dreams. *Don't think about that!*

'. . . couldn't get my purse out,' Robyn was saying, 'and before I knew it, he'd paid for my groceries. And I forgot to pay him back! I now owe a strange man, about whom I know nothing but his name, £78.34. What d'you think I ought to do, Debs?'

Deborah put the pieces together and came up with a picture that made sense. She thought she could even produce the right answer. 'Well, if you saw him shopping in the supermarket at a certain time one day, might he not be there at the same time on another occasion? You could organise your shopping for a few days so that you're there at the right moment, and hope he is, too.'

Robyn was grinning. 'I could, couldn't I? Better than ringing all the Preston, R entries in the phone book, which was what *I* thought of doing.'

Deborah hardly heard. Her mind had reverted to Malcolm. 'Yes,' she said absently.

Robyn, she noticed, was looking at her. 'Debs? Are you feeling bad again? You've gone pale.'

'I – Robyn, you know I said I sometimes have a drink with a friend after work?'

'Yes?'

'Well, he's a man. Malcolm Teague. He's the first man I've been out with since – oh, for ages, and I think he wants us to get more involved than we are at the moment.'

Robyn's face had taken on a serious look. 'And what do *you* want, Debs? It has to be what both of you want. You must realize that.'

'I do! Of course I do!' She wasn't sure that she did. 'I want to go on seeing him, that's for certain. He's kind, and he understands what I've been through.' Robyn's expression indicated she didn't find this very likely. 'He does, Robyn! The last time we went out, just before I got ill, he was terribly sympathetic when I sort of hinted at what it had been like, when I was married. You know.' Robyn nodded. 'Honestly, he looked quite – oh, I don't know how to describe it! Sort of upset. Disappointed, that anyone could behave like that.'

'You didn't tell him the details, did you?' Robyn asked gently.

'No! Of course not! You know how I am over that.' She gave a brief laugh, unconvincing even to herself. 'It tends to make me rather hysterical.' Robyn, when Deborah had unburdened herself to her, had kept on saying, Debs, you don't have to say any more, I've got the picture. Don't distress yourself! 'He was so kind, Robyn. And – well, I can't stay in my nunnery for ever!' She realized she had used Malcolm's words. 'Can I?'

'You can if you like, Debs,' Robyn said. She smiled briefly. 'If celibacy's okay for Stephen Fry, it's okay for you.'

Debs smiled too. Oh, dear Robyn, she thought, but you don't know, can't know, what my subconscious mind has just thrown up. If you did, you would realize, as I am having to do, that celibacy isn't entirely okay for me.

'Why not ask him to supper?' Robyn said suddenly. 'That'd be a nice way of furthering your friendship without committing yourself to anything you're not ready for. Wouldn't it? We could all eat together, if you feel it's too intimate to entertain him up here. Then, if things are going well, you can offer to give him coffee up in your own flat.'

Deborah considered. It was a good idea. A *very* good one. 'Thanks, Robyn. I just might do that. But what about the others? Phoebe, and the Harpies in the sewing room?'

'It's perfectly possible to dissuade them if you don't want them,' Robyn said. 'I'll simply tell them it's a private party and they're not invited. It's still my house,' she added, with some heat.

'I know,' Deborah said soothingly. 'I don't mind Phoebe – she's a bit like animated wallpaper, isn't she? She doesn't exactly contribute.'

'Rather less useful than wallpaper,' Robyn commented. 'But it would make us four rather than three, and your

Malcolm might feel less as though you've brought him round to show him off to your friend.'

'He's nice,' Deborah said. 'Really.'

'I'm sure he is.' Robyn got up to go. 'I look forward to meeting him. Soon as you're better, yes?'

'Yes,' Deborah agreed.

And, when Robyn had returned to the other side of the Great Divide and closed the door behind her, she lay down, closed her eyes and gave herself up to her dreams.

CHAPTER FOURTEEN

On the day Malcolm Teague came to dinner, Robyn still hadn't made contact with Rory Preston to return his £78.34, despite having become a frequent loiterer outside the super-market. Ten days had now passed – the matter was preying on her mind.

She'd actually shopped there for the dinner. Had taken £30 from Deborah – 'Yes, Robyn, I can *see* you don't want to take it, but unless you do, the whole thing's off. There's no reason why *you* have to be out of pocket to entertain *my* friend!' – and gone out to buy supper ingredients remarkably similar to those which Rory Preston had been buying That Day.

I must pull myself together, she thought as she carried her shopping to the Peugeot. A pair of dark blue eyes and an infectious laugh – 'I was a star with the blow-up dolly', indeed! – and I'm thinking about the bloody man all the time. Haunting the supermarket like some pop fan waiting for a Gallagher to appear. I'm *far* too old for this sort of thing.

She was already feeling disgruntled when she got home. Became more so when she noticed that Andy, or Cliantha, or both, had put an enormous wash on and had left the damp clothes inside the machine. I'm expected to sort through their T-shirts, towels and smalls – or, in Andy's case, bigs – and put them out to dry, am I? Buggered if I will! Angrily, she raked the tangle of washing into a clothes basket and kicked it to the corner of the room.

How many days, she wondered, constituted a few, as in, you can stay for a few days? Surely not as many as the twelve that Cliantha and Andy had now been under her roof. It was proving virtually impossible to develop any closeness to Cliantha – for one thing, Robyn hardly saw her. For another, Robyn was increasingly disturbed by her suspicion that some last and most destructive row between Cliantha and Zach had precipitated his final stroke.

There was no sign of the Harpies now. They were either out or bonking, and Robyn didn't much care which.

She was listening to a play on Radio 4 and had almost managed to forget about them – she was grating Parmesan cheese, a much harder job than she had anticipated – when the back door burst open and Cliantha bounced in, Andy hard on her heels.

She stopped in the middle of the kitchen, and, when she was sure she had Robyn's attention, said dramatically, 'We go! We are here to pack, then we go! The flight is tonight! Aaah, to go *home*!' She spun round to Andy, caught hold of her hands and swung her in a circle in a fairly clumping dance.

'Run that by me again,' Robyn said. 'You're leaving? Going back to Athens? But I thought you said you'd had to leave the flat?'

'Not Athens, Crete,' Cliantha panted. 'My *real* home. I talked to my grandmother today on the telephone,' – on my bill, Robyn thought – 'and she say to come home, looking for work in England no good, and not to stay here without work.' Good for Grandmother. 'And Grandmother, she let me use her credit card to buy the tickets!' Cliantha finished triumphantly.

Robyn, who somehow hadn't expected Zach's mother to have a credit card, was standing with her mouth open.

Cliantha said something to Andy about their washing, and Andy disappeared in the direction of the machine.

'It's still damp,' Robyn said. It gave her a totally unworthy sense of glee, to think of the two women trying to pack a full load of wet washing.

She was aware of them stomping about upstairs for the next half hour, and she heard one of them use the phone. Then they both appeared in the kitchen doorway, and Cliantha said the taxi was on its way.

Robyn tried to hide her huge relief, and she didn't think she did a very good job.

Neither Cliantha nor Andy said anything in the way of, Thank you for putting us up, it was really nice of you. And there weren't any mysterious little packages with her name on them, nor any bunches of thank-you flowers.

Oh, well.

She hadn't intended to react. Really hadn't. Had visualised herself cheerily waving them off, a friendly smile on her face. But, watching the pair of them stacking holdalls and carrier bags in the hall, watching Cliantha go into the cloakroom and casually help herself to a large wad of loo paper for her runny nose, suddenly her anger rose up and boiled over.

'The hotel's been up to the mark, I trust?' she said icily.

Both women turned blank faces to her. 'Hotel?' Cliantha said.

'I mean this house. *My* house. Where you arrived unannounced and uninvited, bringing a friend, and where you have made yourself utterly at home upstairs for nearly a fortnight.' She took a step nearer to Cliantha. 'You've treated my home exactly like a hotel, haven't you?'

After her initial surprise, Cliantha was rallying. Standing her ground, she put her face close to Robyn's. 'You want me to settle the bill? Huh? Is *that* what you want, for your own stepdaughter to *pay* for staying with you?'

'Don't be absurd,' Robyn replied. 'Of course I don't want that. But you are old enough now, Cliantha, to understand that, in well-mannered circles, we *ask* if we may visit, and we *thank* our host afterwards. Did nobody ever teach you that?'

Cliantha was nodding rapidly, face flushing a dark red. 'Ach, so now you dare to criticise my father!' she shouted. 'You say, stupid Zach, not to bring up his daughter fit for well-*mannered* circles!'

'I said nothing of the sort!' Robyn shouted back. 'I –'

'You did, you *did*!' Cliantha stamped her foot. 'I will not stay here to be insulted by you!'

Biting down the *come back!* which instinctively rose to her lips, Robyn watched as Cliantha wrested open the front door and hurled herself out on to the drive. The taxi was just pulling up; Cliantha flung open a rear door and got in, slamming it behind her. Andy, whose bemused expression suggested she hadn't a clue what was going on, was left to stow the luggage in the taxi's boot; neither Cliantha nor the cab driver got out to help.

Serves you right, Robyn thought childishly. Serves you right for being a great carthorse of a woman and eating me out of house and home.

At last Andy joined Cliantha in the back of the cab. Neither woman turned as the taxi moved off. Standing in the doorway, Robyn watched as the driver took them away to the airport.

Then she went upstairs and discovered the appalling state in which they'd left their room.

She was still fuming when Phoebe came down and offered to lay the table; she didn't even notice what a lovely job Phoebe had done until Phoebe pointed it out.

Paper napkins folded like a bishop's mitre! Good Lord.

The fact that Robyn was cross about something eventually penetrated even Phoebe's thick skin; she made Robyn sit down and brought her a large gin.

Robyn drank that, then had another one.

Angry and more than slightly drunk was not, Robyn later thought, entirely the best way to meet Malcolm Teague.

Or was it?

Robyn had never felt more proud of Haydon Hall than she did that night. The place *looked* superb – her fury had given power to her elbow, so that every surface shone, every carpet was hoovered, and there were fresh arrangements of greenery in every tall vase – but, more than that, it *felt* good.

I have, she thought, half-way down her third gin and feeling decidedly mellowed, made a haven out of my home. For me, primarily, and I have learned to live on my own, in my own way, and relished the freedom of doing things as *I* want. But, there's dear old Debs too, on whom Haydon Hall has also worked a small miracle; she's now not only seeing someone, but about to bring him home for supper. Then there's Phoebe, over there with her knitting like some nest-building wren, sitting safe, snug and secure and with no pressing need to think about the morrow. She's even got herself a job, and, even if it *is* only three afternoons a week helping out in a wool shop, it's a step forward. And there are – no, there *were* – Cliantha and Andy. Thank you, dear God, for taking them away, but they *were* here, they used my house at a time of need, too. Even if I *did* resent it like fury.

It's a good place. I –

At that moment the front door bell rang, and Robyn got up to let Deborah and Malcolm in.

She didn't like him from the first.

It was prejudice, she told herself sternly, trying valiantly to spot his good points. She knew nothing about him – nothing! – so what justification was there for taking against him?

'You live in Southborough, you said, Malcolm?' she said

earnestly over the pre-dinner drinks, as if this were some great feat. 'How fascinating!'

Her voice sounded insincere to the point of sarcasm. He must have thought so, too; he said, 'Yeah, well. Southborough's not everyone's cup of tea, but I like it.'

'I used to go riding somewhere there,' Robyn plunged on. 'A very nice place.'

'*Nice*,' Malcolm echoed. Now it was his turn to sound sarcastic.

'Perhaps you know it?' Robyn made herself smile, despite the overriding temptation not to. 'The horses were all called after wines, and I rode a lovely grey called Chablis.'

Malcolm raised his left eyebrow, at the same time twisting his mouth into an odd sort of half-grin. It was so obviously an expression that he'd spent ages perfecting, Robyn began to laugh out loud. Observing both Malcolm's discomfiture and Deborah's sudden look of pain, she turned it into a cough and offered them another drink.

Phoebe, who had just rejoined them after a fairly lengthy visit to the lavatory – she was complaining now of reduced bladder capacity – said her usual bit about not drinking alcohol, thanks all the same, but a small glass of juice would be lovely, and Robyn escaped to the kitchen.

Reaching into the fridge for the fruit juice, she heard Deborah behind her.

'What do you think, Robyn?' she asked in a whisper.

It must have been perfectly obvious what Robyn thought, especially to someone as sensitive as Deborah. But Robyn merely said, attempting a reassuring smile, 'He seems pleasant.' This clearly wasn't enough. 'Nice looking, isn't he?'

'Mmm.' Deborah was nodding furiously. 'He – actually, I think he's a little tense. It matters to him, I expect, that you like him.'

Robyn had detected in Malcolm absolutely no sign of either tension or of any desire for her approbation, so she just said, 'Right.' Then: 'Debs, you couldn't take those plates of nibbles, could you? My hands are full.'

Deborah opened her mouth to say something, then, apparently changing her mind, picked up the dishes of crisps, nuts and gherkins and led the way back to the sitting room.

She doesn't like him, she doesn't like him. The words rang out in Deborah's head as she offered the savouries first to Phoebe, who said a pretty thank you and took a fistful of cashew nuts, then to Malcolm, who, busy telling Phoebe how his superior knowledge of the minor roads of the South-East had allowed him to avoid a mega hold-up on the M25, took an even bigger handful and didn't say thank you at all.

Deborah returned to her seat on the sofa, and Robyn sat down beside her. Malcolm finished his conversation with Phoebe and, turning to Deborah, raised his replenished glass and said, 'Cheers, darling. Cheers, Rachel.'

'Robyn,' said Robyn and Deborah simultaneously.

'I love your house,' he went on, waving the hand holding the drink in Robyn's direction. 'Terrific, these high-ceilinged rooms. And the wood-burning stove's great. They chuck out so much heat, these cast-iron jobbies.'

'Yes, that's such a plus point in a stove,' Robyn murmured. Sitting so close to her, Deborah could feel the antagonism. It prickled, like some sort of force field.

'Had the place long?' Malcolm went on. Had he noticed? Deborah did so hope not.

Robyn, with a quick penitential look at Deborah, said pleasantly, 'Quite a while, yes. It's been a family home for all my boys.'

'How many sons do you have?' Malcolm was smiling, looking so dishy . . . Surely Robyn must see there was more to him than she'd originally thought?

'Four,' Robyn said.

'And they've all left home?' Malcolm was raising his eyebrow again. 'You don't look old enough to have four grown-up sons,' he said gallantly.

Robyn stared at him for at least seven seconds – Deborah knew, she was counting – then said quietly, 'How kind.'

Malcolm, who didn't seem to have noticed the faint irony, said suddenly, as if remembering something, 'What's this place called?'

'Haydon Hall,' Phoebe piped up. 'Grand, isn't it?'

But Malcolm didn't respond. Frowning, he repeated, 'Haydon Hall.' Then, face clearing, gave a shout of laughter.

'Won't you share the joke?' Robyn invited icily.

Malcolm was still laughing. Oh, Deborah prayed, let it be something really funny! Let him make Robyn laugh, because that would do more than anything to make her take a second look at him.

The merriment still apparent in his voice, Malcolm said, 'Do you have a couple of foreign women living here? One of them a big piece?'

Oh, Lord. Was that good or bad? Deborah knew Robyn hadn't reckoned much on Cliantha and her pal, but to have Andy described as a big piece might be pushing it . . .

'My stepdaughter and her friend were staying with me, yes.' Robyn's tone was neutral. 'They have in fact left.'

Malcolm was chuckling again, and Deborah found herself smiling. Really, he did have the most attractive laugh. 'Thought so,' he said. 'I remembered they lived somewhere around here. They were angling for a lift home.'

'A lift home?' Deborah tried to make her voice light and interested. 'Where from?'

Malcolm glanced at her. 'The rugby club. They turned up on Saturday, around five, and asked if they could get a drink. The little one was quite a looker, if you like that sort of thing, and a couple of the men did the honours. Several honours – they both had at least four drinks.' He was laugh-

188

ing again. 'It just goes to show that booze isn't really the universal leg-opener. When the boys suggested the four of them went on somewhere – a curry, then some nice quiet out-of-the-way pub – the girls went all sniffy and said they didn't go for fellas.' He was snorting with remembered hilarity. 'Christ, you should have seen Chris Hughes's face! And when Pete Clarke said did they mean they were a couple of dykes and the little one said, "we prefer the correct title of lesbian", you could have cut the atmosphere with a butter knife! Ha, ha, ha!'

Belatedly, Malcolm realized he was laughing alone. 'I mean,' he said, 'what a coincidence! Two of the inmates of this all-women household pay us a visit at the club on the Saturday, and less than a week later, I – a mere male! – get the great honour of an invitation!' He sat back in his chair and took a large mouthful of his drink. 'Small world, eh?'

Deborah thought that the earnest smile must have frozen on to her face. She didn't dare look at Robyn. She was wracking her brain for something defusing to say when Robyn beat her to it.

'My stepdaughter's sexual orientation is really her own business,' she said, with an almost total lack of expression. 'However, I must correct your misapprehension about the remainder of my household.'

Malcolm stared at her. From the sidelines, Deborah had the sudden impression that he and Robyn were aiming guns at each other. Malcolm's lips were moving, as if he were repeating Robyn's remark and working it out. 'You're all straight, you mean?' His eyes roamed to Phoebe and to Deborah, then returned to Robyn. 'Well, as the token male, let me say how glad I am to hear it!' He waved his almost-empty glass to the three of them. 'Bottoms up, girls!'

Robyn got to her feet. Then said, 'If you'd all like to come through, I'll put the starters on the table.'

Deborah, following her, reached to take Malcolm's proffered hand. She felt quite sick with relief; although it seemed absurd *now*, for a dreadful moment she'd thought that Robyn had shot up to leap on Malcolm and punch him.

Robyn sat at the head of the table, trying to make herself concentrate on the three-handed conversation going on around her. Phoebe, smiling and slightly flushed, was being quite superb, talking wittily about university days and keeping the conversational shuttlecock flying back and forth over the net. But then Phoebe almost certainly didn't realize there was anything wrong; her blunted antennae wouldn't have picked up the bristling antagonism that had flared up in the sitting room. And Deborah – oh, I'm sorry, Debs! – was doing her best, matching Phoebe and Malcolm's cheerful anecdotes with a few of her own.

I was out of line, Robyn thought. It had just been bad luck, that he'd hit a nerve. A nerve she hadn't been aware of; if someone had asked her beforehand if she was worried about her all-female household which, until recently, had included two out-of-the-closet lesbians, she'd have said, of course not! On the contrary, I *like* the company of women!

No. That wouldn't have been what she'd have said. She didn't actually like Cliantha and Andy's company. Not that she'd had much of it; they had kept to their room except for meals. Rather like a pair of very superior pedigree cats, who only deigned to reward their owner's devotion at the rattle of the food bowl.

But she did like living with Debs and Phoebe. Well, with Debs, anyway. And to have this thick, insensitive, self-satisfied man pour scorn on the Haydon Hall set-up, to disparage all of them, tar the three of them with the chauvinistic brush which the whole rugby club had apparently used on Cliantha and Andy, was just too much.

She looked at Malcolm. He was leaning back, fully at his ease, and had draped a casual arm along the back of

Deborah's chair. Deborah, Robyn noticed, kept shooting little nervous glances in Robyn's direction. Catching one of them, Robyn smiled. Deborah's anxious face cleared, and she smiled back.

'If everyone's finished,' Robyn said when there was a gap in the conversation, 'I'll stack the plates and fetch dessert.'

'I'll help,' Deborah said.

'Phoebe and I will amuse ourselves while you ladies are gone,' Malcolm said. Yeah, no danger of *you* leaping up to lend a hand, Robyn thought sourly. 'Great meal, Rachel,' he added, sending her what he no doubt thought of as a suitably rewarding grin. 'Your meat was cooked just right.'

Robyn saw Deborah bend down to whisper, 'It's *Robyn*.'

Robyn said, 'Thank you, Malcolm. I do my best.'

Then she picked up the piled plates and marched out to the kitchen.

Phoebe excused herself and went off to bed soon after the meal was over. Malcolm, refusing another cup of coffee – they had drunk it back in the sitting room, as there had, after all, been no suggestion that Deborah take Malcolm up to her flat – said he ought to be going, too, early start in the morning.

He thanked Robyn for her hospitality, and again praised her cooking. Then Deborah went out with him to see him to his car.

She was gone for some time.

When she returned, Robyn heard her close and bolt the front door, then begin to cross the hall. There was a pause, as if she were hesitating to come any further, then she advanced slowly into the sitting room.

She sat down opposite Robyn, in the chair Malcolm had just vacated. She said, 'You don't like him.'

Robyn sighed. 'Not much, no.'

There was a brief silence. Then Deborah burst out, 'You haven't given him a chance! And he did say how much he liked your cooking!'

The absurdity of this apparently struck them at the same moment. Robyn grinned, Deborah looked stricken.

'And that's meant to make it okay that he's a bumptious, opinionated shit who thought he was doing us all a favour just by *being* here?' Robyn demanded. 'Debs, you can do better than that! You don't need *him!*'

'Don't, oh, don't!' Deborah's voice was slightly unsteady. 'Robyn, he's not like that, really, he's not! He's been so kind to me, and patient. I told you, he guessed about my – well, about what happened, and he's being so sweet! Really, I honestly believe he wants to prove that all men aren't the same – he wants me to see that he's one of the good ones, prepared to bide his time until I – you know.' Deborah's cheeks flushed suddenly.

'Yes, all right,' Robyn said. She waited while her instinctive and possibly cynical reaction faded, then said quietly, 'I hope you're right, Debs.'

Deborah got up and came to sit beside her. She took one of Robyn's hands and squeezed it. 'Robyn, I know what I'm doing,' she said with touching urgency. 'Do you think that I, of all people, would risk getting involved with a man I was unsure about?'

Robyn almost said yes, that's exactly what I do think. But it wouldn't have done Deborah's fragile new self-confidence any good at all, so she just shrugged.

'I'm not going to hurry into anything,' Deborah went on. 'Mentally, I'm not ready, although . . .' She trailed off.

'Well, that seems wise.' Robyn tried to sound encouraging. Tried to make herself believe there was in fact a future to Deborah's relationship with the bastard who had just left. And why shouldn't there be? she demanded angrily of herself. Am I so all-seeing that I can tell from just a few hours what a person's really like? Whether they're worthy of Deborah's affection? Of her love?

No. Of course I'm not.

Still holding Deborah's hand, she returned the squeeze. 'I'm sorry if I was a bit unwelcoming,' she said, forcing out the words. 'It was just – he caught me on the raw, talking like that about us.'

'He didn't mean any offence,' Deborah said soothingly. Oh no? Robyn thought. 'He can be a bit blokeish sometimes, and I suppose that, in fairness, it *was* a bit daft of Cliantha and Andy to parade their lesbianism in a rugby club.'

'Maybe they didn't realize,' Robyn muttered, annoyed at being backed into a position of having to defend the Harpies.

'Wouldn't they have recognised the goal posts, or whatever they're called?' Deborah said innocently.

'They don't play much rugby in Greece. The girls probably thought they were for something else.'

'Like what?' Deborah persisted, the smooth brow creased in a puzzled frown.

'*I* don't know!' Robyn burst out. 'For supporting a ten-metre-high washing line!'

There was a stunned silence. Afraid Deborah was mortally offended, she turned to her. 'Debs, I didn't mean to yell at you, I –'

She didn't go on. There was no need, since Deborah's face was alight with silent laughter.

Robyn got up. 'On that note, I think we ought to call it a day,' she announced.

'Right. So do I.' Deborah stood up beside her, and gave her a brief but intense hug. 'Thank you for this evening, Robyn. I appreciate it.'

'Has it helped you decide? About –' She almost said, about whether to go on seeing him. But that was perhaps wishful thinking. 'About how to handle it from now on?'

'Yes.' Deborah's face was angelic. 'I'm going to let us go

on to – well, to the next step. You know.' Robyn was all too afraid that she did. 'He's earned it, Robyn!' Now she was intense again, eyes fixed on Robyn's as if she could transmit her faith in Malcolm – in her own ability to make a good relationship with him – by sheer force of will. 'He was prepared to come here tonight, even though he knew it was a very female household,' – hang on! Robyn wanted to protest, he didn't realize that till he got here! – 'for my sake, because he knew it mattered to me, and I wanted my friends to meet him. Doesn't that outweigh any small gaffes he made with you?' *Small* gaffes! 'Robyn? Doesn't it?'

Suddenly Robyn was tired of the whole thing. 'Yes, Debs, if you want it to.' Realizing how dismissive that sounded, she put an arm round Deborah's thin shoulders as they crossed the hall. 'Give him another chance.' That wasn't right either; it was Robyn, if anybody, who needed to do that. 'It's up to you, anyway, whatever you decide to do.'

There was no reply from Deborah as they climbed the stairs. But, as she was about to go through the Great Divide to her own flat, she turned and, for a moment, caught Robyn's eye.

With trepidation evident in her expression, she said, 'I know. That's just the trouble.'

CHAPTER FIFTEEN

The concept of Haydon Hall being some sort of female commune was not one which much appealed to Robyn. She had vague misgivings over this being how people were viewing the household, but then dismissed them. Was it really likely that anyone except Malcolm could believe a pregnant woman, a woman going out with a man like him, and one who had been married twice – with four much-loved sons to show for it – were actually anti-men?

And what the hell did it matter, anyway?

She was out shopping a few days after the fiasco of the dinner party when she spotted a familiar leather jacket. Its owner was leaning into the cabinet that contained fresh pasta; it had to be him.

Coming up behind him, she said, 'I owe you £78.34.'

She was just thinking how silly she was going to feel if it *wasn't* him, when the person straightened up, turned round, and it was.

'It's the back lady!' he exclaimed.

'Bag lady?'

'*Back* lady. How is it? Better, I hope?'

'It's fine.' She was responding to his smile. 'And I also owe you an apology – I rushed off the other day without repaying you. You must have thought I was awful.'

'I didn't think that at all.' He was watching her intently. The dark-blue eyes were affecting her rather pleasantly. 'I did wait until you were out of sight, in case you remembered at the last minute, but then I realized that it must have slipped your mind. I put it down to shock,' he added charitably.

'Did you do shock on your first-aid course?'

'Oh, yes. Cold, clammy skin, rapid pulse, pale sweating face.'

'Good grief. What a picture. And you *still* stayed around to help me.'

'I was hoping I might be called upon to loosen your clothing.'

She could hardly believe she'd heard right. And in the middle of the supermarket! 'I'm not feeling at all faint today,' she said reprovingly.

But he was undeterred. 'Shame,' he murmured.

She got her purse out. 'Cheque or cash?' she asked.

'Hm?'

'The £78.34,' she said patiently.

'Ah. Oh, a cheque?'

'Right.' She found her chequebook in her pocket, and he turned round so that she could use his back to press on.

'Will you put your name and address on the reverse side?' he asked over his shoulder.

She didn't think she'd ever been picked up with such swift efficiency. It was quite taking her breath away.

'Do you spell your name as one would expect?' she said, not answering his question.

'Absolutely.'

She wrote 'Rory Preston' where the cheque said 'Pay . . .'. Then the date and the amount. Then she signed it and, tearing it out, turned it over and wrote her address. And her telephone number.

She waved it over his shoulder. 'My name's printed on the front, if you can't read my signature.'

He looked at the flourish with which she had signed her name. 'Rayne Euthymol,' he remarked. 'Interesting name.'

'That's a K, not an E. It's Robyn Kazandreas, as you can see very well from where it's printed underneath.'

'Foreign?'

'Of *course* foreign. When did Kazandreas ever sound English?'

'Foreign.'

'My late husband was Greek. From Crete.' Oh, Zach. What would you think of me, standing by the pasta cabinet, having such fun with a handsome stranger?

Rory Preston was folding up her cheque and putting it away in his wallet. 'Have you much more shopping to do, Mrs Euthymol?'

'No. Amazingly little, as it happens.'

'Nor have I. Shall we meet the other side of the checkout and have a coffee?'

She hesitated only for a couple of seconds, and that was only for form's sake. 'Good idea. First one there gets them in.'

Over the moustache-making cappuccinos, he told her he was a freelance journalist. Not that she'd asked outright; the conversation was on far too frivolous a level for such a sensible question. She had in fact asked why a man well below retirement age – 'Thank you for the "well",' he said wryly – was always hanging around in the supermarket during working hours, and he said he never hung around anywhere, and the fact that he had time off during the week was purely because he usually worked during the weekend. 'I prefer' – he fixed her with a stern look – 'to have my time off when everyone else is hard at it.'

Then she said, what sort of work do you do?, and he told her.

'Newspaper journalism or magazine?' she asked, interested.

'Both. Either. I've just sold an article to one of the broadsheets on the Dungeness nuclear power station, and I'm in the middle of a series of pieces for a Canadian environmental magazine on European forests.'

'Is it always green issues?'

'No. Well, yes, but not really.'

She grinned. 'Forget I asked.'

'I could demand the same of you,' he said, the stern look back in place.

'Hm?'

'Why you're always loitering in the supermarket in working hours. Oh, did it improve?'

She was at a loss. 'Did what improve? I already said, my back's fine.'

'Not your back. Last time we spoke,' – last time! there'd only been the once, although already it was beginning to seem as if they'd known each other much longer – 'you said there had been a setback on the employment front. I just wondered if you'd got on top of it.'

How flattering, that he'd remembered. 'Thanks for asking, but no. I'm still where I was.'

'Unemployed?'

There was nothing like calling a spade a spade. 'Quite.'

'What do you do?'

She hesitated. What *did* she do? Very little, in the way of paid work, was the honest answer. 'I was a singer, aeons ago.'

'A singer? What, opera?'

She laughed. 'No. I was a backing singer. Do you remember the Stove Pipe Boys?'

He frowned. 'Had a few hits in the seventies? Irish, weren't they?'

'Their PR said so, although only two out of the six really were. The drummer was a Londoner and the other three were from the Midlands.'

He was frowning again. 'What was their big one? Something to do with the moon, wasn't it?'

'"Emerald Moon". The lyrics went, "Midnight cat with a mouse in its claws, Get me to her, open the doors, Midnight cat with the stars in its eye, Get me to her, make me fly".'

'Deathless prose.'

'Right. The backing lyrics were even better – we got an "oooeee, oooeee, oooaaaeee", then a "get me to her, get me to her, oooeee, get me to her".'

She had, without actually intending to, started to sing. Embarrassed, she had forgotten how powerful her voice was. 'Sorry.'

'Don't be. I'm full of admiration.' She shot him a grateful smile. 'Actually, I sing too. In a choir that's only recently been formed, in the town. I was about to ask if you'd thought of joining, but I think you'd blow us out of the hall.'

She was embarrassed all over again. He must have realised; he put out a hand and, for a moment, grabbed her wrist. '*Sorry*. I don't know you nearly well enough to tease you, because you won't yet have any way of knowing when I'm doing it.'

His remark was so full of suggestion that she couldn't think how to answer.

'Will you give it some thought?' he said after a moment.

'The choir? Yes. I will.' If she wasn't going to get paid singing work, it would be a good idea to do something else, to keep her voice exercised.

He was writing on a paper napkin. 'If your thinking results in a positive, here's the chap to contact.' He handed her the napkin; it wasn't *his* name and address, which was slightly disappointing. 'What happened to the Stove Pipe Boys?' he said.

'They disbanded. Hiram Kelly – it wasn't his real name, by the way – went back to Dublin and formed another band. I don't know what happened to the rest, except for the drummer, who has a wet fish stall in Acton. He slips me a nice piece of cod if I'm in the vicinity.'

Too late, she realised the *double entendre*. Rory was being gentlemanly and making a very obvious effort not to smile; she hesitated, then put him out of his misery. 'I didn't phrase that very well. Actually I usually ask for haddock.'

Recognising that he had been given leave to laugh, he did so. Then he said, 'You seem remarkably cheerful, if I may say so, for someone who's out of work.'

'I don't seriously *have* to work. My –' No. In this mood of flirtatiousness and fun, it wasn't right to mention Zach. It would make her feel disloyal. As if she included his memory in the things she could laugh about. And that was so far from being so that it didn't bear contemplating. 'The house is mine, and I've found myself a tenant, so the heat's off for the moment.'

'Ah yes, you mentioned the annoying people you live with.'

Again, she was impressed at how accurately he'd recalled their earlier conversation. Perhaps it went with his job. 'Debs isn't annoying,' she said. 'She's a lovely person. Troubled, and going out with a right shit, but then it's no reflection on her judgement, she's had a rotten time. She –'

She pulled herself up. This was not the place to bring up Debs's secrets. And she hardly knew the man she'd been about to discuss them with! What had got *into* her?

Tactfully, he changed the subject. 'Would you like another coffee?'

She didn't want one. But, if she said no, then there would be no excuse for them to go on sitting there together. She looked up at him, and found he was watching her closely. 'Not really,' she said. 'What about you?'

Slowly he shook his head. But, bolder than she was, he said, 'Although I do want to go on talking to you. Would a suggestion that we have dinner this evening be unforgivably forward?'

'Totally. But it won't stop me accepting.'

He looked very pleased. 'Mrs Euthymol, I'm delighted. What about the Italian place, next to the cinema? About eight?'

She bent down to pick up her shopping, taking a moment because she was sure she was blushing. 'Eight's fine,' she said when she was facing him again.

He was looking at his watch. 'I must go. I'm expecting a fax from Nova Scotia.'

She couldn't resist it. 'Pretentious? *Moi?*'

Later, getting ready to go out, she felt so happy that it spilled over into remorse that she'd given Deborah a hard time over Malcolm. Especially since, on her doorstep when she got back from shopping, there had been a generous bouquet of flowers and a card that said, *Many thanks for a great evening, best wishes, Malcolm.*

'I probably misjudged him,' she said to Deborah, who, having come into her bedroom to lend her some hair mousse, had sat down on the end of the bed. 'He was nervous, I expect. And the flowers are lovely – a man who chooses bronze lilies can't be all bad.'

Deborah's face lit up. 'Oh, Robyn, he's always doing things like that! He had to go to Paris last week, and he brought me some Chanel Number Nine from the duty free – he'd actually remembered that I'd said I liked it!'

Robyn, touched that Deborah's experience of men had led her to believe that such a gesture was so extraordinary, shot her a smile. 'How kind,' she said. Then, afraid that, despite her best efforts, it had sounded sarcastic, 'It's great when men actually make a mental note, isn't it?'

'*Wonderful,*' Deborah breathed.

There was a brief silence. Then diplomatic Deborah, as if thinking she might have trodden on delicate ground, asked softly, 'Was your husband good at presents?'

'Brilliant.' Robyn, who had turned back to the dressing

table, met Deborah's eyes in the mirror. 'Well, my second husband was.'

'*Second?*'

In all their conversations, had she never mentioned to Debs that she'd been married before? Apparently not. Briefly she told her, and, when she finished, noticed that Deborah was nodding.

'I remember now,' Deborah said. 'Phoebe said something about your oldest three not being called Kazandreas, and that your youngest was only a half-brother of the one she's pregnant by.'

Robyn had been bumbling along quite happily not thinking about that. To have such an unequivocal reminder was a bit unnerving.

'God, so she is,' she muttered. Then, more emphatically, '*Christ!* The baby's due in April.' Again she met Deborah's sympathetic eyes. 'Debs, I'm going to be a grandmother in less than three months!'

Deborah came to stand behind her, putting her hands on Robyn's shoulders. 'There's nothing you can do about it,' she said, her tone kindly. 'You'll just have to accept it.' Then, brightly, 'You were telling me about Zach, and the presents.'

For the second time that day, Robyn was grateful for someone changing the subject. She held out her left hand with the diamond eternity ring. 'He gave me this. Left it, in fact, in his desk, wrapped ready for my birthday. I found it after he died.'

She had thought she had grown used to the poignancy of that. Had imagined that, four months after Zach's death, she was on top of things, coping, adjusted to living without him. The time of tears and of open grieving was behind her; she had picked up the reins and was getting on with her life.

Why, then, was Deborah's gentle expression making her heart hurt? Why were the warm hands still on her shoulders, hands whose touch seemed to say, I understand, it's okay to be sad, making her eyes prickle with tears?

I never really cried for him, she thought suddenly. I was upset, there were bad days, yes, but I always managed to hold back. I thought I was doing so well!

But now it occurred to her that she hadn't done well at all. Had, because dear old Zach's irritating qualities had of late outweighed his lovable ones, actually forbidden herself to be too distressed. Told herself, don't be too sad, life without him won't be as dreadful as all that.

Her heart hadn't had its say.

Now, her streaming tears ruining the careful makeup she'd put on for her dinner with Rory Preston, it seemed her heart was making up for lost time.

Turning round, she leaned her wet face against Deborah's stomach. Deborah's arms went round her, Deborah's hand stroked her damp hair. And Deborah's quiet voice, sounding quite unsurprised, said softly, 'You go ahead and have a good cry.'

When she felt better, she and Deborah went downstairs and made themselves a self-indulgent – and rather late – supper. Deborah had telephoned the Italian restaurant and left a message for Rory Preston; displaying a steadfast determination which had quite surprised Robyn, she had said it was absurd for Robyn even to *think* of going out tonight, and that, when she finally had the chance to explain, if Rory were as nice as Robyn thought, then he'd quite understand.

Deborah's logic was faultless.

And it was comforting, Robyn found, to sit huddled in her old robe with cheese on toast to eat and, afterwards, cocoa to drink. I feel purged, she thought drowsily as she watched Deborah cut slabs of gingerbread cake to go with the cocoa. All this time I'd been carrying that sorrow inside, and I never knew. And Debs was right – what a terrible moment it would have been to go out on a first date with someone else!

Zach. Dear Zach. Smiling, she felt the tears fill her sore eyes again. I'm sorry, Zach, if I appear to have forgotten you. I haven't. I won't, ever. You always said I was strong, and I think I've been believing you a bit too readily. But I'm not actually so strong that I don't mourn you, that I don't wish I could go back to those great days we had together.

She knew – as, indeed, he surely would have done were he there – that the great days had been a long, long time ago.

Phoebe joined them for a cup of cocoa; she had been to an antenatal class, and gone out for a meal afterwards with two of the other young expectant mothers. Preoccupied with telling them about how the class had done relaxation and breathing exercises, she didn't seem to notice Robyn's red eyes. Nor the fact that, usually talkative, Robyn was quiet.

You had the nerve to remark that Stevie wasn't very good husband material, Robyn said silently to Phoebe. And, although I have to confess that you might have been right, I do wonder if someone as preoccupied with herself as you are would actually make much of a wife.

Tired suddenly – too much emotion, over too many issues, and she was, underneath everything else, genuinely sorry that she hadn't turned up for dinner with Rory – Robyn gave a huge yawn. When there was a break in the conversation, or rather, to be accurate, a pause in Phoebe's lecture about the three stages of labour, Robyn put down her cup, got up and announced she was going to bed.

Deborah met her eyes as she left the room. As Phoebe prepared for the next part of her talk, she mouthed, 'All right?'

Robyn nodded. 'Thanks, Debs,' she whispered. And, as an afterthought, bent to bestow a swift kiss on the top of Deborah's head.

The least I can do, she reflected as she wearily climbed the stairs, under the circumstances. When I'm so grateful to her for her tact and her understanding.

Lying in bed, she remembered Deborah as she'd been when she'd first arrived at Haydon Hall. Compared it with how she was now. Was pleased at the change.

Wondered if it was, after all, due to the benign influence of Malcolm Teague. And – the thought came to worry her dreams – decided she was quite sure it wasn't.

CHAPTER SIXTEEN

Robyn couldn't find any Preston, Rs in the telephone book. It occurred to her that possibly he was ex-directory; perhaps investigative journalists covering green issues feared too many calls from cranks to broadcast their numbers.

But she didn't have to resort to hanging around the super-market this time. She found the paper napkin Rory had given her in the supermarket, and the following evening telephoned the number. The man who answered sounded friendly; she said, without preamble, 'Rory Preston gave me your number. About the choir. I wondered if you could return the favour and give me his number?'

'Certainly. Hold on a mo –' He was soon back, and read out a local number. 'Are you going to join us?'

Hardly thinking – she was mentally forming what she was going to say to Rory – she said, 'Oh, yes.'

'Great!' he said enthusiastically. 'Rehearsals are on Thurs-days, seven-thirty PM, Saint Nick's hall. What are you?'

She was, it seemed, committed.

'Alto. Right, I'll come if I can. Thanks.'

Before he had a chance to ask for her name and address, she thanked him and hung up.

When Rory answered, she said, 'I'm ringing to apologize for not turning up last night. I don't usually act like that, there were mitigating circumstances.'

There was a fairly lengthy silence, which made her fear the worst. Then he said, 'Umberto called when you phoned him, so I didn't actually get as far as the restaurant.'

'It wasn't me who called.' Shouldn't that be I who called? She should have got it right, especially since she was speaking to a journalist. 'It was Deborah, my tenant.'

'Oh.'

With any luck, he might conclude that she had been too ill to come to the phone, which, in a way, was true. 'I really am sorry,' she said earnestly.

'Oh.' Then after a pause, 'Are you feeling all right now?'

'Yes, perfectly. I would like to explain, some time.'

She waited for him to absorb the repercussions of that. He said guardedly, 'What had you in mind?'

'What about same time, same place, next week?' She said her pre-thought-out speech quickly, before her nerve failed. 'I'll book the table this time, then, if you want, you can do the same to me.'

'I wouldn't be so petty.' Thank goodness, there was some warmth in his voice. 'Okay, then. Next week.'

She opened her mouth to say more, to tell him the reason for standing him up, but discovered it wasn't actually what she wanted to do. I'm forty-nine, she reminded herself, I don't have to do what other people expect of me any more. And I've already apologized. 'See you next week,' she said.

'Yes, okay. Bye, Robyn.'

He hadn't called her Mrs Euthymol. She hoped it didn't indicate he wasn't going to be lighthearted with her any more.

Deborah was going out with Malcolm after work. He was taking her somewhere special, he said, but, contradictorily, told her not to dress up.

After a drink at their usual pub, he drove her to his house.

'I thought, Deborah my sweet,' he said as he pulled up

beside a front door in need of a coat of varnish, 'it would be nice to be alone tonight.'

Her heart was hammering. Calm down, she told herself. He's been hinting at this. Suggesting that a more private venue might give us the chance to relax together. Relax. It sounds fine. Doesn't it? Don't I *want* to relax?

She got out of the car and joined him at the front door. He opened it, admitting her to a narrow hall in which a sideboard covered in old newspapers, letters, a cap and several plastic carrier bags took up much of the space. He held out a hand for her coat, which she took off and gave to him. He put it on a peg on the wall.

'Squeeze by the sideboard,' he said, reaching past her to open a door off the hall, 'and go into the drawing room.'

Drawing room, she couldn't help thinking, slightly overstated the case. But the little room was warm, subtly lit, and there was a long Habitat sofa under the window. The curtains were drawn.

She went to stand in front of the fireplace. There was a gas fire, which Malcolm lit. 'Sit down, sit down,' he said, waving an arm at the sofa.

It was the only piece of furniture in the room. She sat down at one end, knees together, back straight. Malcolm, watching, started to laugh.

'Darling Deborah, you look as if you've come for an interview!' She smiled with him. It *was* rather funny. He bent down and gave her a kiss. 'I'll fetch us a drink – I've got something nice . . .'

He came back with a bottle of chilled sparkling wine and some Kettle crisps in a plastic dish. He opened the wine, poured some into two glasses, handed one to her and sat down beside her.

Right beside her.

For a while they just talked. Ordinary, day-to-day conversation, just the sort they would have had in the pub. He had his arm round her, yes, but then he often did that in the pub.

He refilled her glass. She hadn't been aware of having drunk so quickly. She took a sip, nervously, telling herself to slow down.

His hand on her shoulder was making small circling movements. With each one, the ends of his fingers got slightly nearer to the collar of her blouse.

He was still talking, telling her about having beaten somebody at squash that lunchtime. His mouth right by her ear – when had he got so close! – he said, 'I was knackered afterwards, I can tell you.' The hand darted inside her blouse. 'But I'm fine now.' His fingers went under the edge of her bra. Gently kneaded the flesh of her breast. 'Raring to go.'

She made herself sit absolutely still. His hand was gentle, and the sensation was actually most enjoyable.

Why did she feel so apprehensive! Was it only to be expected, after Br—?

He was murmuring in her ear, something about wanting to help, wanting to unlock her . . . Then he cupped her chin in his free hand, turned her to face him and began to kiss her.

That felt nice, too. Tentatively, she kissed him back.

'Deborah, that's so good!' he said huskily, removing his mouth from hers. 'Now, what happens if I undo these little buttons . . . ?'

He undid the next four buttons of her blouse, and they both looked down at her small breasts in the plain white bra. '*Very* schoolmarmish,' he said. 'We'll have to get you into something more adventurous, won't we?'

The alarm bell was only faint at first.

He reached behind her and unfastened her bra, instantly swooping forward to kiss her breasts, taking each nipple in turn into his mouth. She felt the slight pain of his teeth, nipping delicately.

It began as delicate.

He pushed her down so that she lay on her back. Still being gentle, although there was a firmness in his hands which made the alarm sound again.

'Deborah, talk to me,' he said urgently, lying beside her, one hand on her breast and the other roaming around her waist. 'Is this what you like?'

'I – oh, yes. It's lovely.' She sounded unconvincing, even to herself.

He laughed quietly. Then, without warning, swung one leg across her thighs. 'There, my darling,' he murmured, 'pinned you down at last. That's what you like, isn't it? To be held firmly under a man?'

Wherever had he got hold of that idea? 'Well, I –'

'Tell me what he did, Deborah!' Malcolm's voice was hoarse with lust. 'You're longing to, aren't you? You'd never have hinted at your secret past if you didn't want to talk about it. What did he do? Tie you up? Was that it, is that what you like? Tell me, I'm on to try *anything!* Bit of low-grade beating? Little whips, something like that, and you dressed up in some kinky leather outfit with a thong and chains? D'you want me to tie you up now, while you tell me?'

'No!' Dear God, no! She tried to lever him off her – she could feel his erection pushing into her thigh as if he had a courgette in his pocket. 'Malcolm, please, get off!'

He was laughing again. 'Great! Fight me, yes, come on, baby, fight me all the way!' She raised her hands to shove at his shoulders and he grasped her wrists, one of his hands easily holding both of hers. Then, when she opened her mouth to shout at him – plead with him – he began to kiss her again.

The earlier, sweet fledgling feelings of arousal were driven out by her panic. Wriggling, writhing beneath him, she heard him moan with pleasure. 'Baby, oh, *yes!*', he gasped, before plunging his mouth back on to hers.

She closed her lips together, pulling them in. Wrenching her head violently, she managed to get free of his searching mouth.

'Malcolm, stop it!' she cried. 'You've got it all wrong!'

Her right leg was suddenly free of his weight; to reinforce her words, she bent her knee and kicked him sharply on the backside.

'Ouch!' He sprang away from her, sitting up. 'That bloody well *hurt!* Your heel hit my arse!'

She took her chance, leaping to her feet and buttoning her blouse. 'It was meant to!' she shouted. 'Malcolm, the *last* thing I wanted was to *tell* you what happened to me!' Suddenly furious, she bent towards him, almost spitting at him. 'Are you entirely thick? Can't you begin to comprehend that someone who's been tied, beaten and abused doesn't actually want to repeat the experience, even verbally?'

He seemed quite stunned. His mouth was hanging open and he reached up to run a hand through the tousled hair on top of his head. He looked like Stan Laurel saying, with pretend tears in his eyes, 'Oh, Ollie!'

Absurdly, she wanted to laugh. But then, as abruptly as they had come, the feelings both of amusement and anger went away, leaving her shaking with the aftermath of revulsion and fear. And, beneath that, sadness. She was so very sad, because she had thought she was cured and now she knew she wasn't.

Before the powerful emotion could overwhelm her, she turned, picked up her bag, collected her coat and ran out of the house.

Robyn was in the kitchen when she got back to Haydon Hall. Thank God, Phoebe was in the living room, eyes fixed on the TV.

Deborah pulled out a kitchen stool, sat down at the table and dropped her head on to her folded arms.

She felt Robyn come to stand behind her. 'What's up, Debs?'

She shook her head. She didn't think she could bring herself to say anything at all, never mind trying to tell Robyn what had happened.

Robyn moved away. 'I'm making tea, if you'd like a cup.'

'Please.'

A little later, a cup was placed gently in front of her. 'Why don't you take it up to bed with you?' Robyn suggested.

'Mm.' Deborah got up and made for the door.

'I'm here if you need me,' Robyn said quietly.

Deborah didn't answer.

For the next few days, Robyn watched Deborah move like an automaton through her comings and goings. She didn't seem to be eating, she didn't talk much. She was pale, and sometimes seemed to be muttering to herself.

There was no sign, nor even any mention, of Malcolm Teague.

Robyn said on Sunday night, 'Debs, if I'm out of line, tell me, but do you think it'd be an idea to talk about this? Whatever it is?'

'I *can't!*' Deborah cried. 'That's the whole problem! I just *can't!*'

'You've already told me things about your past,' Robyn persisted, not sure if she was doing the right thing. 'You managed very well, then.'

'That was different! You're – you're you.'

'Oh.' She took a breath, then plunged on, 'You could talk to me, but you found you couldn't talk to someone else. Was that it? Was it Malcolm?'

Deborah turned a livid face to her. 'He tried to make me tell him all about it! He was ranting on about whips and leather thongs! He was getting *off* on it!'

Oh, Debs, Debs! Of all the men in all the cars in all the

towns in the world, you had to accept a lift from Malcolm Teague. Robyn went to sit on the floor at Deborah's feet and reached out a hand. 'I'm so sorry.' It wasn't really adequate.

There was a long, painful silence. Robyn could feel Deborah's distress; the air seemed to reverberate with it.

She said, 'Deborah, why not see someone? A counsellor, I mean.' Deborah made a sound which might have been expressive of either interest or rejection; assuming the former, Robyn hurried on. 'Zach and I knew someone whose brother went to a chap in Hawkenbury – apparently he was very good. Our friend said his brother really rated him.'

There was a pause. Then Deborah said, 'What would I have to do?'

'Debs, you don't *have* to do *anything!*' Robyn bit down hard on the flare of irritation; it wouldn't help in the least to get mad at Deborah. 'I mean, dear Debs, *you* must put yourself in the driving seat. There's no law that says other people must tell you what to do and you tamely go along with it!'

Deborah's voice came from over Robyn's head; she sounded very distant. 'Is that what you think of me? That I'm tame? Do what I'm told?'

'I – no, not entirely.' Was it better to tell a convincing lie or to proceed with something nearer to the truth? 'I think you've been conditioned to think your own wishes are secondary. If that's really at the root of it, then maybe talking it through to a professional counsellor might help.'

Deborah was quiet for so long that Robyn was beginning to think it was terminal. She said tentatively, 'Debs? Have I mortally offended you?'

Deborah said vaguely, 'No.' Then: 'I was thinking. You may have a point.'

Then, quite calmly, she got up and left the room, closing the door quietly but firmly behind her.

*　　*　　*

She asked Robyn for the name and number of the counsellor on her way out to work in the morning. Just as she was leaving; she didn't want to stay and talk. Robyn might gloat.

No, she wouldn't. Deborah berated herself for even thinking it.

At lunchtime, she rang the number. A quiet, male voice said, 'Sean Duncan.'

Deborah tried to speak, found that her mouth was dry. Swallowed, tried again. Heard herself say, with admirable composure, 'I have some quite serious emotional problems, resulting from a bad marriage to a man who mistreated me. I've heard that you counsel people, and I wondered if you could see me?'

Sean Duncan said, still in that quiet, unexcitable tone, 'I can see you, yes, of course. When would you like to come?'

'As soon as possible, please.'

There was a brief pause. Then – perhaps he imagined she might think he was having second thoughts – 'I've just got my diary out, and I'm looking through. Next week . . . Oh! I see I've got a cancellation at five this evening. Any good?'

Good Lord, it was like arranging a dental appointment! Before she could lose her courage, she said, 'Fine.'

She was about to put the phone down when he said – and she was sure there was faint humour in his voice – 'Hadn't you better tell me who you are?'

She had no idea what to expect. Half of her was worried that she'd made this crucial appointment with a man; would it not have been better to ask around and see if she could have found a female counsellor? Weren't men – *a* man, really – the whole cause of her trouble?

But she couldn't cancel her appointment. You couldn't cancel a cancellation. She smothered a laugh, and wondered if she were becoming hysterical.

*　　*　　*

Sean Duncan lived in a small terraced house in a quiet side street. There were what looked like dark velvet curtains at the front room window, and, when he answered the door, a pleasant smell of coffee and baking.

'Come into the front room,' he said. 'Make yourself comfortable.'

'Thank you.' Other than in its size, it couldn't have been more different from Malcolm's room. There was a small table with two chairs at one end. A two-seater settee sat on one side of the fire, an armchair on the other. Deborah sat down in the armchair. The fire – an open fire – was burning merrily, and there was an occasional crackle of igniting wood.

She stared at Sean Duncan. Arranging a pad of paper, a file and a pencil on the table, he was half-turned from her, so he didn't see her looking. He was about her own height, or only a little more, and slimly built. His fair hair was in need of a trim, but so clean that it was floppy, like a child's. He was wearing jeans and a navy pullover over a white collarless shirt. His feet were bare. As he pulled out one of the upright chairs and turned to face her, she saw that his eyes were a sort of hazel colour.

He looked young. He looked – she sought for the right word – innocent. As if he'd hardly come to grips with the world. It was unexpected, considering what he did for a living. Was he any good? she wondered. Was this whole thing another bloody mistake?

As if he knew what she was thinking, he said, 'I'm not as young as I look.'

Feeling awkward, she said, 'No, I'm sure you're not.' That didn't seem right. 'I'm sorry, I didn't mean to be rude.'

'You weren't. And, even if you were, it's all in a day's work.' He smiled suddenly, and his face seemed to fill with light. He looked even younger.

Disconcerted, she said abruptly, 'May I ask how old you

actually are?' instantly following it up with an agonized, 'No! Forget I said that!'

He was still smiling. 'I'm forty-six.'

'Oh.' Same age as me. 'Oh, I see.'

He tapped his pencil a couple of times on the pad, as if calling a meeting to order. But the gesture was so quiet, so unobtrusive, that it couldn't have been a very big or important meeting. No high-powered men with long-winded titles and florid faces, shouting a lot. For some reason, suddenly she began to have confidence in this rather unprepossessing, totally un-pushy, soft-spoken person. When he said why didn't she, in her own time and in her own way, see if she could start to tell him why she had come, it didn't really seem difficult at all.

Deborah, pursuing a theme, says, 'It's so easy to be swept up by someone, to believe, with what you think is your rational mind, that they are the very person for you, yet, in the fullness of time, discover that you were wrong.'

Robyn, still frowning, has the distinct air of someone who doesn't actually want to go on talking about this, thank you very much. She says, 'I know. I *know*.'

Deborah, however, is not to be deterred. 'I speak as one who has had experience, as you will no doubt realize.'

Robyn turns to look at her, eyes screwed up against the brilliant light bouncing up off the sea. Her face briefly registers an expression of – what? Can it be admiration, that Deborah is sticking to her guns?

It matters a lot to Deborah what Robyn thinks of her, so she very much hopes she is right about the admiration.

But: 'You're stating the obvious,' Robyn said flatly. And quite forcibly.

Deborah, who understands Robyn far better than Robyn is aware, is not dismayed. For Robyn has used her no-holds-barred, confrontational voice. The one she reserves for heavy-weight adversaries.

The one which, for months, she *never* used when talking with Deborah.

Inside Deborah's head there silently begins to sound a small victory song.

'Perhaps,' she says. 'However, it doesn't alter the fact that you – both of us – have almost certainly been married to someone who wouldn't have been the first choice of partner proposed by a marriage bureau.'

'*Marriage* bureau? Ha! What do *they* know?'

'Quite a lot, I would imagine,' Deborah says spiritedly. 'They – well, the good ones, anyway – go into the subject of compatibility quite extensively. And isn't that – compatibility – what it's all about?'

'Hm.' Robyn is frowning again. Then she bursts out, 'But you don't stop to think about whether you're compatible when you fall in love! You just get swept up in it, and you think you're doing the right thing, whereas, often . . .'

She trails off. It is perfectly clear to Deborah why she has not gone on; she would have repeated pretty faithfully Deborah's initial premise.

Deborah knows better than to say, QED, or, I rest my case. Instead – for it is dear old Robyn she is talking to, and she does not wish to crow – she says humbly, 'I always found it so very difficult to make rational judgements when I'd fallen for someone. I was aware of the tendency to get my initial assessment all wrong, but I didn't seem to be able to change. And it can make for such mistakes – you think someone is one thing, you get all steamed up because you don't like what you seem to be seeing, then you find out they aren't it at all.'

What a tangled sentence, she thinks. But Robyn, who has been at her side through her recent tribulations, nods. 'Right,' she says. Then – as if she's had enough of high-flown philosophical stuff – 'It's a bugger, isn't it?'

Deborah is compelled to make one more attempt. 'Robyn, dear Robyn, will you just promise not to dismiss it out of hand?'

'Dismiss what?' Robyn asks gruffly, picking small pebbles out of the short grass and flinging them viciously towards the edge of the cliffs. More than half soar straight over and, presumably, drop into the sea: Robyn has a strong right arm.

We are, thinks Deborah, on delicate ground here. And she doesn't mean the nearby, crumbling cliff edge. 'Dismiss the idea of admitting someone into your life.'

'My life's full of people!' Robyn cries. 'Overflowing, in fact! Stepdaughters, stray past flings of my sons and their offspring, parents, mothers-in-law, ex-husbands, grown-up sons . . . have I left anyone out?'

'Friends?' Me, Deborah means.

Briefly Robyn smiles. 'You're special. I don't count you among the people who seem constantly to want me to do things for them.'

The silent little song turns into a mighty chorus. It is perhaps the nicest thing that anyone has ever said to Deborah. After a quick pause to get her bearings – for it is heady stuff, getting used to a new self-image – she says, 'I think you might possibly have exaggerated the number of people on your list. When did Paddy ever ask anything of you?'

'Okay, not recently,' Robyn concedes. 'If you don't count him *still* ringing up occasionally to check when the boys' birthdays are. Good God alive,' she adds with heat, 'he rang up last year to ask me when his *mother's* birthday was.'

'Even that's only a minor demand,' Deborah points out.

'Yes. Well.'

'I'm concerned because the time may well be not far off when you have Haydon Hall all to yourself,' Deborah says quietly.

'Alleluia!' Robyn shouts. 'Hurry the day!'

'Robyn, you'd hate it!' Deborah swiftly counters. 'You of all people, so used to the light chatter of your loved ones, so good at looking after them, and –'

'Don't tell *me* what I would or would not hate!' Robyn is shouting again. She looks really angry. 'I've had years, *years*, of all that! You only think it's what suits me because you've never seen me any other way! Bloody hell, Debs, haven't I earned a bit of peace and quiet? I want to please *me* now. It's my fucking turn!'

The echoes of her powerful voice carry across the meadow. On a footpath a couple of hundred yards away, a couple in matching jade and purple cagoules turn to stare. The larger figure – it is impossible to tell, under the woolly cap, if it is male or female – calls to a little terrier which has its nose in a pile of sheep shit, summoning it closer as if it might be contaminated by someone shouting 'fucking' on a peaceful cliff-top.

'Sorry,' Robyn mutters. 'It's just something I feel strongly about.'

'You don't say,' Deborah murmurs.

Robyn grins. 'We're not going to agree on this, Debs.'

'We don't need to. I just want you not to close your mind to the possibility of happiness.'

'Debs, that's exactly how *I* feel about *you!*'

They sit staring at each other. Deborah senses that Robyn feels the same affectionate frustration that she is experiencing.

After a moment, Robyn says, 'We could always change the subject.'

'And talk about the weather?' Deborah suggests.

Robyn lies down again. 'Which just happens to be fabulous.' She gives a full-lunged sigh of pleasure and closes her eyes, as if to say, ah, feel the sunshine! And, more to the point, shut up, Debs, I've had enough of this argument.

It *is* an argument, Deborah thinks, turning on to her stomach and watching the cagoule couple negotiating a stile. The terrier, which has run on ahead, is crouched in that unmistakable canine pose that indicates it is having a crap. It is doing so right on the footpath, and Deborah hopes one of its unconcerned owners treads in it. Serve them right. It's hell getting dog shit out of the treads of walking boots.

Robyn and I sit on opposite sides of the fence, she thinks,

turning back to look at the more satisfying picture of the wide sea, and neither of us wants to accept that the other may have even a *smidgen* of a valid viewpoint. Yet we should, really we should – we both want what's best for the other, so at least the other ought to listen.

Since Robyn has clearly declared she wants no further part in the discussion right now, Deborah goes on by herself.

Marriage. The case for and against. Which, as one would expect, varies with the person under discussion. Because some people are born for it, and some are not. The important thing is to work out who is and who isn't.

She smiles faintly. A few years ago – a few months ago – the concept of marriage would have conjured up such dark images, that she would instantly have shied away from it. Even if it was not she for whom the idea were being suggested. And she would have shied from the very word, never mind the actual institution. How sick I was, she thinks. It was no wonder I reacted like I did. The smile threatens to turn into laughter, but if she laughs out loud, Robyn will want to know why, and then the discussion will begin all over again.

But it *is* funny, Deborah thinks. She can look back at that evening in Malcolm's house now and see it for what it was.

She wonders if his bottom went on hurting for long.

She hopes not.

PART FOUR

Decisions

CHAPTER SEVENTEEN

Life at Haydon Hall seemed to enter a plateau phase; for some weeks, there were no departures, no new arrivals. Phoebe got progressively bigger, and increasingly more self-absorbed; once or twice Robyn tried to introduce the subject of the Future – it seemed to demand a mental capital letter – but Phoebe always evaded the issue.

'At least ring your parents!' Robyn urged one day. 'Yes, I *know* you're not ready to tell them,' – for Phoebe's face had assumed the truculent expression it always did when someone was trying to make her do something she wasn't prepared to do – 'but you did agree to have a nice uncontroversial chat with them from time to time!'

Robyn often tried to imagine what it would be like to be a parent with whom a child failed to keep in touch. It must, she concluded, be hell. She had, in the few days prior to her little speech to Phoebe, had a visit from Will (okay, he'd brought a load of dirty washing, but it was still lovely to see him; and anyway *she* hadn't had to do it, she'd merely pointed silently to the washing room and left him to it), a phonecall from Tim (he was still going out with Kazuko, and there was talk of them travelling to Japan together in the summer), and a letter from Jerome (he'd written a whole paragraph in Greek, which was admirable if a little pointless, for Robyn's Greek had never been really up to *reading*).

Was it significant, Robyn wondered, that the only son not to have been in touch was Stevie? He couldn't possibly know about Phoebe – could he? – so it was odd, that he was the one who was out of communication.

There was going to be a day of reckoning. *Dies Irae* – she had joined the choir, and they were doing Verdi's *Requiem*, which on the face of it seemed a tall order for a newly formed amateur choir – although who was going to judge whom, she wasn't quite sure. But, since there didn't seem to be anything she could do, for the time being at any rate, she made herself put it to the back of her mind.

She was loving the choir. It was therapeutic to be singing again – doing her as much good, she thought, as that counsellor chap was doing old Debs.

Part of the benefit of her own therapy, she admitted, was the fact that Rory Preston was there.

They had both enjoyed their postponed dinner at the Italian place. She had found the words to explain why she had let him down the previous week; 'A domestic drama,' she'd said. 'Something set off a reaction, and the shock of losing Zach – he was my husband – suddenly seemed brand-new again.' She hadn't said that she had been floored by grief. It was too private, when she and Rory hardly knew each other.

Her revelation had, nevertheless, had the desired effect, even if she wasn't aware of it in her conscious mind. Rory, evidently picking up that the loss of Zach was quite recent, had followed Robyn's lead and kept the evening on a friendly, amusing note; he'd made her laugh a lot, and she had kept her end up and made *him* laugh as well. He hadn't mentioned a wife, a live-in lover or a girlfriend, even by implication, and Robyn began tentatively to believe that she might have found that rarest of beings, an unattached man. They had parted with, of all things, a hand-shake.

After that, she saw him every week at choir practice. Sometimes he'd suggest a drink afterwards, in the pub or at her house, and, once he had her phone number, he'd ring up now and then and say, don't eat before rehearsal, we'll go out for supper when we've finished.

They progressed to exchanging a friendly kiss on the cheek when they went their separate ways home to bed. He was, she thought, waiting for her to give him a cue.

It was a heady thought.

They went to the pictures together one Friday evening. The film was quite good – more so if you were a particular fan of Julia Roberts – and, like a teenage couple, she and Rory held hands and he bought her an ice cream.

Also like a teenage couple, he put his arm round her. And, ten minutes before the credits, leaned over and kissed her. Did a thorough job, too, so thorough that she felt suddenly, vividly aroused.

It had, as it always does, put their relationship on a new footing. Intimacy grew, and she believed she welcomed it. She wanted him – he was attractive, excellent company, independent, with his own interests and, perhaps most importantly, his own life to lead and his own place to live in. When he suggested they might go away for a weekend together to Suffolk, she thought it was a pretty good idea.

They were going to stay in a pub he knew, in a village inland from Dunwich. She didn't know the area, but was encouraged when he said they'd be doing a lot of walking, some of it on the coast paths, so make sure to bring boots and outdoor kit.

She didn't dwell on the deeper implications of going away with him. On what he – she – might be expecting.

Which was, perhaps, just as well, since on the Wednesday before they were due to set off, he cancelled.

'I'm ringing from my bed,' he said in a voice thick with cold. 'I'm really sorry, Robyn, but I'm so ill I can't possibly make it.' As if to emphasize the point, he coughed, sneezed a couple of times, and followed that little demonstration with a pathetic, 'Oh!', as if he couldn't quite believe how unwell he was.

'Oh, dear.' She wondered if she should have tried to sound more sympathetic. 'What is it? A cold?'

''Flu,' he said firmly. She remembered the old line, that a man with a bit of a sniffle has 'flu and must go immediately to bed and be cosseted, whereas a woman with a sky-high temperature and aching all over, who ought to be in bed instead of cleaning the house, doing the shopping, fetching the kids from school and cooking the evening meal, only has a cold. 'Is there anything I can do? Get some shopping for you, perhaps?'

'I don't want to give you this,' he said mournfully, as if he had dengue fever instead of a runny nose and a slight cough. 'But I haven't got any more Lemsips.'

'Lemsips.' She was writing as she spoke. 'And honey? Tissues? Vitamin C? Olbas Oil?'

'What's that?' He sounded alert suddenly. Then, as if worrying in case his ability to take an interest implied he wasn't as ill as he'd made out, he emitted three more little coughs and another 'Oh!'

'You put drops of it on your hankie, breathe in, and it clears your nose. It's great stuff.'

'I don't think it could clear *my* nose,' he said sadly.

'Why? Have you a special line in nasal catarrh?' It was out before she could prevent it; guiltily, she said, 'Sorry. Anything else?'

'Oranges? Grapes?' he asked optimistically.

'Fruit,' she said, writing it down. 'Cans of soup? Bread? Milk?'

'All of those. Robyn, you're a life-saver.'

'Don't mention it.' She forbore to say, no I'm not, nobody ever *died* of a cold, although a million men have a close-run thing every winter. 'I'll be along in an hour or so.' She already knew where he lived; they'd popped in together one evening so that he could run upstairs to fetch a book he'd promised to lend her. 'Leave the door open, then if you're asleep, I'll just leave the shopping where you won't miss it.'

'Thank you,' he said, on a faint sigh.

Wondering why she was thinking of *La Dame aux Camellias*, she put the phone down and went to find her purse.

Rory's flat was in a tall Victorian house near the Common; he had half of the first floor. It was a large flat and, Robyn discovered as she pushed open the door and went in, strangely devoid of furniture. The front door led into a parquet-floored hall, with several doors leading off it, all closed. At the far end of the hall a short flight of stairs led to a half-landing, from which three more doors led. One of them was ajar.

She called out softly, 'Hello? Rory?'

Faintly he called back, 'In here. The open door.'

She crossed the hall, her shoes making distinct echoing sounds, and went up the stairs. Pushing open the bedroom door, she saw him, propped up on pillows in a double bed, wearing a thick navy blue guernsey over his pyjamas. Music was playing softly on a cassette player on a bedside table loaded with bottles and jars; she recognised Sibelius's violin concerto.

He looked up at her, face assuming an expression of bravery under duress. 'Hello, Robyn. You *are* plucky to come.' He sniffed, coughed, and tried a smile.

'Hi.' She dumped the carrier bag down on the end of his bed. 'No problem. Want me to make you a Lemsip straight away?'

He looked at his watch. 'Let's see . . . yes, please. It's four and a quarter hours since I had one.'

'Honey in it?'

'Please. Kettle's over there. I moved it in here.' He pointed to a power socket near the door, into which was plugged an automatic kettle.

She crossed over to it. This floor, also only partially carpeted, again echoed her steps. 'Nobody could accuse you of going in for clutter,' she remarked, bending down to check the water in the kettle.

'Clutter?'

Realizing belatedly that it was rather a personal thing to say, she tried to make light of it. 'I mean, there's a lot of light, airy space in your flat.'

He laughed, and it turned into a cough. When he stopped, he said, 'Thank my ex-wife for that. She took it rather too literally when the vicar at our wedding spoke of me endowing her with all my worldly goods. When I left home, she not only sat tight and refused either to sell the house or buy me out, she also chained herself to all the antique furniture I'd inherited from my grandparents.'

'Good grief.' Robyn stopped in the middle of stirring honey into the Lemsip to stare at him. 'Why didn't you fight her?'

He sighed. 'I'd been fighting her for years. I didn't have the heart.'

'But your own things! How could she – how could *anyone* – do that?'

'You don't know my ex-wife,' he said grimly.

'No, and I don't want to!' She went back to the bed and handed him the Lemsip. 'Here. I didn't let the water boil.'

'Thanks.' He clasped his hands round the cup and sipped at it. He only needs fingerless gloves, she thought, to complete the image of Hobo at the Brazier.

He was staring round the room. 'It does look bare, doesn't it? I suppose I should think about buying some new bits and pieces.' He didn't sound very keen. If, as seemed likely, he would be replacing beautiful, valuable antiques with modern veneered chipboard, then she could see why.

'You could make bareness a feature,' she said encouragingly; she had a sudden powerful sense of the poignancy of his situation. 'Go Scandinavian, with pale pine furniture, lots of off-white and one absolutely dazzling painting on that wall.' She waved a hand towards the bare expanse opposite the door. 'And long, floaty, cream curtains in some light material that blows in the breeze.'

He was still staring round. 'You know, that's not a bad idea.' He turned to her. 'Thank you, Robyn. Is that one of your talents?'

'Decorating? Not really. I do like it, but I'm self-taught. Like most of us. I've done what became necessary, and learned by my mistakes.' She remembered Zach's deep blue lavatory; it had taken three coats of gold-tinged white to cover the turquoise, and it still showed through in places.

Zach.

Rory had finished the Lemsip and was trying to put the cup down on the crowded bedside table. She hadn't thought there were that many proprietary cold remedies on the market. 'Here, let me take it. I'll go and wash it.' She took the cup from him, glad to have something to do to take her thoughts away from feeling shaky about Zach.

'You're being so kind, Robyn.' The pitiful tone was back in Rory's voice. 'I do appreciate it, especially when I've had to let you down about the weekend.'

'You're absolutely sure you won't be able to make it? It's still two days away.'

He shook his head. 'Ouch! That makes my ears hurt. No, I know I won't. It'll be well into next week before I'm fit again.'

It seemed unduly pessimistic. Perhaps he really did have 'flu. 'Have you taken your temperature?' she asked.

'I've lost the thermometer.'

She put a hand on his forehead. Bringing up four children had given her the experience to detect a temperature at a

231

touch. 'I don't think you're feverish,' she said. He felt quite cool.

'Oh, I'm sure I am.' This clearly wasn't what he wanted to hear. 'I always know.'

So do I! she wanted to say. But it seemed a little unkind. 'I'll leave you to sleep,' she said, heading for the door. 'Phone me if you need anything. Or if you just get lonely.' She smiled at him.

'I will. Thanks again, Robyn. You're being so good to me.'

She went on staring at him. He had turned one of his pillows end on, and the upper end was flopping over on top of his head. The pillowcase had a deep, lace-trimmed frill, which framed his face so that he looked like a huge baby in a bonnet.

It was so absurd that she knew she was going to start laughing. So as not to offend him, she hurriedly said, 'Cheerio!', shut the door, bolted down the steps and out of the flat.

Sitting in the car, the laughter burst out of her. When she had recovered, she started the engine and set off for home, only to see an image of his frill-framed face when she stopped at the traffic lights. Think about something serious! she ordered herself. Think about something moving and senti-mental!

She suddenly saw Tim, aged ten, at a primary school Christmas show called *An Evacuee's Christmas*. He'd been dressed as a soldier, wearing Paddy's old parachute smock that he used for gardening and a tin hat found in a neigh-bour's shed, and he held aloft a Union Jack while all the children sang 'Keep the Home Fires Burning'. There hadn't been a dry parental eye in the house, and most of the teachers were sniffing.

It did the trick, so thoroughly that, instead of laughing, she felt more like shedding a reminiscent tear.

*   *   *

When she got back to Haydon Hall, there were anxious voices coming from the living room, Deborah's and – Phoebe's, was it?

What was Debs doing at home in office hours?

And why did Phoebe appear to be crying?

She flung her keys into the bowl on the camphorwood chest and ran into the room.

Phoebe was on hands and knees in front of her usual armchair, and Deborah, one hand rubbing the small of Phoebe's back, was leaning over her, saying, 'You've got to let me go, Phoebe, or I won't be able to go to phone for the ambulance.'

Only then did Robyn notice that Phoebe had hold of Deborah's free hand.

It was perfectly obvious what was happening, even if it was happening a couple of weeks too soon.

Robyn said, '*I'll* phone the ambulance. Don't worry, Phoebe, you'll soon be in good hands.'

'I'm scared!' Phoebe wailed, and the hand grasping Deborah's gripped tighter, making Deborah wince.

Robyn exchanged glances with Deborah; Deborah mouthed, 'Hurry up!'

She ran back into the hall and found the hospital number; she'd got Phoebe to write it on the pad for just such an eventuality. A reassuring nurse said they didn't usually send ambulances, could Robyn drive Phoebe in?

'Yes, right,' Robyn said, trying to sound confident and capable.

'You know where to come?' the nurse asked.

'Yes.' After four babies, I certainly do, Robyn reflected.

Back in the living room, she told Phoebe they were going in by car. Phoebe wailed again, and said, 'I *can't!*'

'Yes you can,' Robyn said firmly. 'Come on, up you get – Debs, you hold her other arm, that's right – now, best foot forward – there! Not too bad, is it?'

'The baby's coming!' Phoebe moaned.

'I'm sure it's not, they take ages, especially first babies.' It wasn't the most tactful thing to say, so Robyn hurried on. 'Have your waters broken?'

'I don't *know!*'

'You would if they had,' Robyn said. 'Debs, how long has she been like this? Has either of you timed the contractions?'

'She phoned me at work,' Deborah said, panting slightly with the effort of supporting Phoebe. 'And no, sorry. I haven't done any timing.'

'Phoebe? How often are they coming?'

'I don't *know!*'

'Bloody hell,' Robyn muttered. She heard Deborah give a smothered laugh. 'Where's your bag, Phoebe? Have you packed your things?' And if you say, 'I don't *know!*' again, I shall thump you.

'In my room,' Phoebe gasped. 'But I can't make the stairs, I can't, I *can't!*'

'Nobody's asking you to, I'll fetch it,' Deborah said tersely.

'Great. I'll get her in the car . . . come on, Phoebe, down the steps – good!'

Deborah came back with the bag, flung it in the car and sat in the back with Phoebe. Driving as steadily as she could, telling herself that haste wouldn't help and probably wasn't necessary, Robyn got them to the hospital.

Robyn and Deborah took it in turns to sit with Phoebe, who seemed to panic at the thought of being left on her own, although it could hardly be called that when a steady stream of nurses and various other medical people kept coming to check on her. She panicked even when they were both there, as the afternoon turned to evening and then to night, until someone arrived and gave her a shot of pethidine.

'I had pethidine with Tim,' Robyn said quietly to Deborah as they watched Phoebe's tense, tear-stained face gradually relax. 'Wonderful stuff, I felt capable of flying. You can see how people get addicted.'

'It's done the trick for our little Phoebe.' Deborah was stroking one of Phoebe's hands. Her own hand, Robyn noticed, was purple with bruising.

'What happened to you?' she asked, nodding at the injury.

Deborah glanced down and smiled ruefully. 'Phoebe's labour happened,' she whispered. 'I'd been down on the floor with her for nearly half an hour when you got back.'

'Oh, Debs!' Their eyes met across the hump of Phoebe's stomach, and Robyn felt a surge of affection for her, this nervy, frightened woman who seemed to have turned, before Robyn's very eyes, into someone else.

There was peace for a while, until, shortly before midnight, Phoebe's contractions speeded up and intensified. Robyn and Deborah were allowed to go into the delivery room with her, where, at 11:49PM on the last day of March, with Robyn cradling her lovingly and dropping encouraging kisses on her sweaty forehead, Phoebe gave birth to a healthy, seven-and-a-half pound boy.

CHAPTER EIGHTEEN

'I'm not going to marry Stevie. It's just – it's completely what I *don't* want to do.'

Phoebe spoke firmly, as if Robyn had been urging her into matrimony.

'I know that, Phoebe.' Robyn hung on to her patience. With difficulty. 'If you'd just listen, you'd realize I'm not suggesting that.'

Phoebe was sitting up in her bed at Haydon Hall, struggling to get one of her nipples into the baby's mouth. Her breast was hard with milk, and the baby was grizzling because it – he – was hungry and nobody seemed to be able to do anything about it.

'Come on, oh, *do* come on!' There was a faint note of despair in Phoebe's voice. Robyn, who could see what needed doing but hesitated to get involved in so intimate a way, was worried that matters might swiftly go from bad to worse.

'Can I help?' she said tentatively. 'Only I can see what you're doing wrong, and –'

'I'm doing *everything* wrong!' Phoebe cried. 'Absolutely everything! Oh, dear, I –'

'No, you're not.' Robyn spoke calmly. Leaning forward, she put a firm hand on Phoebe's breast, very gently squeezed it so that the nipple and aureola made more of a point, and touched it lightly against the baby's cheek, just beside his mouth. Instantly he turned, latched on to the engorged nipple and began to suck.

'Ouch!' Phoebe said. 'It hurts! Oh! No, it doesn't.' Then a slow smile spread across her face. 'I'm doing it, Robyn! Aren't I? Even without the midwife helping me!'

Robyn was smiling too. 'You are, Phoebe. Clever girl!'

Phoebe looked down at the baby, who was making tiny sounds evidently expressive of pleasure. 'How did you know what to do, Robyn? Oh – well, I suppose you would.'

'Quite.' It wasn't just Phoebe being Phoebe that made her so self-absorbed, Robyn thought, it was fairly typical of all brand-new mothers.

They sat staring down at Phoebe's son. After a few minutes' enthusiastic suckling, Phoebe gently detached him and moved him to the other breast. Soon after he had started to suck from that one, he stopped, and, small features taking on a beatific expression, produced what sounded like a rather liquid fart.

Robyn was on the point of offering to change him, but held back. And, since it wouldn't help Phoebe to have Robyn breathing over her while she got to grips with baby wipes and nappy fastenings, she got up and quietly left the room.

That, she had been led to believe, was the positive side of grandmotherhood; being able to leave the room when the smelly bit started. She wasn't sure, yet, whether the positives were going to make up for the negatives.

While Deborah was having a session with her counsellor early the next evening, Robyn got up from *The Times* crossword to answer the phone. She was greeted by Cliantha.

The second surprise, having accustomed herself to the first, was how pleasant she sounded.

'I am in my father's house, here in Rethymnon,' she said, 'and I am calling to ask is this okay.'

Stunned, Robyn said she supposed it was.

'I lived with my grandmother, but her house is small, and I felt that I was crowding her,' Cliantha explained, further confounding Robyn by this revelation of sensitivity to the needs of others. 'Grandmother, she said it would be good to air Papa's house, but only if you do not mind.'

So you moved in and *then* asked my permission? Robyn thought. Ah. No true change in the leopard's spots, then. 'I agree,' she said calmly. 'It's better for houses to be lived in than to stand empty.'

There was a fairly long silence; Robyn was just being glad Cliantha had instigated the phone call when she realized that, since the call was originating in the Rethymnon house, she'd probably get to pay for it anyway.

'What can I do for you, Cliantha?' she asked, to expedite matters.

'Oh. Ah, yes.' Another costly silence. Then: 'This is very difficult. I want to ask you to come out here, to visit.'

Good grief. 'Whatever for?'

'I – Robyn, I am sorry for how I behaved. When I was with you at Haydon Hall. I need to see you, and I can't afford another trip to England.'

That was putting it on the line. 'Okay. Why do you need to see me?'

When Cliantha answered, it was in a tone that Robyn hadn't heard before. 'There are many things to say. I – it's not possible to tell them over the phone.'

'If it's about the house –'

'No. That, yes, is part of it. There is much more.'

'But –'

'Robyn, *please*.'

It was also the first time Robyn had ever heard her say 'please'. That, combined with quite strongly aroused curiosity, made the request all but irresistible.

She said, 'All right.'

Having missed out on her weekend in Suffolk, Robyn felt she was entitled to a pleasant little break in Crete. She phoned

Rory to tell him she'd be away for a few days, and that he'd have to get someone else to do the ministering to the sick.

'I'm almost better, actually,' he said.

'Oh, good.'

'And you're off to the sunshine?' Was he angling for an invitation to go with her? 'Lucky you.'

'I am indeed.' If so, she wasn't going to issue one; tempting though it was to imagine the two of them lazing around in the Cretan spring weather, this wasn't the moment. For all sorts of reasons. 'I'll send you a postcard.'

Phoebe wasn't very happy about being left all on her own, as she called it. Robyn's attempts to boost her confidence by mentioning that she could always phone the health visitor with any problem, and that anyway Deborah was around, didn't seem to help very much.

'Could I ask your mother to stay?' Phoebe asked, eyes wide like Bambi's, which for some reason made Robyn want to shake some sense into her.

'My mother prefers to sleep in her own bed.'

'But couldn't I invite her in the daytime?'

Frances, Robyn decided, was quite up to saying no if she didn't want to be involved. On the other hand, she might quite like to get some hands-on experience with her great-grandson. 'I'll leave you her number,' Robyn said. 'You can ask her yourself.'

The person she would have liked to take with her to Crete, if she were going to take anyone, was Deborah. Sitting over a drink the evening before departure, telling Deborah about the many attractions the island had to offer, Deborah's intelligent interest made Robyn think what an excellent travelling companion she would be.

But Deborah was very busy at work – she was tackling more and more of what Maria Fletcher referred to as the 'really shitty stuff' – and, in addition, appeared to have reached some sort of a target with her counsellor. It was not,

Robyn could see, the moment to take off on a carefree trip to Greece.

So she went on her own.

The first happy surprise was being met by both Cliantha and Jerome. The fact that she would be able to see her youngest son had not been totally irrelevant to her decision to make the trip, and to be greeted at the airport by his tanned, smiling face – he'd grown, she was sure he had! – and his muscle-creaking hug had in itself made the visit worthwhile.

Cliantha drove them from Heraklion to Rethymnon, keeping up her end of the conversation while simultaneously driving at a fairly hairy speed. Fortunately, it was a good road. Jerome sat in the back, hand on his mother's shoulder while he gave her what sounded like a blow-by-blow account of everything he had done since he arrived.

It became apparent that he and Cliantha got on well. Very well. Sometimes they spoke to each other in Greek – usually one of them would remember to make sure Robyn had understood – and they seemed to have quite a collection of shared jokes. When the car pulled up outside the Rethymnon house and they all went inside, it was further revealed to Robyn that Jerome and Cliantha must be sharing the place, at least some of the time; Cliantha had adopted the master bedroom – Robyn didn't really blame her, it was by far the most comfortable – and quite a lot of Jerome's stuff was spread around the smaller spare room.

'I have put fresh sheets on the bed,' Cliantha said, showing Robyn into the master bedroom. Good grief, she'd moved out of the main bedroom without being asked! A cynically suspicious part of Robyn's mind asked, what's she after? What am I being soaped up for? 'I hope you don't mind that my clothes are in the cupboard?'

Robyn murmured that she didn't. It was lucky, she thought, that she hadn't brought much with her.

While she was unpacking, Jerome came to join her. 'Is it nice to be back?' he asked, sprawling on her bed.

'It's lovely,' she said with total honesty. She glanced up at him. 'It's really average to see you, darling.' He grinned.

'What's it like for you, love,' – she turned back to her holdall – 'living here, in the house?'

'I'm not here all the time,' he said quickly, as if she might mind if he were. 'I still live mainly at Aunt Sophia's, only I like to keep Cliantha company sometimes.'

'I think that's great,' Robyn said stoutly.

'You do?' He glanced towards the door, then whispered, 'I thought you'd be cross.'

'Why?' she whispered back.

'Oh – you don't like her.' He jerked his head towards the stairwell, where the sound of Cliantha, banging pots and pans around down in the kitchen, could be heard.

'Did *she* tell you that?'

Jerome nodded, anxious eyes on hers.

'Oh. Well, she's never given me much reason to like her.'

'Mum, you've got to –'

Whatever he was about to say, he didn't; Cliantha's voice, suddenly sounding very near, summoned them down to a pre-supper drink.

They let Robyn sleep on in the morning. When she finally woke, she found that Jerome had gone to work. Cliantha was in the kitchen doing the ironing.

The *ironing*.

Robyn, helping herself to coffee – the taste of a Cretan cup of coffee brought back such vivid memories of Zach that it seemed for an instant he was right there with her – reflected that she'd have put money on Cliantha not even knowing how to erect an ironing board.

Perhaps it was the peaceful domesticity of the scene there in the kitchen, Cliantha quietly working, Robyn sipping at her coffee and thinking, with love, about Zach, that finally allowed Cliantha to relax sufficiently to say what she needed to say. From the moment she began – 'Robyn? May I talk to you about my father?' – Robyn had a strange presentiment that what followed was in some way going to be beneficial.

And, for both of them, it was.

'It's more my mother that I have to explain to you,' Cliantha said, eyes on her ironing. 'You didn't meet her?'

'No. She had left quite a long time before I met your father.'

Cliantha was nodding slowly. 'Yes. My father, you know, exaggerated. In fact it was not so long. The breakup, the divorce and my mother's return to Sweden happened within a year, and she went in the spring before you came to Crete.'

Robyn thought back. No, Zach had never actually *said* his wife had gone years ago, she'd just sort of picked it up. But she couldn't see what difference it made.

Then, suddenly, she did. If Cliantha had only just been robbed of her mother – because that was no doubt how she'd see it – then it explained why she had been so hostile to Robyn.

'I'm sorry,' Robyn said quietly. 'I didn't realize.'

'No. I see that, now. Then, I thought you didn't care.'

I probably wouldn't have done, Robyn thought honestly. I was so wild for Zach that very little would have held me back. 'It hit you hard, your mother's departure. Didn't it?'

'I was fifteen! Of course it did!'

'But you saw her, didn't you? There were holidays, she took you to exciting places . . .' It didn't sound very much.

'Twice to Spain, once to London,' Cliantha said stonily.

'That was it?'

'That was it.' Suddenly the dark eyes were filled with tears.

'She said she would send for me! She said I had to give her time to settle, to make a nice home, then she would come to fetch me.' The tears spilled down her cheeks. 'I used to lie awake listening for her. I had the idea she would come in the night. God knows why.' She wiped angrily at her nose. 'I need not have bothered.'

'But you stayed in touch.' Say you did! Robyn urged silently. Surely you did!

Cliantha shrugged. 'Birthdays, yes. I always send her a card and a present, and usually she sends me something for mine. Once she forgot, or maybe it went astray, I don't know.'

'And letters? What about visits?'

'She does not like writing letters and she says she cannot afford to travel.'

'So how long since you've seen her?'

Cliantha said, head down, 'I went to see her in Sweden. Her boyfriend didn't like me.'

'And that was how long ago?'

'Six – no, seven years.'

Robyn put down her cup and walked round to the other side of the ironing board. Then, not allowing herself to stop and think, put her arms round Cliantha and, for the first time ever, hugged her.

The grief erupted out of Cliantha as if it had been stored under high pressure. Robyn, her own poignant reaction to being back there in Zach's house – in the place where they had first slept together, fallen so passionately in love – already making her highly emotional, found that she, too, was crying. Crying for Cliantha, for Jerome, for the whole complicated business of love between parent and child, for the joy and the despair, for the pain when, for whatever reason, the parent is no longer there to give or to take it.

Her own tears ceasing, she fetched a clean tea-towel and began on the task of mopping up Cliantha.

* * *

'You see, I blamed him for my mother not being there.' Cliantha, calmer now, was sitting on a kitchen chair nursing a strong coffee. 'It was not fair, but he was the one who was available.'

'Yes.' That was understandable. 'Did you know why she had left? Why the marriage broke up, I mean?' She wasn't sure it was right to ask. Did Cliantha's need to talk extend to events that far back?

'Oh, I know, yes. My mother did not like being an outsider, and she stopped doing things with my father. So, he went alone, and, being what he was, he began to see other women.'

In a sudden flash, Robyn remembered the toiletries she'd found in the Athens flat. Yes. She'd known full well that Zach had had other women. What she hadn't known – or, possibly, hadn't let herself think about – was that he'd had them while he was still married.

'Then my mother moved into her own room,' Cliantha said starkly. 'Which finally made my father realize he was not to have a son.'

'I have only one child,' Zach had said. 'And she is a girl.' And, later, 'My wife did not want other children. She refused to have sex with me after my daughter was born.'

Then, Robyn had seen it only from his point of view. In the whirlwind of her feelings for him – especially, it had to be admitted, the physical ones – she had overlooked how the daughter would have reacted. What it must have felt like to know that your father had wanted a son, and, now that it was certain he wasn't to have one, to believe that he would be even more resentful that his only child was a girl.

If I'd *liked* you, she said silently now to Cliantha, it would have been different.

'I believed he hated me,' Cliantha said, 'and so I hated him as well. I did my best to make him angry.'

'You succeeded.' Robyn smiled and, reaching out, briefly touched Cliantha's hand, to indicate no malice was intended.

Cliantha laughed, a short, hard sound. 'Remember Dimitri?'

'Dimitri. Not the one at the party, with the knuckles that swept the ground?'

This time the laughter had some humour in it. 'No, that was Zeno. Zeno! God, I can't believe I went out with him! No, Dimitri was the one I lived with, in the little house. The peasant, as Papa called him.'

'Ah. Dimitri.' Robyn hesitated. Was now the moment to mention Andy? And her own dread suspicions that it was Zach's agonized fury over Cliantha's relationship with Andy that had led to his stroke?

She watched Cliantha. Saw the softness in her face, which, for reasons best known to herself, she was only now revealing to Robyn.

No. Now wasn't the moment. There probably would never *be* a moment, for something like that.

'I always wanted to make him take some notice of me,' Cliantha was saying. 'I would see him with this pretty woman, with that pretty woman, and I wanted to say, hey, Papa! *I'm* here! Look at *me!*'

'And you thought you could only make him look if you were bad?'

'Yes! No, I didn't *think* that, I knew it. Because I had *been* good. I was good all the time he and my mother were married, I was quiet, I worked hard at my studies, I kept my room neat, and what happened? My mother started to hate my father and my father didn't notice me because I wasn't a boy.'

She had spoken without self-pity, which made her words the harder to bear.

'And then your dad married me, and we had Jerome,' Robyn said.

Cliantha met her eyes. 'Yes. I hated you, and I hated Jerome, too, although I hardly ever saw him.'

245

'You could have come to England,' Robyn said. 'We invited you. We asked you about sixth form college, remember?'

Cliantha sighed faintly. 'I remember. But did you really think I'd come? Didn't you do all that just to make yourselves feel better? My father said once on the phone to me, Cliantha, it is your own fault, you bring all these troubles on yourself. When I said, how did he work that one out?, he said, you have a home, with my son and me, but you choose not to accept it.'

'Oh, Cliantha! He didn't mean it like that, didn't mean to make you feel shut out! I'm sure he didn't!'

'He did, Robyn. But it's okay, I wanted him to react like that. If he went on treating me like the bad girl, I could go on behaving like her. I thought it was what I wanted, that way of life. The drink, the drugs, the boyfriends, I thought it was great, but it was only great because it made my father so angry.'

Robyn said, feeling her way very carefully, 'He was angry because he was hurt. He didn't give up on you.' Cliantha's eyes held pain. 'My love, he never would have done that,' she said, leaning close to Cliantha in her urgency to make her see. 'He knew you were there – the real you – and he was waiting till you came out and found him.'

'You think so?'

'I *know* so.' She wasn't sure she did know it, but whoever was entirely certain of anything? 'He would have left you the Athens flat, I think, had he lived to see you –'

'To see me come to my senses?' There was a wry smile on Cliantha's mouth. 'Yeah, well.'

Maybe Cliantha ought to have it, anyway, Robyn thought.

If, that was, she wanted it, which surely she would. It was clear to Robyn that Zach would probably have left the house to her and Jerome and the flat to Cliantha. Had he not died when he did.

The flat was so bound up in Robyn's mind with Andy that she almost mentioned her name. Andy, she thought. God, Andy. Maybe she shouldn't make any decision about the flat just yet . . . she waited to see if Cliantha would talk about Andy. She didn't.

'I really love Jerome,' she said instead. 'I'm glad he's here. And I'm glad I didn't get to know him sooner, because the hatred would have got in the way. Now, meeting up here in Crete, at the relations' houses, it's like we are two strangers getting to know each other. But we're not strangers, we have the same father, and it has made us close. We are alike, you know?'

Robyn didn't. She could see absolutely no resemblance at all between her youngest son and her stepdaughter. But it wouldn't be tactful to say so. 'You must have a lot in common,' she said. 'Because of sharing Zach.'

'Sharing Zach,' Cliantha repeated. 'I like it.'

There was a short contemplative pause while they both thought about that. Then, with a strangely shy smile, Cliantha said, 'You called me "my love" just now.'

Robyn felt awkward. 'I did? Well, fine.'

'I used to hear you call them things like that – your sons, Papa,' Cliantha said, speaking fast as if this were the most difficult thing of all. 'I used to feel so sad, because *my* mother wasn't there to call me sweet names, and even when she was there, she didn't. And Papa, oh, when I was small he did, but later, no. And there you were, with your pet names so full of love.'

The emotion was threatening to overcome her again, Robyn could tell. 'Often it was only because I couldn't get the right name out quickly enough,' she said, defusing it. 'It was easier to say "darling" or "sweetheart" than work my way through all four. Five, if you count Zach.'

'It's good,' Cliantha said softly. 'It makes you realize that people care about you.'

Sensing that Cliantha wanted to tell her, Robyn asked, 'What did your father call you when you were small?'

Smiling, face full of love, Cliantha said, 'He used to call me his Little Flower.'

CHAPTER NINETEEN

Robyn stayed on another five days in Rethymnon, days which passed in a whirl of visits to relatives, outings with Jerome, stomach-bloating suppers in local restaurants, quiet evenings in the old house with Cliantha. When, a couple of days before she was due to go home, Robyn asked Cliantha if she'd think about another visit to England, when she could afford it, Cliantha said she'd love to.

Jerome took his mother back to the airport. He had recently passed his test, and Cliantha was generous about lending him her car: 'It is Papa's car, so it's as much yours as it is mine.' She said it would be good experience for him to find his way to the airport and back.

He seemed very cheerful as he drove Robyn back along the coast road to Heraklion.

'You're enjoying life here, darling,' she said. It was a statement, not a question; it was perfectly obvious that he was.

'Oh, yes. The work's hard – they're really determined to make me learn every little thing – but I like it. The season's starting now, so all the stuff I've been taught is going to get tested.'

'You'll cope,' she said serenely.

He was quiet for a few moments. Then: 'Mum, it's okay if I stay, isn't it?'

'Of course, if you're sure it's what you want.' The picture of him with a university scarf and a carrier bag of washing appeared briefly, waved its hand in farewell and vanished.

'It is.' He was nodding as if to emphasise his determination. 'No offence to you, but I really feel at home here.'

'None taken.' Was that strictly true?

'Mum, did Dad ever – I mean, when you talked about my future, that is *if* you ever did, did he – was he . . .'

She knew what he was asking. 'We never actually discussed the possibility, darling, because it didn't arise. But I think I can promise that nothing would have tickled Dad more than to have his son follow in his footsteps.' She reached over and gently punched his arm. Aware that it would only be she who understood the truth behind the lightly spoken words – and ignoring the rights and wrongs of it – she added, 'He always wanted a son he could be proud of.'

Robyn had a sense of *déjà-vu* as the taxi dropped her at Haydon Hall; Frances's car was in the drive.

But, this time, there wasn't any panic. Frances emerged as Robyn got out of the cab, and, responding to Robyn's hug and her greeting, announced she was just leaving.

'Stay for supper? A drink, anyway?' Robyn said.

Frances glanced at her watch. 'Sorry, darling, got to dash.' The smile she shot Robyn looked – although this seemed unlikely – rather sheepish. 'Dad will be waiting, he never unscrews the gin bottle until I'm there, although really I don't know why. See you soon!'

Wondering, Robyn went into the hall, waved her mother off and closed the door. She called out, 'Hello?'

From the living room, three voices responded. She crossed to the partly-open door, pushed it. Saw Phoebe, Deborah. And, nursing the baby as if he'd always done it, Stevie.

She said softly, 'Oh, Lord.' Then, since nobody else seemed to want to say anything, she turned to Stevie. 'Who told you? Or is your sudden appearance after quite a lot of silent months entirely coincidental?'

'Gran told me.'

'*Gran?*' No wonder Frances had looked sheepish.

But, confounding her, he said, 'Yes. She told me some time ago.'

'She told you.' Robyn sank down on the sofa, vaguely aware of Deborah's glance of sympathy. Deborah got up and, without asking, mixed Robyn a gin and tonic. A strong one, as Robyn discovered when she sipped it.

'I didn't know!' Phoebe piped up. 'I didn't *ask* her to, if that's what you're thinking!'

'Not at all. I –'

'If you remember, Robyn, I said I *didn't* want Stevie to be told, because if he came back, it'd mean it was only because of the baby.'

Robyn turned to Stevie. 'So why have you come back, if it's not to obey your grandmother's summons?'

'To see my son,' he said promptly. He was, Robyn noticed, looking exceptionally proud of himself. 'Isn't he great, Mum? We were just discussing names, and Pheeb and I think Jake Patrick is pretty cool.'

'Jake,' she echoed. 'Jake Kingswood.'

'Jake Parry,' Phoebe said firmly. 'I keep telling everyone we're *not* getting married!'

There was a reflective silence in the room. Breaking it, Robyn said, 'So, having brought this young man into the world, what *are* you going to do?' She felt like saying, you can't go on living here, but it would have sounded harsh. But why shouldn't I be harsh, for God's sake? she asked herself angrily. *I* didn't ask them to sleep together. *I* didn't beg Phoebe to go ahead with her pregnancy because I was just dying to be a grandmother.

'We don't want to marry,' Stevie was saying, 'but we are actually pretty good friends. Aren't we, Pheeb?' Phoebe nodded. 'We're sort of thinking along the lines of Pheeb coming up to Ipswich and maybe having a room in the house where I'm living – there's three of us, but it's a big house. There's usually quite a lot of people around, so we thought Pheeb might be able to work part-time, perhaps bar work or something in the evenings, when I'm at home. That way, we could sort of share looking after him.'

From being furious at a situation so far out of her own control, Robyn suddenly felt near to tears. It was something to do with the way Stevie was holding his baby son, something to do with the mixture of pride and awe in his voice when he said, 'We could share looking after him'. She cleared her throat and said, 'It's right that you should share the responsibility, I agree.' She kept her private thought – that this was actually a bit rough on Stevie, who hadn't had a say in whether or not the baby should actually *be* here – to herself. 'You do realize, though, both of you, just what bringing up a child entails? It's not just a question of buying disposable nappies and a pushchair and getting a friend to babysit when you want to go out for a drink. It's for life. Like they say about puppies and Christmas, only more so, since people usually live longer than dogs.'

Phoebe and Stevie clearly picked up her anger, which was hardly surprising considering that she had raised her voice and was waving her hands around. A deaf imbecile would have picked it up. Quietly Deborah got up and poured her another drink.

Stevie said, with a note of desperation, 'Mum, I'm doing my best!' and Phoebe, with an injured sniff, remarked that she didn't need a lecture on responsibility, thanks all the same.

It was too much. Rounding on her, Robyn said, 'Phoebe, that's precisely what you *do* need. Or, even if you don't, I'm going to give it to you anyway!' Phoebe began to protest, but Robyn was in her stride, heading for the first hurdle and not to be stopped. 'You came to me because you weren't prepared to tell either Stevie or your own parents that you were pregnant – okay, I accept that the getting pregnant was down to both of you – and you have sat here on your backside, bone-idle apart from a very undemanding part-time job, for the remainder of your pregnancy. Stevie's only here *now* because my mother had the good sense to tell him what you or I ought to have told him as soon as you arrived here! Debs and I got you to the hospital, Debs and I held your hand through the birth, Debs and I brought you back here and looked after you!' Leaning over Phoebe, she demanded, 'Just when the hell do you propose to start taking care of yourself? Or are you planning to spend the rest of your life allowing others to take responsibility for you? Like Stevie, for example? *You* decided you were having this baby, Phoebe. Don't you think *you* should be planning his future?'

Phoebe, red in the face, opened her mouth, but nothing emerged. Feeling a hand on her arm, Robyn shook it off. 'All right, Stevie, you don't have to hold me back, I'm not going to hit her.' Although, she thought, it's terribly tempting.

She turned to give Stevie a reassuring smile. But it wasn't Stevie, he was still sitting nursing the baby and looking faintly shocked by his mother's outburst. It was Deborah.

'Come and finish your drink, Robyn,' Deborah said.

'I don't want a drink!' She glared at Deborah, who bravely stood her ground. 'Well, I do,' she smiled briefly, 'but this has got to be sorted out!'

'They're sorting it out,' Deborah said. 'Didn't you hear?'

'You can't bring up a child in some Ipswich squat!'

'It's not a squat,' Stevie said, 'it's actually quite a nice house. Paul and I have done some decorating, and Angie's good at sewing, she's made lots of curtains and hangings and things.'

'Angie?' Robyn and Phoebe spoke together, and, as if that instant of identical reaction briefly united them, exchanged a brief grin.

'She's not my girlfriend.' Poor Stevie sounded quite hounded. 'She's nobody's girlfriend. Well, she *is*, but he's not one of the tenants of the house.'

Robyn had sat down again. She felt very weary, and she could feel the tightness on the top of her head that usually heralded a grade-one headache. 'You've got to tell your parents, Phoebe,' she said quietly. She put a hand up to massage her right temple. 'You really mustn't keep this from them any longer. It's not fair.' She didn't feel up to thinking out and explaining who it wasn't fair to, but fortunately nobody asked.

Waiting to see if Robyn were going to say more, Deborah eventually said, 'How about this for a plan of action?'

Robyn, Phoebe and Stevie all turned to her expectantly. Robyn heard her mutter, 'Oh, Christ.' Then, more authoritatively, she went on, 'Robyn and I can go on looking after Phoebe and Jake for a week or so, while Stevie goes back to Ipswich and talks over with his co-tenants the idea of Phoebe having a room in the house. Provided they agree, he can get on with making it ready for her. Well, actually, them, Phoebe and Jake. Again providing the tenants agree, Phoebe could then go up to Ipswich for a few days and see about getting a job of some kind, and – or, perhaps, or – sorting out what benefits she can claim. Then, and only then, when the questions of accommodation and income have been tackled in a nice, responsible, adult way, can she get in touch with her parents.' She looked at Robyn, then at Phoebe. 'Wouldn't that go down better, to reveal it to them only after sensible steps have been taken?'

Phoebe, who seemed to have been holding her breath, let it out in what sounded like a relieved sigh. Stevie was smiling, and Robyn could see he saw the sense of Deborah's plan.

'Got it in one, Debs,' Robyn said. 'Brilliant.'

She hadn't meant to sound sarcastic.

Into the awkward silence, Deborah said, 'It means Robyn

will have to go on providing you with a home, Phoebe, when really she'd rather be here on her own. So it might help if you showed a willingness to lend a hand now and again. You could cook an occasional evening meal, couldn't you? Do the ironing?'

Robyn, overwhelmed at having Deborah speak for her when she'd just rubbished Debs's careful proposal – albeit unintentionally – closed her eyes and put both hands over them. She could see jazzing lights in the darkness behind her eyelids; it was time for goodnight, Vienna.

'Of course, if Robyn wants me to do things, then I . . .'

Robyn didn't hear any more. With a vague wave to the assembled company, she got up, walked as steadily as she could towards the door, and headed for the stairs and bed.

She was awoken by Deborah and a cup of tea. The morning sun was shining in through the gap between the curtains.

She sat up, and reached for the tea. 'What time is it?'

'Half-past nine.'

'Why aren't you at work?'

'It's Saturday.'

'Oh, yes. So it is.'

Robyn drank her tea, eyeing Deborah sitting on the end of the bed. 'I don't suppose, by any miracle, I imagined the last few months, and there isn't really a young woman who I don't actually like very much downstairs with my son's baby on her knee?'

Deborah shook her head. ''Fraid not. She's there, large as life. She's sent Stevie into town to buy some baby lotion and a pineapple.'

'A pineapple?'

'Don't ask.'

Robyn drank some more tea. Then: 'Debs, I didn't intend to sound so mean-spirited about your plan last night. Actually I think it's great.'

Deborah smiled. 'I know.'

'You know I didn't mean it or you know I think it's great?'

'Both.'

'Oh, Debs, life's a sod, isn't it?'

Deborah considered that. 'Yes, it can be. But *your* life isn't.'

'God, if you're going to tell me to count my blessings, you can bugger off.'

'I wouldn't dream of it,' Deborah said mildly. 'I was going to go on to say that your life *would* be great, if you could just get rid of all your responsibilities.'

'I thought I had,' Robyn muttered. 'I suppose it's nature abhorring a vacuum.'

'Hm?'

'Word got out that I was living in a big house all on my own and on the point of relishing my freedom, so instantly someone came along clamouring to be looked after.'

There was a short, embarrassed silence, as Robyn realized what she'd said and Deborah hoped she hadn't meant what it sounded as if she'd meant.

One of them had to break it; Robyn said, 'I'm talking about Phoebe, Debs. As I bloody well should hope you know.'

'I do,' Deborah said softly. 'I do *now*.' She shot Robyn a smile. 'Okay. I did *then*.'

Robyn laughed suddenly. 'I've just thought of something!'

'What?'

'Even when we get rid of Phoebe, there's Cliantha.'

'Cliantha? Oh, Lord, she's not coming back here, is she? I don't think I can cope any more with bouncing beds and tripping over Andy's huge boots in the hall.'

'She *is* coming back. Debs, I invited her.'

Before Deborah could proceed with her protest, Robyn told her what had happened in Crete. And, when she had finished, Deborah was nodding in sympathy.

She got up, taking Robyn's empty tea cup. 'Do we know when she's coming? Or is it they?'

Robyn shrugged. 'No idea. When she asked me to go out there, she said she hadn't any money, so I don't imagine it'll be just yet. No need to air the sewing room right this minute!'

But she was wrong. Cliantha put yet another air fare on to the bottomless pit of her grandmother's credit card, and arrived back in England two days later.

Stevie had gone back to Ipswich, and so Haydon Hall was once more an all-female enclave, if you didn't count an infant boy. And Cliantha came on her own, so there wasn't even the presence of Andy's masculine clothes and overwhelming personal possessions.

Contrary to expectations – to Robyn's expectations, anyway, since the happy week in the Rethymnon house hadn't fooled her into believing everything to do with Cliantha would from henceforth be plain sailing – the four of them had a wonderful fortnight. The company of the other women was, just then, so supportive, so strengthening, that when, one evening, Robyn went out to dinner with Rory, it seemed quite strange to be with a man again.

'We have a postponed weekend to rearrange,' he reminded her when he dropped her off at home, only a little put out that she didn't ask him in.

'I know.'

'Still want to go?'

'Yes. But –' But not right now, was what she wanted to say. 'I can't at the moment. Too many things to sort out.'

'Soon, then?'

'Soon.'

Cliantha made herself at home in the sewing room, although there wasn't all that much room in it even for one. Now that Robyn was liking her so much more, she actually felt a little guilty that the best accommodation in the house was spoken for.

'I do not mind, I like it in here,' Cliantha said when Robyn mentioned it; Robyn had taken up a vase of spring flowers, which Cliantha received with a gratitude that implied people didn't often bring her vases of flowers.

'Er – is Andy going to be joining you?' Robyn put the flowers down on the windowsill, deliberately avoiding looking at Cliantha.

'Andy?' Cliantha laughed briefly. 'No.'

'Ah.'

Cliantha was sitting on the bed, braiding a section of the tasselled fringe on the end of the bedspread. 'I do not think I want to live with another woman, not any more.'

'Oh. I see.'

Cliantha did not speak, and Robyn turned to look at her. 'Do you see, really?' Cliantha asked.

'I imagine so,' Robyn said. 'You needed to explore your own nature. You did so, and discovered that something you believed was true wasn't.'

Cliantha put her head on one side. 'My own nature. No, Robyn, I do not think it was much to do with that. And nor, I think do you. Am I not right?'

Robyn met her eyes. She seemed to be demanding the truth, so Robyn decided she ought to get it. 'You are. I think, if you really want to know, that having a female lover was your last and greatest bad-girl trick.' She grinned, and, to her relief, Cliantha responded. 'I think Andy was a bigger and better version of – what was it again? Zeno? Okay. Of Zeno and Dimitri. Your swan-song in the annoying-Papa stakes. And, now that he is not here to be angry, you find there isn't much point. Yes?'

Again, Cliantha had adopted her considering pose. 'I guess, yes. Although we had some good times, Andy and me.'

'I can imagine.' She couldn't, but it seemed the thing to say.

'I am not a lesbian,' Cliantha announced dramatically. 'This I know for sure.'

'Oh. Right.'

'You're not going to ask how I know?'

'No, I'm not. I think it's pretty self-explanatory.'

She wondered if Cliantha understood self-explanatory, but it didn't seem to matter as she was ploughing ahead anyway. 'It is the little one, you see.'

'What, the baby? Jake?'

'Jake, yes. He is so cute!' Cliantha's face was alight. 'So adorable! I say to myself, Cliantha, you stay with women and you're for sure not going to have anything like *that* little boy! And, you know, Robyn, I think I want that? Maybe I'll get pregnant, maybe that's what is next for me.'

'Fine,' Robyn said. 'As long as you don't do it *here*.'

But Cliantha wasn't listening. She had got up and was touching the flowers, rearranging them slightly so that a huge yellow daffodil was centre front. 'There. Daffodils are my favourite.'

'Oh, good.'

'A baby,' Cliantha said softly. 'A little boy, like Jake. Maybe a little girl, to dress up pretty?' Her face softened; for a moment, she looked quite beautiful. 'No, no more women,' she repeated. 'No more Andy.' She looked up, caught Robyn's eyes on her. Smiling, she said, 'Anyway, Andy has gone to Amsterdam with an enormous Dutch woman in dungarees. Robyn, how long may I stay?'

PART FIVE

Coming to Terms

CHAPTER TWENTY

Deborah took a final look at herself in the mirror – honestly, she didn't know why she was bothering, since it was only Sean, but, on the other hand, it was good if he thought she was sufficiently self-regarding to want to look nice – and left her room. From the other side of the Great Divide she could hear Jake crying, and Phoebe's muttered, 'I'm coming, I'm *coming*, don't be so impatient!'

With some relief – it really was high time Phoebe made herself scarce, poor old Robyn was looking as if she was at, or, more accurately, just past, her wits' end – Deborah quietly let herself out of the flat and ran down the drive. She had stopped going in and out through the main house because Phoebe had developed the habit of calling out to anyone passing and getting them to do things.

Deborah was in good time, so she walked the mile and a half to Sean Duncan's house. The May evening was warm, and quite a lot of people were out and about. It was, Deborah reflected, a good world. She hoped Robyn was enjoying her dinner with Rory Preston. Robyn had brought him home a few weeks ago, and introduced him to Deborah. She had rather liked him.

She rather liked quite a lot of men nowadays. Not in *that* way – hastily she corrected herself – but just in general. Now that, with Sean Duncan's help, she was putting her own past into perspective, understanding, at last, that the things that had happened to her had been just that, things that happened *to* her and therefore not her own fault, life was getting better in many ways. Her attitude to the male sex was only one of them.

Striding out in the bright evening light, she was able, even, to think about Br—. About Bruce.

'Turn it around,' Sean had said, in his quiet voice that seemed to reach out across the room and wrap itself around her, giving her the confidence to say the unsayable. 'Think not of yourself as the recipient, but of him as the one who was dishing out the aggression.'

She had done so. Despite her grave misgivings, she had let Sean take her metaphorically by the hand and walk her back into the hell that had been her marriage. To see, as surely he had intended she should, that Bruce's need to dominate had been in existence long before he had met Deborah. Had led him to the sort of woman that Deborah was, had made him determined to court her, flatter her, win her, wed her. Because he *had* to.

Sean had led her further back than her marriage. Had asked her, always in that impersonal, distant voice from across the room, about her childhood. Memories of her father, whom she hadn't thought about in years, indeed, whom she would have said she barely remembered. About how he had left them, Edith and Deborah, to cope on their own in what Edith – and therefore, following her example, Deborah – believed to be a hostile, threatening world. 'Of course he didn't really leave us, I know that now,' Deborah had said with an apologetic laugh.

Only to have that disembodied voice, speaking as if its owner could see far further inside her than she would have imagined possible, say, 'You perceived it as leaving you. That is what is important', which of course made having said 'left us' when she actually meant 'died' perfectly all right.

In retrospect, it seemed to Deborah that Sean had actually said very little during their dozen or so sessions. It had been she who had done all the talking. It had been a first in her life to talk at such length about herself, and to begin with she had found it extremely difficult.

'Tell me what you want to tell me,' he had said. 'There are no right things and wrong things here. No strict order. No order at all.'

So she began with what she'd said when she phoned to make the appointment. The fear that, because of what Bruce had done to her, she had mucked up the new relationship with Malcolm Teague. The worse fear that it would always be like that.

It had been a long time before they'd got back to Malcolm. Many sessions had been spent on Deborah's early years, and she told him happy things, sad things. Spoke about Edith – a lot about Edith – and about how the two of them, timid, unconfident mother, nervous daughter, had virtually closed themselves off from the world. She once heard herself say, 'Of course, I can see *now* that Mother should have had help, that her extreme introversion was virtually pathological, certainly not the reaction of a normal woman to being widowed with a very young child.' It was only later, going over the session in bed that night, that she'd thought, how extraordinary that I should come out with all that, as if I'd been talking psycho-speak all my life! And how even more extraordinary, because she had certainly not got those expressions from Sean. He rarely ventured an opinion about anything, let alone calling Deborah's poor mother pathological.

Sean had allowed her to see herself, for the first time. She knew that now, understood that this was how it worked. You poured out your troubles, the unobtrusive listener absorbed what you said, thought about it, worked out why you were so troubled, made gentle hints to nudge you into suggesting how *you* might help *yourself*.

An odd by-product of all this navel-gazing was, Deborah had discovered, a violent upsurge in her dreaming.

They say you dream every night, she thought, waiting to cross the road and set off on the last half-mile to Sean's house. Well, that might be so, but she had never recalled her dreams as she was doing now. Some of them were bad dreams – once she had been back in the bedroom in the Worcester house with Bruce standing over her naked body, a carpet beater in one hand and a rubber glove on the other one. He was shouting at her, telling her she had made a hash of washing the carpet, and anyway she should have beaten it first. She had tried to get up, tried to take the beater from him because she had known he was going to use it to beat her. But her hands were tied behind her, and, using the hand with the glove, he had turned her over on to her stomach and whacked her buttocks until she screamed.

She had woken, sweating, terrified that she had screamed aloud. How did you find out a thing like that? Did you go and knock on Robyn's door, on Phoebe's door, and say, Please, was I screaming just now? I was? Oh, sorry, only I was having a nightmare in which my dead husband beat my bum to a pulp with a carpet-beater.

No. You didn't do that.

That particular dream, fortunately, had been at the time when Cliantha and Andy were ensconced in the sewing room. Loud nocturnal noises floating along the landing weren't actually then a rarity.

It was, Deborah thought, surprising that she hadn't had more nightmares of that sort, bearing in mind that she was in the process of turning out all the dirtiest rubbish from the very back of her subconscious. Most of her dreams, vivid though they were, were more or less pleasant. And often, if not always, had a strong sexual content.

She wanted to ask Sean Duncan about that. Knew she must, for surely it must be important? She was going to tell him today. It wasn't going to be easy, but she had made up her mind. And, nowadays, when Deborah made up her mind about something, she didn't easily change it.

'I thought I ought to mention it,' she said to Sean fifteen minutes later. 'I wonder if it was relevant?'

'Are you referring to this particular dream that you had last night, or the fact that you're remembering so many dreams in general at the moment?'

'Oh – both.'

He was silent for a few moments. Then he said, 'It's by no means uncommon for people undergoing counselling to dream more than they usually do. You are, after all, thinking about events and aspects of yourself profoundly relevant to how you function as a person, and often this seems to have a stimulating effect on the subconscious.'

Stimulating. Oh, dear, what's *wrong* with me? Deborah wondered, for, instantly, her mind had leaped to *sexually* stimulating, which of course he hadn't meant at all. Had he?

'Tell me about last night's dream,' Sean suggested.

Grateful for the distraction, she began. And only after she had done so thought that this, too, led straight back to the dangerous areas she had sought to avoid.

'I was on a hillside, in a lovely, wooded area. Below me I could see an imposing château-like place, where I knew I lived. It was a mountainous region, very beautiful, with a great ice-green river racing along in the valley. I was out walking at night, aware that I was doing something a little unwise – there was a sense of threat, but it was by no means unpleasant. A runner went by, and he blew me a kiss. Then I met a group of women, sort of forty- to fifty-year-olds, wearing bathing costumes and sarongs. They were going to swim in the river, and they beckoned to me to go with them. They were chanting a psalm of praise. It felt pagan, as if they were worshipping nature, and there was an enormous feeling of joy.'

267

She paused, glanced at him. He had his head bent, and was making a note.

'There was a circus in a water-meadow,' she said, closing her eyes to aid her memory, 'but I walked past it – it didn't involve me. I went on to the river bank, and sat down, bending my head back so I could look up at the sky. And – oh, it was so beautiful! All the constellations were brilliant against the black night sky, I could see the signs of the Zodiac, properly outlined, in gold on a vast gold wheel, slowly turning up there, high above. There was the sound of bells, or tinkling metal, and I saw the sign of Libra, tipping over slightly as it danced, changing places with one of the others.'

'Which one?' His voice startled her, although he had, as usual, spoken softly.

'Oh. Capricorn.'

She thought he said, 'Your own sign,' but probably she'd misheard, since she hadn't told him when her birthday was. Strange, though, because if he *had* said it, he'd have been right.

'Then the moon came up,' she went on, 'and with it came the realisation that I was Diana. Artemis. On the river I saw a long, thin boat, and I was invited to step on board. Apollo was there, looking like Rutger Hauer when he was in the Guinness ad, and he was lying in a sort of bower, attended by two women, or perhaps they were goddesses. They were all so loving, so kind, including me in their embraces, presenting the pros and the cons of getting involved with them. It was a risky business, they said, but I knew I would take that risk. It involved him, Apollo, and –' She stopped.

Sean waited, then said, 'Go on.'

'I knew I was going to have sex with him,' she said, speaking fast. 'It was what all this was about – it was some sort of pagan fertility festival, where people not only could but were expected to join in. In any way they liked – anything goes, as it were. And it was so very appealing! It was forceful stuff – I could feel heat coming off Apollo, and in my mind I was saying, sexual heat, he's burning with sexual heat. But, although I knew he had such power – perilous power, in a way – I couldn't stop.'

'In your dream, you let the Apollo figure make love to you?'

'No, I made love to him.' Eyes closed again, she smiled at the memory. 'I took off my sarong, threw it into the river and then I leaned over him and began to kiss him. He wrapped his arms round me, gently pulling me close, and I straddled him and sat down on him so that he penetrated me.'

'You had full sex with him, but on your own terms?'

'Yes! Exactly that. I was in control, I was setting the pace. And, when I knew he was going to come, I held back. I slowed down so that I was scarcely moving, then, feeling his need throughout my body and soul, very gently I began again. Then I made the rhythm increase, faster, faster, pushing down on him so that he was thrusting deep inside me, and then, with a wonderful, thrilling sort of a moan, he climaxed.'

The silence in the room after she finished speaking seemed to hold the echo of her words. Suddenly very embarrassed, she heard her own voice. *Pushing down on him. With a moan, he climaxed.*

Dear God! What must Sean be thinking!

'I'm sorry, I –'

'Please, Deborah, no need for that.' She risked a glance at him, and saw he was smiling faintly. 'I hear far more explicit things than that.' He hesitated, then, as if making up his mind to go on, added, 'And, if I may say so, far less elegantly and affectingly told.'

'Oh.' Then realizing he had paid her a compliment, 'Oh!'

'Have you ever had a dream of this sort before?'

269

She shook her head in vehement denial. 'Never! It was so beautiful! So realistic!' She had spoken rather loudly; deliberately lowering her voice, she said, 'What do you think it means?'

'I'm not an expert on dream interpretation, and I hesitate to draw any specific conclusions, but some of the facts seem to point to some fairly obvious symbolism. Don't you think?'

'Er – the sexual bit, I suppose. I mean, I was actually loving it. Initiating it, really.'

'Quite so. And you were in control. You were unafraid to go ahead when they invited you to, despite the fact that you sensed a certain peril, because you were, physically and symbolically, on top. It's quite amazing how our dreams so often make that sort of pun, you know.'

'Oh.' Unafraid. Yes, she'd certainly been that. And much *more* than that. 'Sean, I was loving it, really loving it! It was ecstatic, just so pleasurable, and –' No. This wasn't her saying this. It couldn't be!

'The intense enjoyment seems to me to be on a par with the beauty of the entire scene,' he said, his voice calm. 'You described the elegant castle, the lovely woodland, the impressive green river and, most vividly, the great golden wheel of the Zodiac. You also mentioned paganism, nature worship – I think all these things, added together, may indicate that you now feel positive where once you felt negative.'

She understood. 'About sex, you mean.'

'About sex, yes. Also about other people, and how they view you – the women in the sarongs invited you to join them, the goddesses on the boat were affectionate and loving.' He smiled suddenly; it was rare to see him smile so broadly. 'If goddesses are loving to you and Apollo himself wants to have sex with you, on your terms, then you must be a very entrancing and loveable person indeed!'

'I'm sorry, I didn't mean to brag.' She was ashamed.

He said forcefully, 'Deborah, *why not?*'

'Oh! Well, because . . .'

'Boast,' he said. 'Tell yourself you're okay. That's what your dream told you, so obviously that's just fine with your unconscious.' He waited. 'Go on!'

'Go on?' Lord, was he expecting her actually to *say* it? He was.

'I'm okay,' she muttered.

'I didn't hear that.'

'I'M OKAY!' she yelled, then burst out laughing.

He laughed, too, then said, 'I shouldn't really have done that, but I couldn't resist it.'

Not done it? She wondered why. Perhaps it was unprofessional. If so, *she* certainly wasn't going to complain. 'My birthday's January 6th, so Capricorn's my birth sign,' she said, remembering the dream vision. 'The sign in the dream, which danced with Libra.'

'I know.'

'Did I tell you?'

'You didn't need to.' He was smiling again. 'Self-conscious, ladylike, small and well-formed with deep, dark eyes and a full mouth. That, actually, isn't my description of you, it's what is recognised as the typical Capricorn woman. But it could have been you.'

She was, she realized, sitting with her mouth open. It had taken her by surprise, that he had actually studied her for long enough to know what she looked like. He usually seemed to have his head bent over his notepad, busily writing.

'Did you know,' – now he was doing just that – 'you share your birthday with Joan of Arc? Your ruling planet is Saturn, the most beautiful planet. Do you know what time you were born?'

'Four in the afternoon. My mother used to joke that I arrived in time for tea.' It was the only joke Edith had ever made.

'Your rising sign is Cancer, ruled by the Moon.'

She said, 'Is this relevant?'

'Not really. I thought you might be interested, bearing in mind the astrological content of your dream.'

'I am interested.' This, too, was a surprise. Beyond the occasional glance at her horoscope in someone else's abandoned magazine, she didn't bother much with astrology. And now look what her secret mind had turned up! 'And you are, obviously.'

'Yes. I know many people dismiss it, but I don't believe in dismissing anything without a good reason. Especially not something which has occupied the minds of man since the earliest civilizations.'

No, you wouldn't, Deborah agreed silently. You're far too thoughtful to do that.

Sean was gathering up his papers. Glancing at her watch, she saw that not only was her hour up, it had overrun slightly. She got up. 'Sorry, I've been talking too much.'

The absurdity of that, when to talk was the very reason she was there, seemed to strike both of them at the same moment. Listening, for the second time, to the pleasant sound of his laughter, she said, 'Sorry. How daft.'

And, perhaps because he knew it was a different kind of sorry *this* time, he let it go.

'Same time next week?' she said as she opened the front door.

'Yes, if you feel you need it.'

That brought her up short. 'You think I don't?'

'It's not what I think that matters. I'm here, any time you want to come again. I'd be glad to see you next week, or, if you like, you could leave it for a fortnight. See how you feel.'

The idea that she might be *cured* – although she was sure he wouldn't have used the word – was heady. It made her feel omnipotent. 'May I ring you?' she asked, turning to look at him.

'Of course.'

He stood in the door as she walked away, and, when she turned to wave, responded. He still had bare feet.

CHAPTER TWENTY-ONE

Robyn and Rory had reconvened their postponed weekend. They had been to see Rory's contact near Dunwich, they'd walked for several hours along the coast paths, then spent the night in a country pub with a big open fire in the bar, excellent beer, a good evening meal and an oak-beamed, sloping-ceilinged bedroom. They had shared the bedroom, and also shared the double bed; the consummation of their relationship had been highly satisfactory for both of them, so much so that they had done it all over again in the morning. There was, Rory remarked as they sat down to a late concoction of fruit juice, bacon, eggs and toast, nothing like a gypsy's breakfast for sharpening the appetite.

Robyn hadn't heard the phrase before, but had to agree to its accuracy.

The weekend away didn't alter their association in any dramatic way; it was more subtle than that. But there *was* a change, and it worried Robyn that she couldn't put her finger on what it was.

Rehearsals for the Verdi were going well, very well, when it was borne in mind how recently the group had got together. 'You have to learn to *listen* to each other,' the choir master kept telling them, 'get to know what you all sound like, so that each of you can blend your own voice in with the whole.'

They were actually beginning to sound like a choir, which was, as Rory remarked when Robyn mentioned it after rehearsal one night, quite encouraging, and better than sounding like numerous other things.

She certainly liked being with him: he was fun, with a lively mind and a way of picking up her own utterances and throwing them back at her. It could be quite annoying, but it was teaching her to be less sloppy about how she phrased what she was trying to say.

She also enjoyed sleeping with him. Why, she asked herself when she was musing about him, do we insist on using euphemisms, even in the privacy of our own thoughts? I don't enjoy *sleeping with* him – we rarely do sleep when we're in bed together – I enjoy us *having sex*.

What, then, was the small and all-but-invisible cloud on the horizon?

She didn't really know. She thought, however, that it could have something to do with commitment. With there being the possibility of an increase in it, now that their friendship had progressed to something more intimate and, as far as both of them were concerned, more exclusive.

There was, she thought, an assumption of a future together.

And that prospect, while part of her welcomed it, was also quite scary.

Also at Haydon Hall, and also, apparently, undergoing major changes in her life, was Deborah.

Robyn was happy that Deborah's counselling sessions had had such a beneficial effect on her, and felt a certain smugness because it was she who had suggested Sean Duncan in the first place. But at the same time she heard increasingly loud alarm bells. Okay, it was great that old Debs was so transformed, wonderful to see her so happy, putting on a little weight, even, so that her beauty intensified. But, oh, surely it was folly to be doing what Robyn was almost certain Debs was doing? By all means go out for a drink with the man – although was that, even wise? – but to contemplate anything more? After all that Debs had been through?

Robyn tried, tactfully, to talk to Deborah about it. Deborah seemed only too willing.

'Oh, Robyn, when I think back to those early days with Malcolm!' she said with a laugh over their pre-supper drinks one warm July evening. 'I was so tense that he must have thought I'd snap in two if he came too close! But I think it's possible, looking back at it now, that I might have been sending out come-on signals.'

It was a new facet of Deborah, this ability – willingness, even – to discuss matters of a personal nature, Robyn thought. Oh, Lord, another euphemism. This willingness to discuss *sex*. 'I remember the up-tight bit,' Robyn said. 'Personally, I didn't notice the sexual signs.'

'Well, you wouldn't, would you? But I'm pretty sure I was making them. Honestly, Robyn, I used to dream about sex, and that must have meant I was secretly wanting to get physically involved, even though my conscious mind didn't want to accept it. Because of what I went through with Bruce.'

If there was nothing else to go down on your knees and thank Sean Duncan for, Robyn reflected, then you had to hand it to him for straightening out Deborah on the subject of her bastard of an ex-husband. Hurrah for Sean Duncan.

'It's logical that you'd have gone for someone who was rather like Bruce, I guess,' she said tentatively, wondering if this was going a bit far.

But, 'Oh, I agree!' Deborah said. 'And Malcolm is definitely the same physical type as Bruce was. Same sort of looks, that same self-awareness, which makes men like them stop to look at their reflections in shop windows. If they'd been old enough in the fifties, they'd have whipped out their combs and adjusted their quiffs.'

'Quiff comes from coif, as in small cap, and hence anything to do with the hair,' Robyn remarked. Rory had told her, when they were in bed doing *The Times* crossword.

'Oh.'

'Sorry. Go on about Bruce.'

'Not much more to say, really.' Deborah stretched, sounding indifferent. Indifference towards one's ex, thought Robyn, is really the ultimate insult. Hatred, being the opposite side of the coin from love, could be regarded as still being over-concerned with them. Not to give a damn about them really does cast them off into the blue.

'Debs, you two seem to be seeing a lot of each other at the moment,' Robyn said, grasping the nettle and giving in to the indulgence of expressing what was uppermost in her mind. 'Are you – I mean, do you really think it's a good idea? He might read too much into it. Well, not too much, if it's what you want as well, but he might start thinking you'd like to get *married*, ha, ha, ha!'

What an absurd idea! she tried to imply. Whoever would want *that*, especially you, Debs!

Deborah, after a silence which Robyn found faintly ominous, repeated softly, 'Marriage.' Then went on, 'Robyn, do you realize that a particular tone enters your voice when you say the word, a tone that is, in fact, reserved exclusively for the word?'

Robyn, who hadn't, and who, furthermore, decided Deborah must be exaggerating, merely said, 'Oh.'

Deborah leaned forward, her expression earnest. 'Robyn, why do you think that is? Is it really such a dreadful concept? After all, you –'

Robyn burst out, 'Debs! What's wrong with staying as you are? You can see each other whenever you want, have all the privacy you need – you've both got your own places! Don't you like it, living here?'

'I love it,' Deborah said, her fervour surprising Robyn. 'You *know* what it's meant to me, coming to live at Haydon

277

Hall, or if not, you ought to. But . . .' She trailed off, a faintly wry look on her face as if something were gently amusing her.

'But? Debs, it'll get better here, I promise you! Phoebe's going next week, so there'll be no more of, "Oh, Deborah, oh, Robyn, would you just . . ." and no more of her mess – honestly, did you ever know *anybody* to spread their stuff over quite such a wide area? I found a dirty nappy in the bath this morning, and she left a pair of nipple shields boiling in a saucepan. Till I took a good look, I thought they were giblets. And if I trip over that bouncing cradle once more, it's going in the bin. The baby's not even *using* the bloody thing yet!'

'I know.' Deborah, who had relaxed back into her chair, smiled. 'I don't envy Stevie, or the others in the Ipswich house. Do you think it'll work out, Robyn?'

'No,' she said honestly. 'I don't think Stevie would have suggested she move in, other than because of the baby. Jake,' she amended. 'I must get used to calling the poor little thing by his name.'

'Why poor little thing?'

'Oh, I don't know.' It was too great a subject easily to be put into words. But she had a go. 'He's been brought into a situation that's not his fault, but he'll probably suffer because of it. Phoebe's a bit feckless, and, looking at it in the hard light of day, eventually Phoebe may be all he's got.'

'Stevie's doing what's asked of him,' Deborah pointed out. 'He's arranged a home for the pair of them, and there's a good chance of Phoebe finding part-time work. She'll be able to put some money by, if Stevie's helping to support them.'

'Stevie won't want her around for ever,' Robyn said bleakly. 'I don't even think he'll want her around for very long.'

'That's a bit harsh! And how do you know?'

Robyn sighed. 'I don't *know*, really. But I do know Stevie has someone else, although he's being very discreet about her. I also think he's being carried away at the moment by the novelty of it all. Jake's a sweet baby, and Phoebe's doing most of the nitty-gritty stuff, so none of it affects Stevie very deeply. I don't think he'll want to settle down with Phoebe, that's for sure. She annoys him.'

'Does she? Did he tell you that?'

'He didn't need to.'

'Oh.'

'Debs, he knew about Phoebe's pregnancy some months before she gave birth. My mother told him.'

'I know. I was there when he suddenly turned up, remember?'

'So you were. But you probably don't know that he actually kept away till Mum informed him the baby had arrived, because he didn't know what he wanted to do and he wasn't prepared to come to see her – Phoebe – until he did.'

'Wasn't that rather irresponsible of him?'

'He didn't *want* her to get pregnant!'

'Then he shouldn't have slept with her.'

There was no answer to that one. Robyn, again reflecting that the old, pre-counselling Deborah probably wouldn't have made such a remark, and certainly not with such vehemence, said nothing.

'Sorry,' Deborah said. 'I know what you think. And, yes, you have a point. Not having had a say in what they did about the pregnancy, it *is* a little unfair to expect Stevie to shoulder the full responsibility. But then life *is* unfair. And, anyway, no-one's asking him to shoulder the lot.'

'Oh, I'm sick of it!' Robyn said suddenly. Fleetingly it occurred to her that somehow they had been deflected from the subject she'd wanted to talk to Debs about – marriage – but this new topic had its own momentum, and wasn't to be dismissed. 'Honestly, Debs, you bring them up, get them educated, see them off on their way into the world, and, just when you think you're at long last going to have some peace and quiet, one of them has an ill-considered shag and before you can say Bob's your uncle, there's a damned baby to be sorted out! *Jesus*, it pisses me off!'

She hadn't realized how much it had weighed on her. She was far more surprised at her own outburst than Deborah appeared to be.

'Crikey, Debs, where did all that come from?' She tried to make light of it. 'He's not a damned baby, I shouldn't have said that.' She couldn't bring herself, at that moment, to retract any other part of her outpouring.

'No, he's not. But it's quite understandable that you should feel angry at the situation,' Deborah said calmly.

Really, she *had* learned a lot from her counsellor chap – perhaps she ought to think about taking up the profession herself. 'Thanks,' Robyn said.

Deborah grinned. 'Don't get sarcastic with *me*.'

'I wasn't!'

'You were.'

'Okay, but only a little bit.'

There was a brief companionable silence, then Deborah said, 'I think, dear Robyn, you are going to have to stand back and let them work it out for themselves. They are, after all, old enough.'

'Phoebe's not old enough for anything except accidental pregnancy. She still needs a responsible adult in charge.'

'Well, she's got Stevie. And she's got her own parents, now, too.'

Phoebe, Stevie and Jake had all visited the Parry parents a week ago. Stevie had been, in his own elegant phrase, shitting bricks. Phoebe, on whom it had fallen to make the telephone call admitting where she'd really been these past months and what had been happening to her, had appeared, after the trauma of the call was over, remarkably phlegmatic.

'It's down to them, now,' she'd said casually, as if having plucked up her courage and told them absolved her from all further responsibility or blame. 'They can take it or leave it.'

Stevie had told Robyn later that Phoebe's mother seemed to take the view that it wasn't her daughter's fault, and that therefore nobody should be cross with her – this, he'd noticed, was directed at Phoebe's father, who looked, Stevie said, less cross than heartbroken. It was obvious, from Stevie's demeanour, that the visit had been something of a shock.

It was likely, then, that, given this choice of taking or leaving it, Phoebe's parents were going to opt for taking it. For accepting Phoebe having produced an unexpected grandchild, for accepting that, although Stevie would do his share in supporting Jake, there was no question of him and Phoebe getting married.

That – the fact that Robyn wasn't going to have to endure Phoebe as a daughter-in-law – was, as far as Robyn was concerned, the one bright spot in the whole thing.

'You'll get to like Jake, you know,' Deborah said. She had been watching Robyn, and had accurately divined the private trend of Robyn's thoughts. 'You really will. He is, after all, your own flesh and blood.'

Robyn went, 'Huh!'

But Deborah did have a point.

'We weren't meant to be talking about them!' Robyn said when she'd thought about that. 'I was saying that Haydon Hall is going to be better – no, let's be boastful, *even* better – once Phoebe and her great travelling nursery are gone.'

'And you were trying to persuade me it'd be much nicer to stay here with you than to dash off and get married,' Deborah finished tranquilly. 'I know. It's a lovely place to live. And it'd be so peaceful, the two of us.'

'Three.'

'Oh, yes. Of course.'

For Cliantha, not slow in observing that once Phoebe had gone, there would be an extra and far larger spare room available, had announced she'd like to stay on at Haydon Hall for a while, 'at least, until I can find a job and get a place of my own.'

'She won't be here for long,' Robyn said, trying to convince herself as much as Deborah. 'Really.'

'How can you be so sure?'

'Oh, Debs, I can't, but I'll damned well *evict* her if it means you'll give up this idea of remarriage and stay!'

Deborah got up and came to sit beside her, taking the hand that wasn't holding a gin and tonic. 'Robyn, steady on! Anyway, that wasn't what I meant.' She hesitated. 'My decision to stay or go wouldn't depend on whether or not Cliantha lives here. That would be quite unfair! No, I was thinking of *you*.'

'Me?'

'You. Dear Robyn, you keep saying you want to live your own life, you're always implying that, with Zach dead, you want to make the best you can out of his loss, and try to develop your own interests.'

'Yes! I do! I've earned it, it's my turn, Debs, I –'

'Of course you've earned it! I'm not disputing that, I'm endorsing it! Robyn, you haven't *begun* to have your turn yet, so how can you possibly know what will be right for you in the long run? You've had Phoebe, Jake, Stevie, Cliantha, Andy, and me, all of us, in our different ways, asking things of you, your love, your time, your advice, your strength.' The hand holding Robyn's squeezed it tightly suddenly. 'Darling Robyn, all you've had is more of the same!'

'I wouldn't want not to have it! Debs, how d'you think I'd have felt if all of them had said, bloody hell, I'm not going to go to old Robyn with my troubles, *she* won't be any damned good! I'd have hated that! They're my responsibility!'

'*I'm* not,' Deborah observed.

'Okay, but I *like* you!'

Deborah laughed. 'Likewise.'

'I know what I'm going to do about Cliantha,' Robyn said, abruptly making up her mind. 'I'm going to tell her she can have the Athens flat.'

'Golly! Talk about drastic remedies!'

'Debs, I was going to before, I talked to my father about it. Only then she went and got herself chucked out, although it was only because the straight-laced neighbours didn't like her and Andy living there together.'

'You think she can live there now?'

'Of course. Nobody'll be able to say a word, if it's her own flat. Anyway, Andy's buggered off to Amsterdam . . .' She leapt up and went over to her desk, where she had stored all those of Zach's papers which had seemed too important to go on the bonfire. 'Now there ought to be some bumph about the flat. I remember seeing a folder when I sorted out Zach's desk, although I didn't go through it at the time.' She found the folder, opened it up.

An envelope dropped out of it on to the floor. It seemed to contain something heavy, which made a faint jingle as the envelope hit the carpet.

Robyn picked it up. The flap wasn't sealed, and there was no name on the front.

She felt inside. Two keys, on a silver key fob.

A sheet of paper, and, written in Zach's flamboyant hand-writing: *These keys, and my flat in Athens, to which they belong, for my daughter Cliantha, at such time as she finally accepts who and what she is and begins to live a better life. With love to my Little Flower from her devoted Papa.*

Her legs suddenly shaky, Robyn sank down on to the floor. Sensing Deborah at her side, wordlessly she handed her the note.

'He knew I wouldn't mind. That I'd do it – let her have

the flat – when the time was right,' she whispered. Oh, Zach! That you trusted me, to give it to her when, legally, it was mine, because you left it to me!

Zach.

He was present with her there in the living room, his quiet shade not deterred by Deborah's tactful presence. Robyn could sense him, felt she could detect that particular scent, a combination of the strong-smelling soap which he loved, and a faint coffee aroma because he always drank so much of the stuff.

Zach.

She closed her eyes and pictured him. Tanned and fit, as he'd been when he'd first tripped over someone's legs and stood on her. Smiling, so sure of his power to attract her. So completely attracted *by* her, and so honest about it.

Dear, lovely Zach.

Dead Zach, gone from her, beyond her reach.

She bent her head over the letter and the keys, feeling the last fleeting aura of his presence on those things that he had touched. Left for his wife to find, trusting her to fulfil his wishes and pass them on to his daughter.

Then, straightening up and opening her eyes, she gave anxious Deborah a quick grin.

'How's that for telepathy?' she said huskily. 'Think I'll tell Cliantha as soon as she gets in, she can rush upstairs and begin packing.'

Then, feeling suddenly shaky, she leaned against Deborah. And felt Deborah's arms – surprisingly strong arms, for someone so fragile-looking – go round her in a wordless, infinitely comforting hug.

CHAPTER TWENTY-TWO

Robyn and Deborah have come to their clifftop meadow today because they are celebrating. This morning, the weather being fine and sunny, they decided to get down to the seaside with a picnic; Deborah went out early to buy smoked salmon to make sandwiches – she has a particular way of dressing the moist orangey-pink fish with lemon and a little cayenne pepper, which makes it totally irresistible even to those who *try* to resist – and Robyn has provided a home-made trifle in a lidded Tupperware bowl. They have brought a bottle of wine and a large bottle of mineral water; Robyn, who is driving, decided it would be okay to have *one* glass of the lovely Muscadet, provided she drinks it as soon as they get there.

They are celebrating because Phoebe has gone to Ipswich, naturally taking Jake with her, and there are no more shouts of, 'Is that you, Robyn? Can you bring me the changing mat? Jake's sopping wet,' no more suspiciously lower-end aromas snaking through the house, no more gritting of the teeth as Deborah and Robyn endure yet another long, rambling, typically Phoebe account of how Phoebe is going to do this, buy that, get a job doing something fatuous and highly unlikely such as being a manicurist on a cruise liner, 'There'll be a crèche for Jake, oh, and I'll do lectures on the places we stop at'.

Has motherhood addled Phoebe totally? This is a woman who got a degree, damn it! What happened to that incisive intellect? Can't she employ it to tell herself she's living in cloud cuckoo land? With hundreds of unemployed manicurists and lecturers who *don't* have illegitimate babies, does she really think she's going to get this wonderful, hypothetical job when she *has*?

It is not, thank God, Robyn and Deborah's problem any more. Well, not in the immediate sense of having to tolerate the woman. And it won't be Deborah's problem in the future. Phoebe hasn't recently given birth to *Deborah's* son's baby.

They are celebrating, too, because Cliantha has also left. In raptures at her father's gift, she was out of Haydon Hall like a rat up a drainpipe, packed and gone within forty-eight hours, winging her way back to Athens (thank you, Grandmother's credit card) to become a serious, responsible owner-occupier. Robyn reflects, thinking about her stepdaughter, that sometimes you just have to take the gamble of dishing out responsibility purely to make people become responsible. Zach must have known this; Robyn feels that she did, too. It is an enduring, warm comfort, that she and Zach, without ever mentioning it to each other – for, naturally, Zach didn't *really* believe he was about to die – conceived exactly the same plan in regard to Cliantha and the Athens flat.

That it was what Zach wanted – Cliantha living in Athens, in comfort, with dignity – makes it okay, if not more than okay, for Robyn to be quite so delighted that her stepdaughter has gone back to Greece.

But, celebration or not, Robyn is still worried about Deborah. She is beginning to think that she and Deborah could sit in the damned meadow for the rest of the day – of the week, or the year – and *still* Debs won't see reason.

My reason, Robyn thinks honestly. Which, of course, is not guaranteed at all to coincide with hers.

Haydon Hall is now only home to the two of them. Robyn has the main house, Deborah has her flat, as much or as little self-contained as she wants. As Robyn wants, too, for their friendship is now strong. Fortunately, the degree of self-containment is one of the many things on which they agree, and that degree is not very great.

Robyn has decided that she is going to ignore Rory Preston's veiled suggestions that they take their relationship to the next logical step, which is apparently living together. No, veiled suggestions is wrong; what Rory does is put a sort of quiet, subtle pressure on Robyn, manifesting itself in things like assuming they'll be spending Christmas together, discussing next summer's holiday as if they'll definitely make joint plans. And, of course, just casually saying, 'Okay if I leave a toothbrush and shaving things here? I don't mind at all if you leave a sponge bag at my place'.

It's all reasonable, and, to a large extent, it's what Robyn wants. Rory is great; she has become very fond of him. Does she love him? The jury is still out on that one. However, she is certain she does not want to lose him. It's a big world out there, and it's a better place when you have an amusing, attractive, fanciable chap to share it with.

Why does she not want to commit herself? Would it be so bad, living with Rory? No, it'd be great!

Is it, then, that it would undermine her position with Deborah?

Although it probably – undoubtedly – would, it's not.

There is something more.

Robyn wants to discuss it with Deborah, but hesitates because the topic is so very sensitive. It is not, however, subtle or complex: it is no more, no less than that Robyn believes Deborah wants to get married, and Robyn doesn't think she should.

'Robyn?'

'Deborah.'

'Dear Robyn, I've been thinking.'

Since she makes this remark after what must have been

at least twenty minutes of silence, Robyn is hardly amazed. 'Oh, yes?'

'Robyn, will you try to tell me, honestly, why you're so against marriage?'

'Debs, my opinion is my business, you must do as you like.'

'Ah, that's easy to say! But it matters to me, what you think. I'd like to know.'

'It's – oh, Debs, you *were* married! It was a catastrophe! I'm just so afraid . . .' Afraid you're going to go under? No, that isn't fair; apart from anything else, Deborah is a different person now. 'I'm worried that marriage might make you give up some of your new strength and independence, before you've really had a chance to enjoy being single.'

'You do have a point, I suppose,' concedes Deborah. She smiles, then suppresses it. 'I *am* enjoying my independence. For the first time ever, I'm in charge of my own life, and it's a heady, powerful feeling. But, Robyn, marriage to the right person doesn't have to stop you being in control. I *know* that, now!'

The right person.

At last, it is time to speak of the man who, according to Robyn, Deborah is proposing to marry.

Robyn is thinking. Back to when she first met him, what she thought then. How, really, she followed Deborah's lead and dismissed him, just like Debs did. How, when he seemed to melt and then reform into something else, first Deborah and then Robyn had to accept that he wasn't what they'd thought he was. Was, in fact, quite different.

'I didn't see him as a possible partner for you at first, that's for sure,' Robyn says now.

'Nor did I!' Deborah laughs. 'I was so obsessed with myself that I didn't spare him a thought, not a proper, deep one, anyway – it was all about me, then, and what I was going to have to do to get better. He was on the edge. The person who was making it happen, but only in the role of catalyst.'

Both of them reflect on that.

On the slimly built, bare-foot, quiet man whose sympathetic understanding of Deborah has allowed her to return to her own past, understand, at last, her own part in what happened to her, and, armed with that understanding, to regroup the shattered elements of her personality and emerge from the maelstrom as a whole, properly functioning woman.

For, of course, we are speaking of Sean. Sean Duncan, who, when Deborah finally remembered to jump off the giddy, confident merry-go-round that was her life after Sean had put her together again and give him a call, asked, with an unexpectedly hesitant voice, if she wanted to book another session.

And, when she said, no, I'm just ringing to tell you how terrific I feel, and to say I don't need any more counselling, said, with very evident relief, oh, that's good, because it means I can ask you if you'd have dinner with me.

Deborah had put down the phone filled with incredulity. Sean wanted to take her out to dinner?

Sean?

He was so different from the type of man she'd been out with – married – before, that, she now realized, she hadn't been looking on him as male at all. Bruce, and Malcolm Teague, and the one or two others there had been before Bruce, had been big men, dark, usually, broad-shouldered, loud-voiced. With hobbies like sailing and rugby, and other things that seemed to demand lots of strength, lots of brave stiffening of the upper lip in the face of rain, wind, danger and bodily discomfort. And lots of being very matey with the chaps in the various pubs, bars and clubhouses after whatever activity it was had been finished for the day.

Without exception, Deborah's previous men had been domineering. Had told her what to do, expected her to obey.

Simply because they were men, they had implied – Bruce had actually *said* it to her – that Deborah was not to worry her pretty little head about things that, as a woman, weren't her concern.

Then there was Sean Duncan. Soft-spoken, not very tall, fair-haired, graceful. Who, from the stacked CD racks and the expensive stereo in his small consulting room, clearly loved music. And books. Books by women, believe it or not, as well as by men! There in his bookcase was Olivia Manning side by side with Anthony Powell. Susan Howatch next to Trollope, the nineteenth- and the twentieth-century commentators cheek by jowl. And Ruth Rendell and PD James sharing a shelf with Buchan, John Grisham and Conan Doyle (Deborah habitually sat with her eyes level with the crime section). Sean went to concerts – she knew because he had to alter the time of one of their sessions when he unexpectedly got a ticket for some brilliant new Russian playing Brahms' second piano concerto – and he liked ballet. He had, as Deborah suspected, many men had in his profession, a strongly-developed *yin* side to his nature, giving him traditionally female traits – being a good listener, having the sort of intuition that allows one to feel another's pain and, more importantly, know how to alleviate it – in spades.

Bearing in mind Deborah's past selections from the male half of the world, was it any surprise that she had failed to recognize the potential of Sean Duncan?

'I like him very much,' Robyn says. 'You couldn't *not* like him. He's a lovely man, and –'

And I can see why you've fallen for each other? Is that what Robyn is about to say?

We shall never know.

Because Deborah, who cannot bear to lead her friend on any longer – even if it *is* in a good cause – calls a halt.

Says, very gently, 'Robyn, dear Robyn, I'm rather afraid I have been misleading you.'

There is a contemplative silence. Breaking it, Robyn says tonelessly, 'Oh yes?'

Deborah takes a deep breath while she gathers her courage – she has a feeling she's going to need it – and says, 'I'm very fond of Sean. We've got a lot of interests in common, and I enjoy having dinner with him and going to concerts and things.'

'I know, but –'

'Don't interrupt. I did think, for a mad moment the other week when we got slightly pissed together and he gave me a kiss, that liking might lead on to something else. But, Robyn, it's not going to. As you so rightly said, he's a lovely man.' She leans closer to Robyn. 'And I'm not going to marry him.'

She waits to see if Robyn will demand to know why. She doesn't. Deborah ploughs on regardless.

'He's cured me, you know. I *could* marry him, if he asked, which actually he hasn't. I'm quite okay again about the concept of falling in love, embarking on a sexual relationship, getting married. Or not.' She shoots a glance at Robyn from beneath lowered eyes. 'Only not with dear old Sean. He isn't, after all, my type.'

'Oh, *Deborah!*' Robyn shouts, reverting in her distress to the full name. 'You're not going to tell me that, Sean having so nobly put you to rights, you're now going on the prowl for some shit of a man like your bloody ex? Like *Malcolm?*'

'No!' Deborah shouts back almost as loudly (she has neither such strong vocal cords nor such capacious lungs as Robyn). 'Just at the moment, I don't want *anybody*. What I want is to go on living in my Haydon Hall flat, with you the other side of the door.'

Silence descends on the clifftop like a honeycomb blanket being spread lightly across a bed.

After a few moments, Robyn says rather coldly, 'Then what the fuck has all this been about?'

Deborah flinches slightly at the profanity. Then, remembering her purpose, rallies and replies, 'I am, as I believe I said, thinking about *you*. I can't remember which one of us first raised the question of marriage, but I think it was you. You seemed to decide all by yourself that I was going to marry Sean, and I admit I let you go on thinking it, even –'

'You did more than let me!' Robyn is outraged. 'You led me on!'

'Yes, perhaps I did.' Deborah remains admirably calm. 'I wanted *you* to think about marriage. Not to rule it out of your future plans quite so thoroughly as you seem to be doing.'

'And why the hell not?'

Deborah faces her. Yes, she was right, she *does* need quite a lot of courage. 'Because you're the sort of person who ought to be married. You've got such a lot to give, it'll all dam up if there's no-one to receive it.'

'Bollocks!'

Deborah smiles. Robyn reserves 'bollocks' for when she's only playing at being angry. When she really is, she says something different. Or even nothing at all. 'Okay.'

Another silence, but this one has a kinder feel to it.

'Is that it?' Robyn asks presently. 'Just okay?'

'It is.'

'But what about the sales pitch? The don't-let-a-nice-bloke-like-Rory-Preston-go bit?'

Deborah smiles, but does not speak.

'Debs?'

'I've said my piece,' Deborah murmurs. 'I know you heard, so I shan't repeat it.'

Robyn makes a few false starts – 'But . . . Aren't you . . . I would have thought you'd . . .' – and then shuts up.

Peace.

At last, peace.

* * *

292

'Haydon Hall *is* nice now,' Deborah says after some time. 'Do you think it'll seem awfully big, being there on your side all on your own?'

'It's going to seem wonderful,' Robyn says stubbornly.

'Yes, okay.' Deborah smiles to herself. Dear old Robyn. 'Anyway, Tim and Kazuko will come to stay, I expect, and perhaps you'll have the challenge of a Japanese daughter-in-law.' Tim and Kazuko's trip to Japan had been, to quote Tim when he and Kazuko came to tell Robyn all about it, 'Really brilliant! We can't wait to go back!' Tim, Deborah thinks, may not get to visit his mother all that often from here on in. 'Stevie will probably call in now and again, preferably without Phoebe but hopefully with Jake, and –'

'*Definitely* without Phoebe.'

'– and Will's attitude to Haydon Hall, that it's a superior hotel where your shirts come back washed *and* with the buttons sewn back on, will doubtless continue. You may get Jerome living with you again, of course, although he *does* seem keen on life in Crete, and from what you say he's doing very well, so –'

'I can go out to see him!' Robyn sounds almost cross. 'Don't forget I have a house there! I can spend half the year in Rethymnon if I want, and see my son every bloody day!'

'Of course you can,' Deborah says serenely. 'And no doubt will. *And* your credit must be good with Cliantha, so you can have a week in Athens on the way.'

'Hm!'

'Robyn, you won't stop seeing Rory, though, will you?' Deborah hopes, by sliding the remark into a more general discussion of future plans, not to raise Robyn's hackles again.

She hopes in vain.

'I don't want to live with the bloody man!' Robyn bursts out. 'No, he's great, I didn't mean that. It's just that . . .'

She does not go on. Deborah, who knows full well what she is trying to say – although she isn't sure if Robyn does

293

– says softly, 'It's you, not me, who is not ready for a new commitment, Robyn. It's you who needs your freedom.'

'I've got it! I'm widowed, on my own, and all my kids and all *their* kids, all one of him, have finally flown the nest, and the nest's all mine!'

'I know. But they've only just gone, Robyn. All these months I've known you, you've been banging on about how it's your turn now, how your main concern is now yourself, but it hasn't turned out that way. Not to date. Has it? Now that it *is*, your prime need is to sit back and enjoy it. Indulge yourself. Have some fun. Look after *you*, just like you've looked after everyone else.' She adds in a murmur, 'Including me.'

'But you just said not to let Rory disappear over the horizon! Told me I was the sort of person who just had to be married!'

'Yes, I know.' Deborah knows she didn't exactly say that, but it's not the moment for hair-splitting. 'There's a middle way, something between saying that, since you don't want to intensify your relationship, you don't want to see him again, and doing what you think he wants and moving in together.'

'What is it?'

Deborah says, 'You *tell* him why you're not ready for a deeper commitment.'

'How can I do that,' Robyn cries, a note of desperation in her voice, 'when I don't know?'

As the echoes float away towards the cliff edge, Deborah says, '*I* know.'

'You do?' Robyn turns a cross, flushed face to her. 'Then why not enlighten me?'

Deborah, who knows her too well to believe in this sudden show of hostility, says quietly, 'You are still too involved with Zach.'

'Zach's dead! I'm *not* involved with him!'

'Robyn, you need to mourn him. To let your feelings for him and your memories of him have their head. To –'

'He's been dead nearly a year! I should be over him by now!'

'Why?'

'Oh, because . . .'

Because what? Because she has *told* herself she should be? Been so occupied busying herself with other people's needs that she hasn't left room for her own?

She can't go on.

Deborah takes her hand. 'You let your true feelings through twice, to my knowledge,' she says gently. 'Once when you were getting ready to go out with Rory for the first time, once when you found Zach's note and the keys to the Athens flat.'

Robyn says, after a moment, 'Mm.'

'You did love him. Didn't you? Very much.'

'I –' Robyn draws a shaky breath. 'He'd got all old and doddery. I used to get irritated, used to think he was being a terrible old woman. I tried to jolly him along.'

'Perhaps you were afraid,' Deborah suggests. 'That he really was sick. That you might be about to lose him. It hurt less to think, silly old sod, what's he making such a fuss about? And that's why you thought it. The inner soul, Robyn, is very vulnerable. We're very good at believing we think something totally different from what we *really* think.'

Robyn, clearly, is going over all that. Picking through it, trying to find the weak spots. Deborah, knowing both that she won't because there aren't any, and that, being Robyn, she will be forthright enough to say so, waits.

Eventually, Robyn says, 'Okay. I need some time with Zach. I accept that.'

'Good,' Deborah says. 'In the quiet of your lovely, healing house' – she knows it's that all right – 'be alone with him for a while. He'll like that.'

Robyn, already close to tears, feels a shiver of emotion go right down her spine. Deborah is right. Robyn knows she is, because what she has just suggested is the very thing Robyn wants.

'What happens after that?' she asks after a few minutes.

'Whatever you want.' Deborah smiles, then goes on, 'It's what *you* want. Remember saying that to me?'

Robyn grins. 'Yes.' Thinks, how odd, that now it's Debs who's saying it to *me*. 'Rory?' she says hopefully.

'Rory, yes.'

'He may not hang around,' Robyn says. She thinks, I'm not at all sure I would, if the tables were turned.

But, 'He will if you explain. Don't you think?'

Robyn looks at Deborah, then turns to gaze out over the sea. The afternoon is passing, and soon it will be time to pack up and go home. Back to Haydon Hall, the home of both of them. For the foreseeable future, anyway, which is about as far as most of us are prepared to plan for.

She is happy about that. The concept of this quiet time that lies ahead is truly wonderful. My turn, she thinks. Really, my turn now. And, at the end of my little retreat, Rory. More of what we have already. And other things, too? Holidays, shared hobbies, shared concerns? Yes, that sounds nice.

Living together? Marriage?

She is not so sure about that.

She will have to wait and see. Hope that he is prepared to hang around while she does.

She turns back to Deborah.

Says, 'Time to go?'

And Deborah, understanding, says, 'Yes. Time to go.'